UNTAMED

UNTAMED

THE CRYSTAL ISLAND SERIES BOOK TWO

LILIAN T. JAMES

Crystal Pages
·Publishing·

Crystal Pages Publishing is an imprint of Aleron Books, LLC

First printing edition 2022

Cover Design : Murphy Rae
Editor : Allusion Publishing
Map Design : Chaim Holtjer
Interior Art : Etheric Tales & Edits

Paperback ISBN: 978-1-7378899-8-4
eBook ISBN: 978-1-7378899-4-6
Hardcover ISBN: 978-1-958763-02-5
Special Hardcover ISBN: 978-1-958763-05-6

To all the people who continue to burn brighter than a star,
even when the clouds seem determined to hide your light.

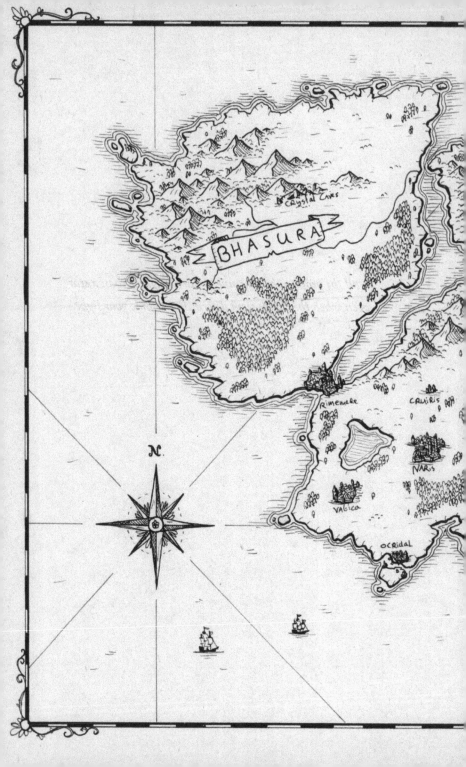

Author's Note

This novel contains content that may be triggering to some readers, including:

Abuse of power, consensual biting, non-consensual biting, child abuse (mentioned, not on-page), mild gore, misogyny, a morally gray love interest, profanity, sexually explicit scenes, suicidal thoughts, torture (mentioned, not on-page), and violence.

Pronunciation Guide

Characters

Alean Arenaris	Ay-lEEn Are-NAIR-is
Alyana Arenaris	AY-lee-AW-nah Are-NAIR-is
Dedryn Barilias	DEH-drin Bar-ILL-ee-us
Doren Panaeros	DOOR-in Pan-AY-rows
Eithan Matheris	EE-thin MATH-er-is
Elric Lesta	EL-rick LESS-tuh
Jaeros Barilias	JAY-rows Bar-ILL-ee-us
Jaren Barilias	JAIR-en Bar-ILL-ee-us
Onas Dornelin	OH-ness Door-NELL-in
Reniya Virnorin	Ren-EYE-uh VER-nor-in
Ryn Hayes	Rin HEY-s
Sulian Matheris	SUE-lee-en MATH-er-is
Taeral Virnorin	TAY-roll VER-nor-in
Trey Gibson	Tray GIB-son
Vaneara Arenaris	Van-EAR-uh Are-NAIR-is
Veralie Arenaris	VAIR-uh-lee Are-NAIR-is
Vesstan Arenaris	VESS-tin Are-NAIR-is
Wes Coleman	Wess COAL-man

Pronunciation Guide

Locations

Aleron	AL-er-on
Bhasura	BAH-sue-da
Cruiris	Crew-EAR-is
Earith	EAR-ith
Matherin	MATH-er-in
Midpath	Mid-path
Naris	Nair-is
Ocridal	OH-cri-doll
Philyra	Fill-EYE-ruh
Rimemere	Rye-meh-mEEr
Slegon	SLEH-gun
Southterres	South-TAIR-is
Vatica	Va-tick-uh

Other

Magyki	Mag-i-KAI
Thyabathi	Tie-yuh-BAW-tee

PROLOGUE

JAREN

His eyes shot open, and he launched up, barely avoiding cracking his forehead against the face that'd been looming over him just a second before.

"Veralie!"

He shifted his legs to stand, but two arms wrapped around his body, keeping him from rising to his feet. He struggled, blindly throwing his limbs out in an attempt to get free.

Veralie. Where was Veralie?

There was a grunt, and a low voice spoke above his head. "Calm down, Jaren. It's just me."

He froze, twisting his body within the confining hold to see his father's face behind him. He dropped his gaze, finally pausing long enough to take in his surroundings.

He was sitting in Jaeros's lap in the middle of the same

hallway he and Veralie had just been attacked in.

Panic clawed up his throat, and he frantically glanced around for the two blond males, but they were nowhere in sight. Other than Jaeros, the only other individual around was his other father, Dedryn, who was currently leaning against the wall, watching him.

Nothing was amiss. If it weren't for his throbbing head and the smell of blood in the air, he might've thought he'd imagined it all. Might've been able to convince himself that Veralie was still safely tucked in her bed.

But she wasn't.

He shoved Jaeros's arms again, squeezing his eyes shut against the last image he'd seen of her. Sprawled on the ground, her curls a wild mess around her face while blood dripped over her neck onto the floor.

She had to have been in pain, but even scared, her eyes had never strayed from his. Their gray depths the last thing he saw before a blinding pain echoed against his skull, and everything went black.

She'd been so brave, and now *he* needed to be brave for *her*.

"Let me up, Veralie's in trouble! We were attacked, and they've probably—"

"Stop thrashing about, Jaren. We know. You have a wound on your head and need to calm down."

The comment only made him thrash harder, digging his elbows into Jaeros's torso, and he slammed his head back into his jaw.

His father cursed, and his hold slackened enough for Jaren to fling himself up and whip around to stare down at him.

"What is wrong with you?" he yelled, flicking his eyes between the two of them. "Did you not hear what I said? She was with me and was taken. Why are you just standing here? She needs help."

His voice cracked on the last word, and he swallowed, wiping angrily at his eyes when neither responded. "I heard two males breaking into the house, so I snuck her out. We ran here to find you, but they followed us."

His eyes stung and tears built in the corners despite how hard he was trying to hold them back. "I couldn't protect her, and she got hurt. She's probably so scared right now."

His heart felt like it was about to pump right through his ribcage at the thought of what she must be going through. Was she calling out for him? Did she think he was hurt, or worse, that he'd abandoned her?

"Jaren."

"We need to find her, right now." What were they doing to her while his fathers stood around staring at him?

"Jaren," Dedryn repeated.

He ignored him, fisting his hands at his sides. He hated that he didn't have the ability to track her by scent yet. Hated that he'd have to rely on his fathers to do it.

He was supposed to be the one who protected her. "She's injured, so if we hurry, her blood should still be fresh."

"Jaren!" Dedryn snapped, gripping his shoulders and

forcing him to look him in the eyes. "She's gone, son."

An answering snarl burst from his lips, and he shoved Dedryn's hands off, half-tempted to risk his father's wrath and spit a curse. "I know she is. I told you; two males took her."

"They're dead," Dedryn said, anger dripping into his words.

Jaren froze at that, his brain taking a moment to catch up with his ears. He looked down at his father's clothes and blinked at what he hadn't noticed before.

Dedryn's hair stuck up at odd angles, his usually pristine tunic wrinkled and hanging loose around his waist. There was even a wet stain on the front, as if he'd grabbed it and wiped sweat off his face at some point.

Jaren's lungs expanded when he looked at Jaeros to see he didn't look any better. He had circles under his eyes, and his long hair had come loose from its tie, bunched and ratted against his head.

He released a heavy breath, the weight that'd been pressed against his sternum easing up, and he nodded in understanding. "You killed them."

"Yes."

Thank the gods. It stung his pride that his fathers had to save her, but he swallowed the bitter feeling down. All that mattered was that she was safe.

"Is she with a healer?"

There was a pause, and his fathers glanced at each other before Dedryn cleared his throat and answered. "No."

Jaren narrowed his eyes. His father was known at court for

his quick, verbal assaults. It's what King Vesstan respected the most about him. Dedryn *never* hesitated. So, why would he—

No.

He whipped his head toward Jaeros, denial already flooding his body, hoping and needing his affectionate father to smile and tell him everything was fine. But he didn't.

Jaeros only gripped one of Jaren's daggers to his chest and looked at him as a silent tear slid down his cheek and disappeared into his beard.

No. No, please, gods, no.

Dedryn opened his mouth, and Jaren's limbs immediately began to shake.

"Don't say it."

"I need you to listen to me, son."

"No. Don't you dare say it."

Dedryn placed his hands on his face, cupping his jaw in the gentlest touch he'd ever given him. "She's gone, Jaren."

His touch felt like a burn, and Jaren yanked out of his grasp, stepping back to glare at him. "I want to see her."

Dedryn dropped his hands, his face hard as stone as he shook his head. "You can't do that."

"*I want to see her, right now!*"

"And I said, no," Dedryn snapped. "You wouldn't be able to handle it."

Jaren hiccupped, another tear slipping out even as he dashed it away. "I don't need your permission. I'll find her, myself. I did it once, I can do it again."

He turned on his heel, but Dedryn flung an arm out, snatching him by the elbow. "Gods damnit, Jaren, she's dead."

Faster than he'd ever moved before, he spun, throwing his fist out and landing a direct hit to the underside of his father's jaw.

"You're lying!" he yelled, cocking his arm back a second time. One hit wasn't enough. He wanted to pummel him into the ground for even daring to utter the word. His chest rumbled, but before he could make contact again, his arms were yanked down and pinned to his sides.

He bucked, finally barking out the curse he was never supposed to say, but Jaeros just tapped into his strength, turning to steel around his body.

"She's dead, son," he whispered, his voice thick and broken. "And I'm so sorry we have to tell you that." He choked at the end, gripping Jaren harder and burying his face into the back of his hair.

No. They didn't know what they were talking about. He'd know if she was dead. He'd *know*.

Closing his eyes, he felt for their bond. It wasn't mature enough for him to understand her different scents or feel her emotions yet, but it'd still been there. It'd still existed.

He'd been able to feel it even years ago when he'd been Veralie's age. Feeling her was like breathing—a natural instinct woven within his soul.

He squeezed his eyes tighter and searched harder, seeking that familiar warmth he'd grown accustomed to. The comfort of her that he'd taken for granted.

But it wasn't there.

Nausea threatened, and his breathing grew ragged. The cold, hollow feeling had him lurching forward, and he gasped, uncaring that Jaeros had released him.

His *aitanta*. His *friend*. The female his fathers had teased he'd fall in love with one day. The story on his daggers, the purpose of his training. All of it was supposed to be for her.

And he'd failed.

His legs buckled, and he dropped to the floor, his knees audibly slamming into the stone. The pain was nothing compared to what he felt inside. It was a poison, taking over his soul and rotting it from the inside out.

Someone called his name, but he could no longer hear them past the hatred spewing in his mind. He curled in on himself, digging his nails into his head, and heaved. Again and again.

She was gone.

She was gone, and it was all his fault.

Agony like he'd never known burned through him, spearing out like spikes along his skin as hot tears streamed down his face. He pressed both hands against his chest, trying in vain to keep his heart from shattering as he threw his head back and screamed.

CHAPTER 1

VERA

Fifteen Years Later

It was impossible to concentrate past the firm ass hovering over her face. The perfectly rounded shape was all she could see, and the temptation to reach out and pinch it was overwhelming. Especially when its owner chose that exact moment to open his giant, annoying mouth.

"Zhumo dzind mbi."

Asshole. She supposed she could always bite it really fucking hard too. She wasn't even sure what pissed her off more, being called a stupid fool, or the fact that even insults sounded sexy in his baritone voice.

"Call me stupid again, and I—"

He suddenly twisted, flinging his leg over her head and missing her nose by a hair. The weight that'd been baring down on her ribs lifted for one blessed moment before he dropped back down, grinding her spine into the salt-slicked wood beneath her.

Locking her jaw to hold in her grunt of pain, she exhaled through clenched teeth and glared at the scruffy, scar-flecked face that'd replaced the firm rear. How could someone so attractive be so gods damn frustrating?

As if reading her mind, he smirked down at her, unperturbed. "And you'll do what? You've yet to succeed at even pinning me once today. I don't think you quite have it in you, *Nlem Snadzend.*"

His tongue curled around the syllables of her title, taunting her, and drawing pinpricks of blood along her pride. But it was the suffocating male arrogance pulsing near her heart that was the last straw.

Tapping into, what she hoped, was a minuscule amount of power, she snapped her head up toward his nose. He reared back to avoid the hit, shifting his weight and removing the bulk of it from her torso.

Using the split second she had before he recovered, she flung her arms into the space between them and shoved against his chest. His breath whooshed out, and she couldn't fight her own smirk when his eyes flashed just before he went flying backward.

She didn't see him hit the deck from her prostrate position, but the *thunk* of his body against the wood was just as satisfying. Maybe it'd knock some manners into him.

Rolling to her least-battered side, she pushed to her feet, mentally preparing for the new bruises that were sure to come from his retaliation. By the time she'd raised her arms, he'd done the same, dropping into a defensive stance.

She took a deep breath, ignoring the stab of pain in her side. If she didn't know better, she'd swear she had the tip of a rib imbedded in her left lung from the last kick he'd landed.

Jaren's eyes immediately latched on to her torso, and he lowered his arms, the muscles of his jaw flexing. "Resorting to cheating when you're angry is a character flaw you should reflect on during meditation today."

"Fuck you," she seethed. She'd barely cheated, and in a real fight, anything was game anyway.

His eyes shot up to hers, flaring in time with the pulse in her chest. "You'd have to actually pin me in order to do that, little star."

Her face heated, and her gaze dropped to his body like her own was physically unable to resist imagining pinning him and doing just that.

Droplets of sweat covered his tanned chest and arms, glistening in the unrelenting sun and drawing attention to each ripple of muscle. His usually sharp jaw was hidden under facial hair that'd grown during their days at sea, and his emerald eyes seared into her under his dark, drawn brows.

They hadn't touched intimately since the day they'd escaped Eithan on Aleron, but it certainly wasn't due to a lack of desire on either's part.

She was more than interested, even when he was being a complete and total ass, and there was no doubt he wanted it too.

She could feel the scorching heat of his desire strengthening every night as he laid on the cot next to hers.

But between how exhausted she was by the time they finished training and their overall lack of bathing, neither had made a move. The constant sound of Vera's gagging and retching the first few days hadn't helped either.

She may not have had a whole lot of experience, but she was pretty sure sex with bile breath and sweaty pits was where intimacy went to die.

His body tensed under her gaze, and he almost seemed to shift forward before he froze, balling his fists at his sides. He glared, looking like he wanted nothing more than to thoroughly kick her ass, but the thick, earthy scent coming off him told a very different story.

"Since you're so keen on using your abilities today, I suppose we'll start your meditation early," he said, practically spitting the words through gritted teeth.

She cringed. Great. She hated practicing with her power. Not because she actively disliked it or anything, but because she genuinely sucked at it.

Since boarding his wretched ship—apart from the first few days when she puked more than she breathed—Jaren had demanded she spar with him each morning and meditate each afternoon.

The sparring she didn't mind, even though it often made her nausea worse and ended with her sprawled on the deck wanting to claw his eyes out. She'd always enjoyed pushing herself physically and knew there was much she could learn from him.

If only he'd lay off the damn meditation.

They'd agreed not to tap into their abilities during their bouts for a few reasons. The main one being that she had zero control over how much power she used, and the second being that Jaren didn't want her exhausting her reserve.

It was the only thing keeping her breakfast in her belly these days, and even that was a struggle. She could caress it like she'd just done with no problem, but she couldn't successfully, and consistently, focus it on any one specific thing.

Experienced Magyki could enhance singular skills like sight or hearing, but her entire body always seemed to turn into a damn beacon. It was hard. Really fucking hard.

The best she'd done was figure out how to heal minor wounds and her seasickness when needed, but even that didn't always work out. The last time she'd attempted it, Jaren had made some offhand remark about her posture and technique, and her flash of anger had fractured her control.

She'd pulled so much up that she'd healed her entire body. Sickness, bruises, sore muscles, all of it. Instead of praising her, or apologizing for being an ass, or literally anything a good teacher would've done, he'd scolded her even more, accusing her of being more of a pampered princess than a warrior.

Of course, she'd responded by punching him in the gut. He'd deserved it. Granted, she'd regretted it a little when she'd nearly sent him overboard, but he'd shut his mouth afterward.

Now, she'd give anything to see him topple over the side. He'd be fine. The asshole knew how to swim.

Ignoring the expectant weight of his gaze, she looked out at the endless expanse of the Dividing Sea surrounding them. The power she'd accessed back on Aleron seemed like a lifetime ago. Like something she'd only imagined.

If she was being honest with herself, *everything* that'd happened since she'd grabbed a sword and sparred Eithan in the training yard seemed like it'd happened to someone else.

She turned toward the stern and squinted into the distance. The coast of Aleron had disappeared long ago, filling her sight with nothing but rippling blue as far as her eyes could see.

It still didn't seem real to be gone. To be heading somewhere where she wouldn't have to hide. Somewhere that would value her for what she could do instead of stone her for it. It was just as exciting as it was terrifying.

"Sit."

The gruff order was accompanied by the snapping of fingers, and Vera's head whipped back, her mouth popping open. He did *not* just command her like a fucking dog.

When he answered her unspoken outrage with only a silent raise of his brow, she immediately darted her gaze around, looking for anything she could launch at his face. How this insufferable male could be her soul-bonded mate was baffling.

She was two seconds from removing a boot and sending it between his eyes when he tipped his head back and released a deep, rumbling laugh. The surprising sound wrapped around her, freezing her in place and snuffing out her irritation like it'd never existed.

She stared along the curve of his neck, latching on to the sound like an emotionally starved woman. And maybe she was. Things like laughter and joy were rare with him. It made him seem younger, less beaten and worn down by the world.

His smile widened farther at her obvious shock, and her body heated. Sometimes it was easy to forget that he wasn't just another human man, especially since his hair now completely covered his ears, and he never used his abilities.

But there was no denying it when his smile revealed two sharp canines. Canines that had punctured her shoulder while his hand had been buried in her trousers, making her climax harder than she'd ever thought possible.

He'd claimed her, marking her possessively without a single hint of regret. She licked her lips, subconsciously lifting her hand to run her fingers along her clothed shoulder.

Jaren's laughter cut off, and he straightened, his nostrils flaring as his eyes zeroed in on her hand. She dropped her arm like her shoulder was on fire, not wanting to draw his attention to what was there.

Or rather, what was *supposed* to be there.

"Fine," she said, hoping her voice didn't give her away as she moved to where he'd indicated and lowered herself to the deck. "But next time, use common courtesy and ask nicely."

"Says the female who was raised by a Weapons' Master but who still cheated during a bout," he said, positioning himself to stand in front of her.

With the way he looked, she'd be convinced he was completely unbothered by their exchange if it weren't for the dark promise swirling in his eyes.

He cracked his neck. *"Thyabathi zhe be."*

"Nlayi," she agreed.

He'd demanded during their first practice that she only use Thyabathi when practicing her abilities to become more comfortable with it. He'd warned that although most Magyki knew both languages, very few used the common tongue.

She hadn't argued. She remembered enough of her native tongue to communicate the basics, but the more practice she could squeeze in, the better. It was like stretching a muscle. She knew *how* to stretch it, but it'd take time and practice to get it loose and natural again.

She was already going to be judged for living in the Matherin Capital, she didn't need another reason to stand out.

JAREN RELEASED A sound that might've been a sigh, had he not sounded like an angry bear as he made it. "You're not trying."

"Yes, I am."

She hunched over her crossed legs, dragging her hands down her face, and wanted nothing more than to curl up and sleep. Why did tapping into her abilities make her so gods damn tired?

He crouched down to her level and rested his arms over his bent knees. "You honed your power just fine on Aleron. What's different now?"

"I don't know," she said, whining more to herself than him. She dropped her hands to the deck, running her fingers along the wood and letting the edges of splinters scrape against her skin. "I'm not sure how I did it then. It just kind of happened."

"Replay the moment," he pressed. "Go through each of your senses one by one and tell me what was happening. What you felt."

Despite her exhaustion, she listened and closed her eyes, forcing herself to go back to that day. How the warm wind felt against her back as they left Midpath, the smell of Jaren that still lingered on her body, the rush of excitement for the future, and then the foreboding sound of hooves charging toward them.

She remembered her shock at seeing Eithan out of Matherin and her horror at what he'd said. Remembered the sadness in Trey's eyes and the hatred in Hayes's. But more than anything, she remembered the exact moment Hayes's arrow had pierced Jaren's body.

Vera's muscles tensed at the memory, and her teeth ground together as she clenched her jaw. She swore she could still feel the residual sting of the wound and the burn in her throat as she'd screamed.

Her fear had been a thick, tangible thing, and she'd plummeted straight into that roiling storm inside her, strengthening her legs to lunge hard and fast. There'd been no thought, no plan, just her naked desperation to save him.

But then she'd been struck herself, forced to watch while Hayes held a sword to Jaren. And then suddenly she wasn't seeing Aleron anymore, and it wasn't Hayes holding the blade to her mate, but a stranger.

She sucked in a shaky breath, taking in Jaren's smell and reminding herself that he was *here*, with her. There was no Hayes and no arrow. They were both alive and unharmed.

"You," she said, frowning. "I remembered you."

His fingers twitched, and he curled them in, clutching his knees. "What do you mean?"

"Not as you are now, but as a child. It could've been my mind playing tricks on me, but it felt real. You were lying in a hallway, and a man—maybe a Magyki, I'm not sure—held a blade to your chest."

She looked up, locking eyes with his now slightly widened ones. "You were reaching for me. I could feel your terror, or maybe it was mine, I don't know. All I remember is when it faded from my mind, something snapped. I didn't feel like *me* anymore."

He swallowed, pain flickering in the green of his eyes before he blinked it away. "Anger and fear are powerful emotions that work well for accessing your ability when absolutely necessary, but they're a crutch. You must mold it to your will without them."

"I understand that," she quipped. "You asked me what I'd felt in that moment, and I told you. What I need now from *you*, my teacher, is to *teach* me how to do it differently."

His jaw ticked. "It's an innate reaction; it's not something I can teach you. You have to feel it and direct it where you want it to go. It answers to you, not the other way around."

"I do direct it."

"Not enough. You have immense power, Veralie. You moved faster than the speed of a fucking arrow. It's there. You're just second-guessing yourself."

She blew out a breath, flicking stray curls from her face. "Why is it so important I learn this before we get there anyway?"

"So you can defend yourself with more than just a sword. Your mother died, Veralie. As you almost did the last time you were there."

"Yes, but the rebellion's over. It's been over for nearly fifteen years. You said so, yourself."

He straightened his legs, towering over her. "I trust no one with your safety, little star. You are the Daughter to the Throne. There will always be a risk of danger. I'll take no chances. Now close your eyes and try again."

JAREN

HE'D BEEN TRAINED FOR YEARS TO WITHSTAND A MULTITUDE of horrific scenarios, no matter the level of pain. The risks he'd taken on his scouting trips to Aleron had required it. Humans may have been weaker, but if enough pebbles balanced on a mountain, they'd eventually cause a rockslide.

He'd never been arrogant enough to believe there was no risk of capture when he was always vastly outnumbered, which was why he'd taught himself long ago to shut out his emotions. He needed to be capable of staying clearheaded no matter what happened to, or around, him.

Then *she* appeared. Gods, that fucking mouth on her. Sometimes he truly wasn't sure if he wanted to kiss it or sew it shut.

The last week had been a torture like nothing he'd ever prepared for. Seeing her every time he opened his eyes until the moment he closed them, feeling her every time he breathed, smelling her, *wanting* her. Fuck. It was maddening.

A throat cleared. "Do you mind?"

His lips twitched, but he somehow fought back his smile, watching her muscles shift as she wiped sweat off her skin from the afternoon bout she'd demanded after her meditation.

"Not at all, little star. Carry on."

Her heart picked up speed, and her cheeks warmed, turning a delicious shade of pink that always drove him fucking insane.

Kiss it. He definitely wanted to kiss that foul mouth. To nibble at her bottom lip and pull it into his mouth, forcing her to open for him. He imagined the feel of her hair wrapped around his fist as he positioned her exactly where he wanted, exploring and tasting at his leisure.

And he wouldn't stop there.

Across the deck, his mate stumbled, clenching the cloth

she'd been using in a death grip. Her flush deepened, and his chest rumbled in answer.

He loved that she could feel his raging desire. Loved that every time he was hard for her, she knew it without even setting eyes on him. But most of all, he fucking loved how much it affected her.

Gods, they needed off this vessel. Almost against his will, he shifted toward her, and she sucked in sharply, flicking her eyes to his trousers and biting that gods damn full lip.

Maybe he wouldn't wait until they were off. He knew their less-than-ideal bathing situation bothered her, but he, for one, couldn't care less if it meant she'd be writhing beneath him.

She made a choking sound and pressed a hand to her chest, taking a step back. "Is there a way to…block this?"

Like a wave smashing against a lone ember, his desire stuttered out, and he froze. A heaviness settled between them, and his fingers spasmed at his sides. "Be very careful what you say next, little star. Block *what*, exactly?"

She tossed her washrag to the deck, squaring her shoulders and standing tall like she was readying for a storm. And maybe she was, because depending on what exited her mouth next, he might just bring one down on her.

"This bridge, or whatever, between us that feeds our emotions to each other all the time. Is there a way to…not do that?"

He gritted his teeth, taking several more steps toward her. If she thought she was going to reject him, she was going to be painfully fucking disappointed. "You accepted our bond."

"I know. That's not what I meant. I only meant—"

Before she could finish whatever excuse she'd conjured up, he lunged. Gripping her hip with one hand, he wrapped his other around the column of her throat, pulling her flush against him and snarling down at her.

"Try to shut me out, Veralie. I'll burrow so fucking deep under your skin, you'll have to carve me out."

She encircled his wrist with both of her hands, her callouses scraping his skin as she squeezed. "I'm not rejecting our bond, Jaren. I'm just not sure how I feel about the lack of privacy. I'm struggling enough with my own emotions without adding yours to the mix."

He shook his head, her explanation doing nothing to calm him. "We are mates. Our bond exists for that exact purpose. So that I may anticipate your needs and see to it that they are met."

"Open, honest communication can do that too," she snapped.

He moved his hand higher, spreading his fingers around her jaw and tilting her head back. "I want to feel you, Veralie. All the time. In everything I do. It feeds me in a way I cannot describe."

Her expression softened, and she released her grip on his wrist, caressing her thumb along his skin. "It's just a lot, Jaren. Sometimes I can't separate how I feel with how you feel. It's confusing."

He inhaled through his nose, saturating his senses with her

star-fire scent and trying to calm the roar in his veins. "I don't know of a way to block our connection without rejecting the bond. If any mated pair has discovered a way, they have not made it known," he ground out.

Her brow furrowed. "I wonder if that's why some Magyki reject it in the first place. Maybe it's not that they're against having a mate, maybe they just don't want the intrusion of it."

He dug his fingers into her hip, lowering his face until it hovered just above her own. "You have no idea how *intrusive* I can be. Tempt me, little star. I will intrude inside your body until we are one and the same. Until you can't tell where I start and you end."

He ran his nose along her jaw, watching gooseflesh pebble down her neck as he whispered in her ear. "You think our emotions are mixed now? I'll meld them together until you can't tell the difference between your pleasure and mine. I'll forge our bond into gods damn steel."

Her throat bobbed, and her heart picked up until it was a thrumming beat beside his own. "You're a lot more possessive than I anticipated," she breathed, pressing closer to him.

He grinned, drinking in the quick flare of arousal that rolled off her in response to his touch. "You have no idea."

And she didn't. Not yet.

The moment the Daughter to the Throne stepped foot on Bhasura, unmated Magyki everywhere would flock to her like starving beasts, desperate to sink their teeth in and lay claim to both her body and her title.

His anger flared, tempting him to mark her again right then and there. Somewhere it could be clearly seen so if anyone so much as thought about taking her, he'd be well within his right to rip out their fucking spines.

He positioned his mouth over the curve of her neck, his jaw aching with the need to clamp it around the tender spot. But something over her shoulder caught his eye, and he lifted his face, enhancing his sight to see out across the water.

Sighing, he released his hold on her throat and gripped her hips, twisting her body so her back was flush against him.

"Consider yourself lucky, little star," he murmured, pointing toward the emerging coastline. "We're home."

CHAPTER 2

TREY

B lood fell to the floor in a steady beat.

Drip. Drip. Drip.

He watched each drop fall, rippling the growing puddle. If he tried hard enough, he could probably force his toes to wade through it, pushing it around the rough, dirty stones like paint.

In his delirious state, he was tempted to write out, *I missed you* in it. With his impaired vision and pounding head, it'd be impossible to write the message legibly, but damn, it'd almost be worth it just to see the bastard's reaction.

His croaked laugh echoed out in the silence, bouncing off the walls and reverberating back at him. *She* would've found it funny too.

He didn't know what time it was. Shit, between how

infrequently he was fed and how often he passed out, he didn't even know how many days he'd been down there.

The last thing he remembered was being strapped to a table with a pair of blue eyes staring down at him, oozing justification every time he screamed. As if he deserved each lick of the inflicted pain.

He'd tried, gods had he tried, to hold it in. But the second that venomous intent focused on his eye, he'd lost all sense of control. Passing out had been a fucking blessing.

His head was killing him, but it was the agonizing pain in his shoulders and wrists that woke him. His arms were secured to the wall above him, high enough that his feet barely reached the floor, and by the level of pain he was in, he'd been like that for at least an hour.

Was his Royal Highness playing with the Weapon's Master too? Trey spat. *His Royal fucking Highness*. He'd never bestow the demon with the title again. The man was the definition of insane, and the worst part was that nobody knew.

Eithan's outer shell was crafted to perfection. There wasn't a single flaw in the disguise he'd created. For years, Trey had looked up to him, believing he could be the future emperor Aleron deserved.

He would've gladly given his life for him had it not all been a cruel lie.

He knew he'd ruined Eithan's trust, knew he'd failed in his duty when he'd supported Vera running off, but this? Eithan wasn't torturing him because he thought he deserved it. He had no qualms admitting he'd rather kill him.

No, Eithan was doing this for the sole purpose of feeding his sick, twisted desires. And by what Trey had heard around him in the neighboring cells, he wasn't the only one Eithan played with.

Footsteps brought him out of his thoughts, and his heart sped up, the throbbing in his head increasing. He couldn't control the instantaneous reaction. Every time he heard those steps, he ended up bleeding and screaming.

In his fantasy world where he survived this, he'd never again be able to hear the clicking of boots on stone without flinching—without expecting pain. He was conditioned for life.

A voice broke the silence, causing his stomach to twist, and bile climbed up his throat.

"I see you're finally awake."

Trey ignored him, continuing to stare down at the floor. He began counting the stones, desperate for anything to keep him from shaking like a weak ass leaf.

Eithan clicked his tongue against the roof of his mouth like he was disciplining an ornery child. "You know, Gibson, all this will end if you just tell me what I want to know."

Trey seethed. Liar. He'd already told him more than he'd have ever willingly done had he been in his right mind, and Eithan had never stopped.

They're mates!

The traitorous words had spewed out of him during one of their last "playtimes" and there was no taking them back.

He hated the stab of betrayal he felt for it. The guilt. He shouldn't feel anything regarding what he'd revealed about Vera. She'd practically admitted it herself when she'd defended Jaren that day.

And honestly, if he really wanted to, he could blame his entire predicament on her. She was the one who should feel guilty, not him.

If she'd never run off, or even if she just hadn't fought him about returning, he wouldn't be where he was. He'd have both his fucking eyes and still be a proud member of the guard.

He wanted to be angry. He wanted to hate her. But he couldn't find it in his heart to feel either.

Maybe he had at first, but after seeing more of Eithan's true nature, he felt nothing but relief that she'd escaped. He couldn't imagine what it'd be like to be this monster's wife.

What he might enjoy in the bedroom.

"I already told you everything I know," he finally said, unable to scrounge up the energy to lift his head. He just continued staring at the floor, watching the rippling reflection beneath him.

Eithan's tongue flicked against the roof of his mouth again, followed by the jangling of keys and the screech of hinges.

An involuntary shudder shot through him, and he bit down hard on his tongue, hating how quickly the bastard had programmed fear into his body. It no longer felt like *his*.

"I don't believe you, Gibson," Eithan said, his voice closer than it'd been before. "You traveled with them for days, and we both know she trusted you. I want to know more about the soul bond you said she has with the Magyki."

"I don't...know," he heaved. The effort of talking was almost enough to knock him out again.

Eithan stepped forward, his polished, black boots entering Trey's line of sight. He felt a sharp pull at his wrists, and then he collapsed to the floor, droplets of blood splashing up his legs and feet.

"That's okay," Eithan said, crouching slowly like he had all the time in the world. He smiled, leaning forward until his pale face was only inches away from Trey's. "I don't mind helping."

JAREN

HOME. AFTER WEEKS OF BEING GONE, HE WAS FINALLY HOME.

Seeing the coastline fill the horizon was always a sight that brought him comfort, but pulling up to the dock with his mate by his side was something else entirely. A sense of rightness that no words in either language could explain.

They'd arrived in Ocridal, a fishing city that was surprisingly clean despite its horrid smell and reputation for its foul-mouthed occupants and drinking. It'd always been more his style than the capital, and he usually spent a few days enjoying its distractions before heading inland. It was an easy place to lose himself and release the tension that always built during his scouting trips.

But things would be different this time around, given he had zero intentions of staying longer than a single night. He was eager to see his fathers, but it was more than that. The longer they delayed, the more eyes would settle on Veralie, and the higher the chance someone might suspect who she was.

He wouldn't have risked staying at all if it wasn't absolutely necessary, but even he couldn't travel much farther without adequate rest and a real meal.

It was about a two-day trip on horseback from Ocridal to the capital, Naris, and if he so much as mentioned going another two days without a bath to his *aitanta*, she was sure to break his nose again.

He chuckled. No, with all the petty fights they'd been having lately and the frustration he felt building inside her, she was more likely to strangle him with his own intestines rather than deliver a quick hit.

Gods, he couldn't wait for his fathers to see her. If they thought she'd been a handful as a child, they were in for a treat with her as an adult. Jaeros, she'd get along with fine, but Dedryn? She and he were going to butt heads even more than Jaren had with him.

Veralie thought her human mentor had been stiff and surly, but Jaren could all but guarantee he was nothing compared to Dedryn. Ded's stoic demeanor made Jaren seem downright sweet and tender.

Luckily, his father had Jaeros, who was ornery and compassionate to a fault, to smooth away his rough edges.

Complete opposites, they were the definition of a perfectly mated pair.

But regardless of their demeanor, they were both going to shit themselves when they saw her. She may have only lived with them for a few years, but they'd accepted her as their own as willingly as they'd accepted him a few years prior.

Jaeros would probably cry while cooking up some ridiculously extravagant meal while Dedryn verbally assaulted her for information about her years on Aleron. Information he, himself, was eager to know as well.

And when they finally disappeared for the night, he'd take her back to his room and cover her in his scent. His body, his clothes, his bed. He'd fucking smother her in it.

Veralie's head whipped toward him, so fast he was surprised she didn't break her neck. He bit his tongue, fighting the sudden urge to laugh.

"Problem?"

She threw her arms out, motioning around them. "Do you plan on doing anything helpful, or am I going to do it all while you stand there daydreaming?"

He tipped his head, trailing his eyes up her body. "If you'd prefer I *do* the things I'm daydreaming about, all you have to do is ask, little star."

Her nostrils flared, and she spun away, mumbling something about ridiculous males as she stomped to the other side of the deck. His pulse picked up as he watched her, delighting in how responsive she was to his own arousal.

She may be apprehensive about their bond and the depth of their connection, but she couldn't fight it any more than he could. They were in tune—two pieces of a whole. And after the sleepless night he had planned for them in Naris, they'd be interwoven forever.

He hummed to himself, watching her lithe body flex and stretch as she worked. How long would he be able to hide her away, to touch and taste at his leisure, before someone inevitably came looking for her?

King Vesstan would obviously want time to get to know the daughter he mourned, but how much? And what would the king say about their mating bond? No queen before Veralie had ever been mated, including her parents. Royal pairings had always been based on their political and offspring potential.

Jaren would gladly see her womb swell with their child if she desired, but he had nothing to offer her through his name. Mating bonds were respected above all others, but given how thoroughly he'd failed at protecting her all those years ago, he wasn't sure how King Vesstan was going to see it.

The unknown of it all caused a dark stir in Jaren's chest. No matter what his standing was, what her name was, she was *his*. King Vesstan could spend all the time with her he wanted, but king or not, if he so much as tried to separate them, they were going to have a big fucking problem.

He'd never actually met him face to face, even with all the times he'd traveled to Aleron under Vesstan's orders, but he'd overheard enough conversations between his fathers over the years to know the king had a thing for control.

Considering what happened to his wife and daughter during the rebellion, Jaren didn't blame him, but he still couldn't help but wonder what he'd do when he realized his daughter didn't respond well to that sort of thing.

HE WAS HAVING as much fun watching Veralie gawk at the figures below them, as she was having watching them all bustle about the dock. Her eyes were wide, lips parted, and her hands clutched the rail tight enough to turn her knuckles white.

Even with her scarred ears and odd mannerisms as a constant reminder, it was easy to forget sometimes that she'd only ever been around humans before now—that she could remember, at least.

She leaned farther over the rail. "Why do they all look like they're panicking?"

He didn't bother following her gaze, too busy absorbing her ever-changing expressions. "They know my ship."

She tore her eyes off the workers to give him a side-eyed look. "You're that important? I thought you were just a scout?"

"I'm not *just* a scout," he said, eyes narrowing. "But no, it's technically my fathers who are important. They likely sent word to Ocridal to keep a close watch for me when I didn't return when I should have. I can almost guarantee a messenger has already left to carry word of my arrival back to Naris."

"You said they're advisors to King Vesstan, right?"

He raised a brow at her formality but made no comment. It wasn't his business to press the subject of her family until she was ready to talk about it. She hadn't known the truth for long, let alone met the male who'd sired her.

"Dedryn is an advisor, yes. He has been since before I was born. Jaeros, however, is more of an unofficial one. He only gets involved to support Dedryn."

"And the king allows that? Just because they're mates?"

"More or less. Jaeros is also well-known and respected."

"Then why isn't he an actual advisor?"

"He's not of noble blood. His parents were cooks in the palace. That's actually how he and Dedryn met. You'll have to ask him about it sometime, it's quite the story."

She frowned. "I guess I didn't realize noble blood mattered that much here. You're all Magyki with the same gifted blood. Why would family lines matter?"

He pushed off from the rail, gesturing for her to follow, and headed for the rope ladder he'd tossed over the side earlier. He was more than ready to have both feet on solid ground.

"*We* are. You have to stop thinking of Magyki as different from you. We're the same, Veralie."

She grumbled behind him but kept her retort to herself as she threw her leg over the side and followed him down.

"Bhasura is not barbaric," he continued, stepping onto the dock and reaching out a hand to help her off. "Unlike Aleron, we do not underestimate our females, and all Magyki are granted the freedom to earn a comfortable living. But do not mistake that for meaning our society is perfect."

Pulling her in, he leaned his face toward hers, his chest rumbling with pleasure when she responded without thought. Her eyes fluttered closed, and she tipped her head back, parting her lips.

He smiled, knowing she couldn't see it, and ran his hands up her arms. Her skin pebbled beneath his touch as he moved along her shoulders and glided the backs of his knuckles over the nape of her neck.

Hovering his mouth above her own, he waited until his breath had just coasted across her lips before gripping her hood and yanking it up and over her head.

Her eyes shot open, and she shoved him back, irritation bleeding into her bright, silver eyes as her cheeks flushed. "You're such an ass."

He smirked, ignoring the challenge in her gaze. Now wasn't the time for one of their battles, no matter how much the feral part of him wanted to egg her on.

"I'll kiss you all you want once we're alone, little star, but for now, we need to move. The inn I usually stay at isn't far from here." He reached up to yank the edge of her hood down farther over her eyes, but she smacked his hand, stepping back.

"Everyone here knows who you are. Our cloaks aren't going to make us suddenly invisible," she snapped, sounding more tired and sulky than actually angry.

"I'm not the one I'm worried about."

"No one is going to recognize me, Jaren. You didn't."

His lip curled at the reminder. Yet another reason he'd been nothing but a shitty fucking mate so far. "Probably not, but we're not taking any chances. We're both too drained to deal with a mob, good or bad. You can take it off as soon as we get to our room," he added, gesturing toward her head.

Her eyes narrowed, and he tensed. He'd bet anything she was weighing her odds at whether she wanted to risk flinging the hood off right there.

Running a hand through his hair, which now reached his eyes, he pushed the matted strands out of his face and sighed. "Gods, why must you be so stubborn? The faster you stop arguing and start walking, the faster you can bathe."

She crossed her arms, tilting her head and sucking on her teeth. "The faster I undress, the faster I can bathe too. Maybe I'll make this even easier and rip all my clothes off right here and strut there naked."

He broke the small space between them, pressing himself flush against her, and slid his hands around her waist. Her body felt so gods damn good molded to his. "Go ahead, little star, I would very much enjoy that view."

She scoffed, but he didn't fail to notice that she didn't pull away. "You're full of shit. You and I both know you'd want to kill anyone who looked at me."

"I can promise you, I would not."

"Is that so?"

"It is," he said, the corner of his lip curling up. "It'd take way

35

too long to clean up that many bodies."

Her eyes narrowed, not believing a word of it, and he chuckled, moving his hands lower to cup her ass. "I'll gladly let every Magyki here admire your naked curves just so they can see how fucking good my mark looks upon your skin."

Her breathing hitched, and he pulled her closer, rolling his hips into her center and watching the way her eyes darkened in time with the heady sensation emanating near his heart.

"Then, while you're safely tucked away, soaking in the tub you're so longing for, I'll track down each and every one of them and pluck their eyes from their sockets with the very daggers that state you are mine."

She blinked up at him from under her hood, speechless for once. He dipped his head, unable to resist brushing his lips across hers.

It was the closest they'd come to kissing since Aleron, and his body screamed for more, desperate for the taste of her. To feel her tongue slide against his. But he swallowed it down, forcing himself to release her. Later. They'd have plenty of time for that after they were fed, washed, and alone.

"*Thyoil?*"

"Yeah...yeah, I'm ready," she replied, her eyes still wider than usual.

He clicked his tongue, putting some much-needed space between them and tapping two fingers to her lips. She groaned and smacked his hand away, but repeated, *"Ye mipoak thyoil."*

"Good girl," he said, turning to make his way down the

dock, fully expecting her to throw something at the back of his head. But after a heavy pause, in which he could only imagine she was contemplating just that, she stomped after him, throwing a colorful expletive instead.

He grinned. At least she'd said it in Thyabathi.

"I DON'T GET it," she said as they walked, continuing to speak in their native tongue. It caused her to speak slower than usual, but overall, he was impressed with how quickly she was picking it back up after only a few weeks.

Not that he'd tell her that.

He glanced down, still half expecting her to smack him in some way, but her eyes were on the Magyki around them.

"You don't get what?"

She swiveled her head side to side, staring at the workers they passed. "All these people raced to prepare for your arrogant ass's arrival."

Gods, he wanted to bite that fucking whip of a tongue. "What about it?"

She rolled her lips in and then popped them out, making a small smacking sound that drew his gaze to her full lips. "So then, why do I feel like everyone is avoiding us? No one seems very welcoming."

"I'm not one for small talk. I've made it well-known." He shrugged, reluctantly peeling his eyes away in time to catch a slight commotion ahead of them.

He slowed his gait, stretching an arm across Veralie's chest and positioning his body in front of hers.

"So, basically, what you're saying is you're a—wait, what are you doing? What is it, Jaren?"

He barely heard her; his focus glued to the male shoving his way through the last line of street-goers and jogging toward the dock with purpose.

Jaren stopped dead in his tracks, refusing to blink, unsure if what he was seeing—*who* he was seeing—was actually there.

Veralie's fingers caressed his back as she peeked around him, sending a shudder down his spine. "Who is that, Jaren?"

He swallowed, every nerve and sense standing on edge. "My father." He could count on one hand the number of times he'd seen either of his fathers leave the capital. What had happened to bring him all the way to Ocridal?

Veralie's fingers stilled. "What? I thought you said they stayed in Naris?"

He didn't answer. He didn't have one. Turning to lock eyes with her over his shoulder, he reached up and gave her chin a soft squeeze. "Stay here."

She blinked, clearly taken aback by the request. Unsheathing one of his daggers—the one that she'd had all those years—he handed it to her, watching her calloused fingers wrap around the script. "Please, Veralie."

Surprisingly, she nodded, tucking his dagger in her belt and shifting to stand out of the way of the crowd. So, she *was* capable of listening, after all. He'd log that tidbit away to taunt her with the next time she argued, which he doubted would take long.

Forcing himself to turn away from her, he jogged toward his father. Jaeros didn't slow as he caught sight of Jaren approaching. If anything, he sped up, barely stopping in time to avoid crashing into him.

"Gods be damned," his father said, "I thought you were dead."

CHAPTER 3

JAREN

His Thyabathi poured out in a rush between heavy breaths as he clutched Jaren's shoulders in a death grip. His scent washed over him, reminding Jaren of freshly baked sticky buns, even this far from his kitchen.

"Your lack of confidence is comforting," he quipped.

Jaeros looked the same as he always did, the only part of his face unobscured by facial hair brightening as he smiled widely. "Maybe if you'd shown even a hint of self-preservation in the last twenty-five years, I'd have more."

Jaren's lips quirked up. "What are you doing in Ocridal of all places?"

He pulled his hands from Jaren's shoulders and rested them on his hips with a huff. "I was waiting for news of you, you fucking idiot."

Thank the gods, he thought, instantly relaxing. "So, nothing's wrong? Deds is all right?"

"Besides the stick he's had wedged up his ass recently?" Jaeros asked, his face practically glowing with mirth. "Yeah, he's fine. Worried about you, though."

Jaren snorted. Dedryn never worried about anything. He had two settings, neutral and angry. Normal feelings weren't his forte with anyone except his mate. They had that in common.

As if reading his mind, Jaeros smacked his shoulder with the back of his hand. "Stop that, he cares. He let me come here to look for you, didn't he?"

He dipped his head, unable to argue. He *was* surprised his father had let his mate travel so far without him. "I'm sorry I worried you both, then. There is..." his lips twitched. "There is a lot to tell."

His father's smile fell, and he hesitantly retreated a step, his humor fading as the creases in his forehead deepened. "That can't be good coming from you. Should I be worried?"

"No. Well, maybe a little once Deds finds out I woke up in an alley, beaten and robbed."

Jaeros's eyes dropped to his mouth, noticing the hint of a smile Jaren couldn't suppress at the memory. He'd been so fucking pissed. Leave it to his star-fire mate to abandon him in a piss-covered alley.

Jaeros raised a brow, clearly confused by his reaction, and muttered, "Maybe it's best you don't tell him that particular story."

Losing the battle, a deep laugh burst from Jaren's throat, and a sense of warmth immediately flickered near his heart in response. "It all worked out. I just got a little distracted."

"Eh, you can tell me all about it while we eat," Jaeros said, placing his hand between Jaren's shoulder blades and giving a gentle push. "But first, a bath. You reek of sea, sweat, and desperate self-pleasure."

Jaren planted his feet, shaking his head minutely when he tried to usher him forward. "Not yet. I have someone I'd like you to meet." When his father opened his mouth to argue, he held up a hand, halting his reply. "It can't wait. *She* can't wait."

He twisted his body to the side to give Jaeros an unobscured view of the dock behind him, Veralie's nerves kicking up as he did. Her heart was like a damn drum inside his chest, beating in time with his own. He couldn't remember the last time he'd felt true excitement.

But rather than take the hint and look behind him, Jaeros hissed a curse, waving a long finger in his face. "That better not mean what I think it does, boy. Because if you worried the shit out of me just to bring back a human woman you impregnated, I will kick your ass."

Jaren's brow lowered over his eyes, his excitement diminishing slightly. It was no secret that he'd taken physical lovers, especially to his fathers, but each one had been Magyki. And even then, he'd never once fucked one without the use of *truik elixir*. Veralie would be the first.

"There is only one female I'd see carry my child," he said,

glaring, "and she is no human woman."

Disbelief flickered in Jaeros's eyes, and he cleared his throat, glancing away sheepishly. His reaction was understandable. Jaren never brought up Veralie to anyone. Ever. He'd never wanted to until now.

"I came across something in Midpath that demanded my attention," he continued, pushing away his irritation. "I decided to track it back to Matherin. That is why I'm late."

His father reared back, holding his chest like his heart might fall out. "*You went into*—may the God of Death take me gently, do you hear my heart, Jaren? Do you know what could have happened if you were caught?"

He grinned wickedly. "I was."

Jaeros gaped at him, but he just raised an arm, pointing to where his mate stood tucked against a crate. As exciting as surprising Jaeros was, he was ready for it to be over so he could be back by her side.

His father followed his gaze, squinting his eyes in a habit he'd always had, even though his eyesight was as good as any Magyki. He looked confused for a moment and the strain around his eyes increased for a split second before they flew open, and he stumbled back.

"Vaneara? No, that's…that's not possible."

Veralie shuffled toward them, her anxiety grating against him. She was so used to hiding who she was that she had no idea what to do or how to act under their attention. What would she do when an entire capital was vying to get just a glimpse of her?

He clenched and unclenched his fists, ignoring the desire to rush to her side. He hated what the years on Aleron had done to her. She was the Daughter to the Throne, and those humans had taught her to feel nothing but shame. Including her mentor.

They'd crushed her self-worth, making her second guess everything she did and was. It killed him, and he was determined to change it. To see her gain it back.

Smiling encouragingly, he waited for her to look at him, but her eyes stayed pinned on his father. Her heart rate picked up exponentially, and he frowned, glancing over his shoulder.

What was his father doing to have snagged her attention so thoroughly? He'd just barely caught sight of Jaeros's pallid face when his scent slammed into him like a fucking hammer to his senses, making his muscles instantly contract.

Fear.

Jaren gripped the pommel of his dagger, taking a step in Veralie's direction, and frantically scanned their surroundings. He threw out his senses, but there were too many Magyki bustling around for him to pick up anything specific.

"What is it?" he asked, tightening his hold. "What do you see?"

He was seconds away from unsheathing it and sprinting to her when his father finally spoke, his words shooting pure ice through his veins.

"Gods have mercy, Jaren. What have you done?"

EITHAN

EXHALING THROUGH HIS NOSE, HE BRACED BOTH PALMS against the floor and shoved up, peeling his face from the cold surface.

He blinked to clear his vision, focusing on the nicks and scrapes in the floor to distract himself from the disgust blazing a path through the remaining sliver of his soul.

He took a slow, steady breath and held it.

One. Two. Three. Four. Five.

His body begged to give out; his head, legs, and ribs trembling under the effort of moving.

One. Two. Three. Four. Five.

The throbbing in his head punctuated each number as he counted, but he ignored it. Pain had been his constant companion for as long as he could remember. It was an old friend he recognized and understood.

It was the humiliation of it all that made him want to rage at the world. To grip it at the roots and pull, making everything around him as dead as he was.

Inhale, hold, exhale. It was nothing he couldn't handle. He just needed to focus.

"You got blood on my carpet."

Eithan glanced at the midnight blue runner to his left. *Yes, Sulian, that's what happens when you order someone to be beaten next to it.* That's why *he* worked in the cells, where there were grates. It was common fucking sense.

"Forgive me, father." He smoothed out his grimace, molding it into a mask devoid of any feeling.

Sulian might very well take insult and opt to teach him another lesson for appearing so uncaring about the carnage of the first one, but he'd gladly take another before giving the fucker the satisfaction of seeing him react.

He pushed up farther, biting his tongue until he tasted fresh blood, and straightened his spine. He slid his knees underneath him, keeping his head bowed and forcing himself to ignore Sulian's amused huff. The fucking asshole was loving this— seeing him kneel at his feet like a disobedient pet.

"Leave us."

Eithan didn't move a muscle, knowing the order wasn't for him. He listened to the lone guard's retreating footsteps, then heard the doors open and close. Yennin. The newest guard to do Sulian's bidding and assist him with Eithan's *lessons*.

He didn't know why Sulian ever bothered sending his men away whenever he wanted to talk. It wasn't like Yennin could reiterate anything he overheard anyway. The man, along with every other one of Sulian's personal guards, was not only illiterate, but also missing their tongues.

They were wealthy beyond measure for it and got away with just about anything on the street. Violence, bribery, rape. Sulian turned a blind eye to all of it as long as they stayed loyal to *him*.

But even so, Eithan couldn't imagine willingly giving up his tongue for a man who wouldn't know how to use his own if a woman sat on his fucking face.

"Some days I wonder if you are worth it. You'd do well to remember you are not my only option."

The words disrupted his thoughts, skittering through him, searching for a crack in his mask to burrow under and exploit. But they'd find no such thing.

There was nothing Sulian could say that he hadn't already said in the last two decades of Eithan's life. His foul words had stopped sticking long ago.

"I understand, father. Tell me what I must do to regain your favor, and I will do it." The words tasted like ash on his tongue, but he meant them. He'd do whatever it took to keep Sulian from looking at him too closely.

There was a pause, the rhythmic tapping of Sulian's fingers on his throne the only sound filling the silence before he spoke.

"I no longer see the point. I order you to marry the Magyki. You fail. I order you to retrieve her. You fail. I order you to bring me your treacherous guard. You fail. An untrained bitch follows commands better than you."

Eithan raised his head in time to see the death glare Sulian was sending his way. It didn't bother him in the least. The feeling was fucking mutual.

"Vera will return, Father. I would bet my life on it."

"For your sake, I certainly hope so." He gripped the arms of his throne, leaning forward to spit, "I want Bhasura under my thumb, and I cannot have that when my sole heir fails at controlling one gods damn female."

"I understand," Eithan repeated, a sense of calm washing over him despite the veiled threat. He may be having to wait longer than he'd originally planned, but he'd have her. He was sure of it. The second Vera received his letters, she'd come running back, and he'd be ready with open arms.

Sulian was determined to use King Vesstan's daughter to put Bhasura on a leash, but what he didn't know was it'd be her very return that would sign his father's death warrant. And Eithan, for one, couldn't fucking wait.

HIS GUARD, WES Coleman waited just outside the doors when Sulian finally released him. Coleman's posture was stiff and angry as one hand white-knuckled the pommel of his sword. But he stayed silent, falling into step with him as he passed.

Eithan rolled his shoulders, trying to unstick the parts of his tunic that clung to him, but he only succeeded in sending spikes of pain up his neck. The tacky film of sweat and blood had him fighting every urge in his body to rip the clothing off. He wanted to burn every gods damn piece of fabric, down to his boots.

The image pulled a sudden chuckle from his lips. Wouldn't that be something? He could only imagine the looks he'd get, strutting through the palace butt naked and beaten. It'd certainly give the snakes in noble's clothing something to talk about.

He felt, more than saw, Coleman side-eye him as they made their way through the palace's maze of hallways. He didn't think the man had stopped frowning once since he'd seen him exit the throne room with a bloodied smile on his face.

"Speak freely, Coleman. I've known you my entire life. I can sense when you're brimming with judgmental opinions," he said, taking pity on him.

His guard rolled his eyes and sighed, removing his hand from his sword to gesture toward him. "I hate seeing you like this. It's my duty to protect you. Every time you enter that room without me, you force my hand to fail."

I order you to marry the Magyki. You fail.

Sulian's words swirled around him, and he ground his teeth together, hardening his shield to keep them out. His mask must have slipped because Coleman snapped his face forward and cleared his throat.

"I apologize for overstepping. It was not my place to say anything."

Eithan shook his head, sidestepping a young servant ladened with an armful of folded bedding. "You have nothing to apologize for, I told you to speak freely. But my business with my father is my own. You need not concern yourself over it."

"It's not usually…"

"This obvious?"

Coleman nodded, pressing his lips into a thin line.

He was right. Besides a few harsher lessons when Eithan was younger, Sulian typically had him punished in ways that weren't outwardly noticeable to the court. As much as his doting father detested him, it reflected poorly to have his heir wander the grounds with a black eye.

"I knew what would happen if I returned without Vera. It's nothing I didn't ask for," he said with a shrug. What he didn't add was that he'd taken the punishment for his entire guard.

"And Gibson?"

Eithan's eye twitched, but he otherwise kept his face neutral. "What about him?"

Coleman rubbed a hand across his jaw, hesitating. "Has his...sentence for aiding her escape been carried out?"

Eithan reached out and grasped the man's shoulder, squeezing once. He may have trusted Gibson, but Coleman had worked closely with him for years. "He died with honor, Wes. I promise."

Coleman nodded again, his face tight. Eithan hated this part of the game, the constant lying and hiding. Especially to Coleman, whom he'd known his entire life and considered a true friend.

He just wanted to be honest about his desires and plans and have his men still proudly follow him. But out of all of them, Gibson was the only one he could completely confide in, and the irony of that wasn't lost on him.

Thankfully, it was about time he checked on the rogue guard anyway. They were due for a chat, and he could desperately use the distraction.

So, when they finally approached his rooms, he paused, nodding his head back down the hallway. "You're dismissed for the afternoon."

Coleman started, turning toward him. "Your Highness—"

"There's no need for you to stand outside my door all day, I'll be fine. I'm just going to rest and clean up, and then seek company much more stimulating than yourself," he lied, giving an exaggerated wink. "So, unless you'd care to join?"

It wasn't a complete lie. He *was* planning on seeking more stimulating company, just not the kind of stimulation Coleman would ever understand.

Coleman's face puckered, but he chuckled, amusement replacing his hesitancy. "I must pass on the offer. I'm afraid I just don't feel the same way about you, Your Highness."

"Shame. I've been told a night with me is quite memorable."

Coleman's eyes darted around his face, no doubt counting the many colorful bruises now adorning it. "I once tripped and landed face first in horse shit. That, too, was quite memorable."

An authentic laugh burst from Eithan's chest, surprising them both. "Fair enough. I suppose I'll just stick to the bath then."

"You'll summon me as soon as you need me?"

"Of course," he said, tipping his head toward the hallway again. "Now, go. Enjoy some down time."

He waited until Coleman rounded the corner, and then he spun away from his doors, heading in the opposite direction.

Moving Gibson to the palace infirmary had been foolhardy and risky, but having a healer tend to him and see Eithan regularly visit was imperative. He'd learned long ago that the key to a strong story was in the breadcrumbs one left along the way.

As the Crown Prince, he couldn't exactly be seen carrying a traitorous guard through the halls—especially one who was supposed to be dead—so he'd had to risk trusting part of the truth to Hayes, but it'd been worth it.

Hayes, of course, hadn't batted an eye, happily marching into the cell to throw an unconscious Gibson over his shoulder. He could be a loose cannon at times, such as when he'd snapped and attacked Vera that day, but he was loyal in the ways that counted.

As a bastard born nobody raised in a brothel, Hayes was well aware that being a member of Eithan's guard was the most power he'd ever have. So, although Eithan would never confide in the man, he at least trusted him enough to keep his mouth shut about Gibson.

Feeling impatient, he picked up his pace as much as his battered body allowed and descended the final staircase leading to the infirmary. He counted each step to distract himself from the stabs of pain radiating up his legs, and rounded the corner, nearly barreling into a young woman racing up them.

She squeaked, backtracking, and tripping down a step before plastering herself to the wall. He noticed the instant her eyes saw past his appearance and took note of *who* he was.

Her blue eyes widened, and she ducked her head, apologizing profusely. By the way her legs shook, she looked seconds away from falling to her knees.

It was a sight he'd have normally indulged in. Trading a few smiles with a pretty woman followed by a night of gaping mouths, spread thighs, and an orchestra of moans. It wouldn't be the first time, or even the twentieth. He had a reputation for a reason.

But he felt no such pull now, pretty though she was. He smiled and tipped his head, turning to continue down without a second thought. He could certainly use a night of pleasure and release, but not from any woman here.

He was a betrothed man, after all.

CHAPTER 4

JAREN

He whipped his head back, confusion swirling as warning signals blared in his head. What had *he* done?

Ignoring the lingering pull to grab Veralie and guard against some unseen threat, he widened his stance and spoke slowly. "What I've done is found my mate. Alive."

The shock he'd expected, the delayed joy and excitement, never came. Jaeros just squeezed his eyes shut as if in pain, and pressed his hand to his chest, whispering, "You damn fool."

"What the fuck is that supposed to mean?" Jaren snapped, moving to stand between them. He wasn't sure if his father had been speaking to him or himself, but either way something was very wrong.

Jaeros hadn't uttered a word about Veralie other than to call her Vaneara. He hadn't seemed even remotely surprised at seeing her, other than seeing her *there*. It didn't make any sense. There was no way his father actually thought she was the late queen. He was just in shock.

"I know it's unbelievable," he said, tipping his head back in her direction, "but that's really Veralie. *My* Veralie."

Jaeros dropped his hand, clenching and unclenching both at his sides as his eyes frantically darted around them. The fear in his scent hadn't diminished in the least.

Starting to feel a sense of unease creep in, Jaren tried again. "She's been alive this entire time, Jae. Living on fucking Aleron of all places."

"And for good reason." His reply was quiet, no more than a muttered phrase, but he might as well have screamed it at the top of his lungs.

Jaren froze, his entire world stopping at those four simple words. Pressure built in his head until everything around him seemed to fade away. The sound of the crowd milling about, the ocean air whipping against his face, the heart pounding in his chest. It all froze in time as his father's words struck him. As they dug in and ripped him open, flaying his skin and tissue as they went.

Jaeros had known where she was? No, that...that wasn't possible. Because if he'd known she was on Aleron that meant this entire time, all these years, he'd also known she'd been—

Horror speared through him, taking every memory, every moment and every word he'd thought to be true, and dousing it all in poison. Black dots spread into his vision, and he swallowed hard, fighting the bile surging up his throat.

Veralie's scent washed over him a second before he felt her approach, her confusion mixing and compounding with his own. Yet his father just continued to fucking stand there, eyeing the Magyki around them, unaware of the soul wound he'd just inflicted. As if he didn't even realize he'd spoken the foul words aloud.

"You knew," Jaren said, his voice thick and hoarse.

Jaeros's eyes snapped to his, blinking back a fog like he'd been so deep within his own thoughts that he'd forgotten he was there. "What?"

Everything suddenly made sense. How she'd wound up on Aleron, the group she'd said had snuck her there and made a deal with Sulian. All the pieces were adding up, forming a spiked truth that was going to tear him apart.

He'd wondered. Wondered how she could have lived when his fathers had been so sure of her death. They'd loved her almost as much as he had. They would've checked her a hundred times, a thousand times, trying everything to save her.

And apparently, they had. He was such a fucking fool. The lump in his throat grew hot, scorching him and turning his words raspy and broken. "You told me she was dead."

Jaeros flinched at whatever he saw in his gaze, and then he looked over Jaren's shoulder to Veralie, who was standing just behind him, tensed like a bow. A mixture of determination and sadness filled his father's expression when he finally spoke.

"This is not the place to have this conversation."

The fuck it wasn't. He lunged, gripping the front of Jaeros's tunic, and glared down at the male he'd respected his entire life. The male who'd followed him into the woods the night Veralie had been born, who'd sat him down and explained what his mating bond would mean, who'd gifted him his daggers and told him how proud he was.

He tightened his hold, desperate to be wrong. Desperate for an explanation, *any* explanation, for what had been done to him. To her. "Tell me I'm wrong. Tell me you didn't know she was alive."

Jaeros's face stayed firm, his soft expressions and playful humor nowhere in sight. "For once in your life, listen to me, boy. This is not the place."

Jaren bared his teeth, snarling down at him. "Tell me the *fucking truth!*"

He tried to shove him off, but Jaren held on to his tunic, refusing to release him until he heard the venomous words straight from the fucking serpent's mouth.

His father's face broke, despair and agony blanketing him, but Jaren only snarled louder. "Say. It."

"Yes," he said, low enough that no one around would hear unless they actively tried. "At least, we knew she left that way. We had our reasons, and I swear on the gods we will talk, but please, Jaren, get her out of sight."

Jaren's fingers released the fabric, his hands dropping to his sides like dead weights as that one word hammered into his skull.

We.

Jaeros stepped back, his body tense and alert, whether in reaction to Jaren's emotions or what he feared from the crowd, he didn't know. He didn't fucking care. He focused on the second beat in his chest, needing to feel her presence and remind himself that she was indeed here, with him.

Veralie's emotions washed over him, and his entire body went taut. There was still confusion, but it was buried under layers of worry, sadness, and pain. Not for herself, but for him. His mate had been cast away by those who were supposed to love her most, yet her heart was breaking for *him*.

As if, after fifteen years, she was so fucking used to males trampling all over her life, Jaeros's admission didn't even surprise her. The knowledge snapped something inside him that he didn't think he'd ever get back.

"You did this to her."

Jaeros's face darkened, his fear dying out as his own, rare anger came to the surface. "Everything we've done was to protect you both."

"Protect?" A hollow sound broke the air as Jaren tipped his head back and laughed. "Were you protecting me when I spent months wanting to ram my dagger through my heart? Did you protect me from the shame of not only killing my *aitanta*, but the Daughter to the Throne? From the shame of furthering the taint of my home?"

Jaeros blanched before slashing his hand through the air, hissing, "Lower your gods damn voice."

A corner of his brain screamed at him, warning him to be careful, but he couldn't obey it. He couldn't tamper down the feral rage building and coursing within him. He was consumed by it.

"Were you *protecting* her when she was abandoned in a strange land? When they held her down and mutilated her?"

Jaeros's eyes shot back over his shoulder, his face draining of color as horror flashed across it. He may not have been able to see her ears tucked under her hood, but he wasn't stupid. There was only one way for a Magyki to blend in on a continent of humans.

The thought enraged Jaren all over again. An image flashed across his mind of a five-year-old Veralie, with her dusting of freckles and mischievous gray eyes, screaming in agony. She swore she had no memory of it, but that didn't keep away the nightmare of her calling out for him while she bled on a table.

Jaeros dropped his voice to barely above a whisper, an almost soul-deep exhaustion replacing any anger he'd had. "We didn't have a choice, Jaren. You would have demanded to go with her, and you were barely more than a child."

"She was my *MATE!*" He roared, gripping his dagger and barreling down into his power with blood-red focus. He was going to fucking kill him.

The rippled blade made it all of an inch out of its sheath before a hand wrapped around his own, squeezing harshly and pushing it back down.

"Jaren," Veralie said, a clear warning in her voice. But it was the erratic thump of her heart that ripped him out of his frenzy. His nostrils flared as he took her in, and he whipped his head around them, noticing the crowd that had begun to form.

"Fuck," he spit, releasing his dagger to link his fingers through hers. The more his head cleared, the more he realized he could hear murmurs as more Magyki stopped, angling to see what was happening.

They needed to go now before he did something even more stupid, like ripping out Jaeros Barilias's heart and gifting it to his *aitanta* in offering. There were many positives to his fathers being well-known, but this was not one of them.

He shot another glare at Jaeros, whose hands were hovering over his own blades as he considered the growing crowd. Jaren hated to admit it, but the asshole had been right about one thing, he needed to get her out of sight. Now.

He inhaled, filling his lungs with fire and iron, and squeezed Veralie's fingers hard enough to make her suck in a breath. If he could bury down his overwhelming self-hatred for fifteen years, he could control his gods damn fucking temper long enough to not publicly murder his father.

Taking a deep breath, he looked at Veralie, the silver of her eyes keeping him tethered to the present. "Keep your head down, little star. We need to go."

She nodded, but before she could open her mouth to say anything, another voice beat her to it, making his eye twitch with the effort to restrain himself.

"Will you be staying at your usual place?"

He clenched his jaw, refusing to answer. The male had a fucking death wish. Did he really think he'd tell him where they were going? But his silence must have been answer enough because in his peripheral, his father nodded once.

"I'll meet you there tomorrow, and we'll talk. Be careful."

Jaren's lip curled, and he started to turn back, but Veralie yanked hard on his arm, catching him off guard and causing him to stumble into her.

Righting himself, he shot her a glare that was meant more for the male behind them than her. Then he exhaled roughly, swallowing down the threat he'd been about to spew, and beelined through the crowd, letting his hatred fuel his steps.

VERA

SHE STILL COULDN'T BELIEVE SHE WAS HERE, ON *BHASURA*. Her real home where she was free to walk around without hiding, without donning her alter-ego's mask and pretending she was a boy named Varian when she wasn't.

Maybe that was why she'd gotten so angry when Jaren had demanded she wear her hood. It wasn't the playful way he'd done it that had upset her, it was stepping foot onto a land where she thought she'd be able to breathe, only to be asked to hold her breath again. It'd stung.

From Jaren's ship, Ocridal hadn't looked all that different than any city or town she'd seen on Aleron. It wasn't until they'd docked, and she'd leaned over the side that she'd become speechless. Where Aleronians wore dull, neutral tones, the diverse Magyki bustling about were dressed in a multitude of colors that she'd only ever seen before on royalty.

The sight of their pointed ear tips, an array of brown, golden, and ivory hues, peeking out through their different hairstyles, had caused her heart to leap. Top that with the sheer number of voices speaking a language she was still trying to grasp, and it'd been unreal. Like a tale straight out of a children's story.

She'd immediately wanted to wander the streets and see more. To take in every sight and see how the Magyki interacted and how it might differ from what she'd seen in the markets of Matherin and Midpath. Even with all the stories Jaren had told her on their journey, she still knew so little about their world and had so many questions.

She'd never realized just how little she knew about her own heritage until now, and she couldn't help but feel ashamed. She didn't even know what foods were popular or whether they drank ale, let alone whether they prayed or what festivals they celebrated. But now that she was here, she wanted to know it all.

However, it was becoming increasingly difficult to take in any amount of detail when she was being dragged at high speed through the city like a misbehaving child.

Jaren was a force to be reckoned with. He darted through the streets, pulling her along and launching curses at any vendors who dared to call out to them. She was honestly surprised when he finally came to a halt at one merchant long enough to purchase them clean clothes. Not that she was complaining.

And even that didn't go smoothly. He'd haggled with the elderly merchant, acting every bit the asshole his reputation claimed him to be. She'd eyed him warily, unsure how long they had before Jaren exploded.

She didn't blame him for his anger, but it also made it really hard to understand how she actually felt about everything that had just happened. All she could feel was Jaren. The turmoil of his emotions had flooded into her until she felt like a minnow within her own body, lost in the sea of his rage.

She felt angry, hurt, ashamed, and broken, yet not a single one of those emotions was her own. It was like nothing she'd ever experienced before.

The only emotion she knew for certain was hers was confusion. She hadn't been able to catch everything they'd said, but what she *had* understood, hadn't helped.

Jaeros Barilias had looked exactly how Jaren had described him. An inch or two shorter than his son, he was tan skinned, with long, dark hair tied at his nape, and a matching trimmed beard, both speckled with gray. Given the lifespan of most Magyki, she could only guess he was much older than he appeared.

His nose was slightly too big for his face, and his oaky brown eyes had practically been mini celebrations in his face when he'd seen his son. Bright, shimmering, and full of the kind of relief she imagined only a parent could possess.

He'd looked exactly like the sweet, nurturing man Jaren had described him as. So why had all that joy died out the instant he'd spotted her? He hadn't acted like someone who'd loved her as much as Jaren had claimed.

None of it made sense, and she had so many questions she wanted answers to, but she wouldn't do that to Jaren. One look at him told her if she even tried to bring it up, he'd fracture right before her eyes.

She didn't know what to do to help him. It wasn't like she could ask him about his feelings right there in the middle of the street. He wasn't much of a talker, even in private.

He loaded up their new belongings and glanced down at her as he snatched her hand again. The anger still in his eyes crushed her. It darkened their hue, making them muddied and dull, and not at all like the bright, fierce green she so loved.

Heading for the closest food vendor, he quickly purchased two meat pies, barely placing one into her hand before they were moving again. He didn't speak a word to her as he tore into his meal and dragged her around the corner, finally spotting their lodgings.

By the time he'd checked them in and led her in their room for the night, he was practically vibrating with everything he was pushing down. It was coursing inside him like a violent storm. All it would take was one thing to set him off, and she knew in her very being that he'd take out everyone around him.

She was overwhelmed just by the echoes of everything he was feeling. She couldn't even imagine how he was coping under its full weight.

She remembered the hurt she'd felt when she'd learned that Elric had kept her identity a secret from her. The way her heart had twisted under the knowledge that he hadn't trusted her or cared enough to tell her the truth. But this was far crueler. Jaren had been betrayed in the worst possible way.

He tossed their belongings near the unlit hearth, not even seeming to notice or care when their supplies spilled out, as he collapsed into the lone chair. He immediately leaned over his knees and began yanking at the ties on his boots.

She approached him slowly, like she might a skittish animal, not sure if he wanted her around or not. It was odd to be irrevocably tied to someone, but still not know simple things about them, like how they preferred to process thoughts, or how they relaxed.

"Let me," she said softly, lowering herself to kneel at his feet.

She set her hands on his much larger ones, prying them away when he didn't budge them on his own. She worked the first boot off, taking her time while she analyzed their bond, searching. Anger was his most potent emotion, raw and sharp. But just underneath that—devastation.

"Take it out on me."

His eyes, which had lowered to watch her hands, flicked up. "What did you say?"

Switching to his other foot, she repeated, "Take it out on me. I can feel it rising in you, Jaren. It's not going to end well for anyone, including you, if it breaks free. Let me help you."

He waited until she'd set the second boot next to the chair and lowered his leg before he leaned over her. He was close enough that his breath fanned the stray curls around her ears, but she couldn't quite place the expression on his face as he looked at her.

"And just how would you like me to take it out on you, little star?"

"I thought—" she felt it then, like a battering ram, as he stared down at her kneeling between his legs. *Need.*

It was desperate and rough, spearing through her and taking hold until her own arousal joined it, and she couldn't breathe around the combined potency.

She lurched forward, her hands landing on his thighs to steady her body. A shiver raced down her spine, and she exhaled jaggedly. She'd meant sparring, maybe trading a few punches to raise his adrenaline and release some of his mindless aggression. It hadn't even occurred to her that sex could have the same outcome for him.

Just because *she* would have sought to grab a sword and train as her way of coping, didn't mean that's what *he* wanted. What he needed.

An image of that night in Midpath flashed through her mind. When she'd touched him. The look of blissful ecstasy that'd taken over his face as she'd stroked him, the arch of his neck as he'd tipped his head back and cursed. The way his throat had bobbed, and his hands had fisted like it'd taken everything in him to restrain himself.

She shuddered, sliding her hands higher, memorizing the way his muscles felt beneath her palms. Then she pushed up, burying her nerves to the furthest corner of her mind, and brushed her lips along his scruffy jaw, smiling when it tightened in response.

"Bathe with me," she whispered, thankful when the words came out steadier than she felt.

But his reply was immediate and harsh. "No."

She pulled back, confused. She could *feel* how badly he wanted her. The desire had been there for days, simmering just under the surface, but now it was pouring out of him in heady plumes, practically drowning her senses.

Her brow creased. He'd told her the point of an emotional bond between Magyki was so that mates could anticipate each other's needs, and she thought she had. But given the way he was glowering at her, she was apparently as bad at that as she was at controlling her power.

Just because he was physically attracted to her, didn't mean he wanted her *right now*. Gods, she was an idiot.

He pressed his thumb on her chin, pushing down until her lip popped out from between her teeth. "You misunderstand me."

He took his time, trailing the backs of his fingers across her cheek and down her neck, leaving gooseflesh in his path. Then he curled his hand behind her neck, gripping her plait and yanking her head back. His other slipped over her throat, squeezing.

"I don't just want you, Veralie. I need you so badly, it's a visceral pain stabbing and twisting every inch of my body. I can't fucking think past my need for you."

She placed her hands on his wrists, whispering past the firm pressure on her throat. "Then let me help you."

"No," he repeated, pulling harder on her hair until tears stung her eyes. "Because I am not in the right frame of mind to be gentle with you, little star."

"I can take it."

As if in agreement, heat flooded her core, and his eyes darkened. "I would hurt you," he said, squeezing harder until spots danced in her vision. "I *want* to hurt someone."

She darted her tongue out to wet her lips, ignoring the way her skin flushed and her heart picked up. Something deep within her raised its head at his words and the threat within them, humming in anticipation.

"I said, I can take it, Jaren. I *want* to take it."

His body lurched toward her, almost against its will, before he suddenly growled, closing his eyes and releasing her. With a curse, he shot up out of the chair, putting several feet of space between them as he stared down at her kneeling form.

"Go enjoy the bath, Veralie," he snapped. His voice was thick, and she could have sworn his hands shook as he fisted them, but before she could formulate a reply, he'd already spun away, practically sprinting to the door.

Vera sat back on her heels, watching him slam the door

behind him as he left—sans boots—like he'd truly rather stand on a city street barefoot than be anywhere near the same vicinity as her.

She swallowed hard, shifting to sit flat on the cold floor. He was going through a lot, she knew that. But try as she might to remind herself that it wasn't about her, she still couldn't completely brush off the lingering sting of his rejection.

CHAPTER 5

VERA

Bouncing on her toes, she watched the innkeeper with intense focus as he picked up the last, empty bucket and trudged to the door.

She tried to seem calm as she gave a quick wave of her hand and thanked him in Thyabathi, but the second he slipped out, she sprinted to the bathing room.

She plunged her hand into the water, squealing at the warmth that greeted her fingertips. She hadn't had a real bath in weeks. Not since before…well, before Jaren.

And even then, she'd been lucky if the water had still been lukewarm by the time she'd finished filling it and climbed in. This was definitely the first time she hadn't had to stand by a hearth, heating it, herself.

Wasting no time, she untucked her tunic from her trousers

and yanked the hem above her head, nearly breaking her neck in her eagerness.

She held the garment out, wrinkling her nose and tossing it to the floor before moving on to her trousers and undergarments. She kicked the soiled pile across the floor, stifling the desire to burn it all. Having a good sense of smell was no blessing sometimes.

Naked as the day she was born, she picked up the new clothing Jaren had purchased her, running her fingers over the soft fabric before setting the stack next to the tub. It was going to feel like a damn cloud compared to the outfit she'd been wearing.

She'd never take clean clothes for granted again.

Twisting to lift her leg over the lip of the tub, she started, losing her balance and nearly toppling backward when she noticed someone moving in her peripheral.

She leapt back, arms raised, prepared to launch herself at the intruder. If that innkeeper came back, thinking he could take advantage of her being alone and naked, she was going to bash his head into the wall. Repeatedly.

But no sooner had she shifted to lunge, her arms fell slack at her sides, and she blinked. Then blinked again. "Holy Aleron."

It wasn't another person. It was *her*. A life-size version, to be exact, reflected at her in the largest mirror she'd ever seen.

She stepped closer, mesmerized. The mirror had to be at least five-feet tall and was tucked against the wall with a gorgeous bronze frame. She shifted and turned, watching in fascination as her image moved along with her.

Growing up with only her small opaque mirror, she wasn't sure what to do with the clarity in which she could suddenly see her entire body. It was like seeing herself for the first time in twenty years. She slid her fingers up her stomach and over her breasts, grimacing at how her dirty, broken fingernails looked against her skin.

No wonder Jaren had rejected her advances. She looked like she'd spent the last year living off the streets. Her fingers trailed higher at the thought of him, tracing the dip of her shoulder.

She could still feel the ghost of his teeth sinking into the flesh there, feel his fingers circling her clit while he did, wringing the most intense pleasure she'd ever had from her body. Her center tightened at just the memory of it. It'd been erotic. A term she hadn't understood until that moment.

She traced her fingertips over the place on her shoulder he'd pierced. A spot that was now nothing but smooth, unblemished skin. Despite his wishes, they hadn't even made it to Aleron's coast before she'd chosen to heal it.

Jaren wanted to advertise their bond to the world, shout it from the rooftops and mark it upon her skin, but she just wasn't quite there yet. She'd claimed him, yes, and she didn't regret it, but she just didn't know how to feel about being branded like some sort of possession.

She might not ever feel like true royalty, but that's what

every Magyki would see her as. Their *Nlem Snadzend* who'd been raised by their enemy.

She didn't want that. She wanted to be seen as strong and confident, a female who could stand on her own two feet and wield a weapon when needed. And she wanted to *earn* it. Not as a Barilias mate, but as herself.

She wasn't a possession that needed to be branded, nor was she some damsel in need of protection. She could protect herself.

Shaking her head, she let her hand drop to her side. Jaren would be furious when he found out what she'd done, but he'd get over it.

Eventually.

When she grew the courage to tell him.

Turning from her reflection, she finally stepped into the tub, lowering herself down until everything but her head sank below the surface. It engulfed her like a warm embrace, and an embarrassingly loud moan slipped from her lips. Gods, that felt good.

She closed her eyes, filling her lungs with as much air as they could hold, and slid the rest of the way down until she was fully submerged. Practically attacking herself, she rubbed vigorously at her face and neck, determined to come out a different color than she'd gone in.

When her skin stung and her chest started to burn, she pushed up, heaving in air. But the second she did, her body seized, and she gasped, slipping back under. It felt like she'd inhaled jagged shards of ice straight into her lungs.

Water sealed around her, ramming up her nostrils and down her throat, and she thrashed, flailing her arms until her face finally broke the surface again.

She choked, spitting water, and snapped her eyes open, blinking away the burn. But instead of the walls of the bathing room, she was met with solid darkness. She kicked, trying to locate the bottom of the tub to hoist herself out, but it wasn't there.

She tried again, throwing her body around as a panic attack clawed at her chest, seeping into her mind, and threatening to take over. This wasn't happening. This wasn't happening.

She spread her arms, slapping at the water as she blindly searched for the edge, but it was like the tub had completely disappeared. As if she'd never been in it to begin with.

She cried out, trying not to vomit as she kicked her legs back and forth, desperately trying to keep her nose above the water. She had no idea how to swim. Elric had described it to her once when she was a child, but she couldn't remember anything he'd said.

Was she supposed to chop her legs and circle her arms, or was it the other way around?

She fought with every ounce of energy she had while tears streamed down her face, blending with the water covering her skin. But no matter how hard she tried, she continued falling under. Again. And again.

Each time she broke the surface, she darted her eyes

around, ignoring how badly they burned, and tried to figure out where the fuck she was. But she couldn't see *anything*. She couldn't even make out her own arms or the water she was surrounded by. Nothing.

It was pitch black. As if every light from every corner of the world had been snuffed out. Her heart beat faster and faster, her panic rising while her body struggled to continue moving in the freezing temperature.

She needed to find shore, or even just a tree branch. Something. Anything. She kicked harder, shoving her head back above and urging her body to move forward.

Her body refused to listen, and her mind started to spiral out of control as the water, again, slipped past her chin. Gods, she was going to die. She was going to die alone out here. She cried out, her words gurgling as more water entered her mouth. "Oh gods, help me."

There was a sudden flare in her chest, a dose of scalding heat that kickstarted her adrenaline and made her feel nauseated all at the same time. She suddenly felt like she was late for something, but worse. Like she was in a nightmare, and try as she might to run, she couldn't get her legs to move fast enough. It was like...

Jaren.

It was Jaren. She couldn't see him or catch his scent on the wind, but she could feel him. His utter panic. He was somewhere out in the void, but she didn't know where or if he was even safe.

"Jaren!"

His name tore from her throat, scratching her vocal cords even as water filled her mouth, muffling the sound. He didn't respond. She could hear nothing but her labored breathing and the sound of water assaulting her exhausted body.

She choked, crying out over and over, her head pounding and eyes bulging from her effort. But no matter how hard she screamed, how hard his heart beat next to hers, he never responded.

As her fear morphed into unfiltered terror, Elric's words began to slam into her, like he was standing over her shoulder, whacking her hands with a sparring sword.

"What are you flinching for, girl?"

She cowered, staring up at the man towering over her with a weapon. "I'm scared," she whispered.

"Good. You should be. Only an idiot or a liar would say they aren't scared of the sharp end of a sword. Are you an idiot?"

She shook her head vigorously, and he bent down to her level, flipping the blade and offering her the handle.

"Fear is a flame, Vera. It cannot be extinguished by will alone. You can let it burn you alive, or you can do something with it."

She closed her eyes, hiccupping back a sob, and searched for her power. The power she was so used to ignoring that she forgot she even had. She tried to coax it out to strengthen her limbs, but her mind was too splintered to focus.

Past the point of caution, she drove straight down into the center. She grabbed at it frantically, ripping it out of every vein and forcing it through her entire body.

There was a pause. Like the heavy silence following lightning, just before the thunder sounds, the frigid air seeming to still in anticipation. Then light exploded from her chest, illuminating her surroundings and pumping wave after wave of adrenaline into her.

The water she was in was not endless after all, but a lake centered in a cavernous room. The surrounding walls were on every side and extended so high that even with her enhanced eyesight, she could barely make out the ceiling.

And everywhere, intermixed among the rocky surface, were what looked like glass shards of every color. They hung from the ceiling and walls, down to where the ground met the shore.

It was the most beautiful sight she'd ever seen. Something that could have been breathtakingly serene, if it weren't for the lake of death trying to drown her.

Knowing her hasty power draw wouldn't strengthen her for long, she began her efforts anew, kicking and slicing her arms through the water, aiming for the faraway shore, even as the light began to fade.

She searched for her power again, but just as she reached in, someone—or some*thing*—circled her waist. And before she could even take a warning breath, the hold on her waist yanked, pulling her under.

Water pressed in on her from every side, choking and trapping her all at once. She bucked and threw her body around, trying to loosen the vise-like hold around her body, but more water shot down her throat, and a voice spoke behind her.

"Hello."

She tried to turn toward it, but her limbs refused to obey, and her eyes began to close even as she fought to open them.

"My name is Alean Arenaris, and I seek entrance."

That voice. Who was—

"VERALIE!"

She lurched up, twisting just in time to vomit water all over the floor. Her chest convulsed as she heaved again and again. She squeezed her eyes shut, digging her fingers into her temples. Her head was pounding, and her eyes felt like she'd poured cleaning polish in them. What the fuck just happened?

"You're all right. I got you, Veralie, I promise. *Yinlanem dupye, a li.*"

She heaved one last time, and her chest burned as her lungs worked overtime to bring in air. Her body was shaky and limp, like every minuscule amount of energy had been siphoned right out of her.

She slumped forward, not realizing she was cradled in Jaren's lap until her forehead hit his body with a wet thud. He didn't say a word. He only held her closer, tucking her legs in and stroking a hand down her spine.

Deep breath in and out. She wasn't drowning. There was no endless void. She was here. She was alive. Taking another wobbly breath, she got out, "Wh–what…happened?"

"I feel like I'm the one who should be asking that," he said, resting his chin on the top of her head.

"You scared the shit out of me, Veralie. I thought someone was attacking you," he added, holding her tighter. "Fuck, I never should've left you alone."

She raised her head, blinking the last few dots out of her vision. "No one attacked me."

He threaded his hands in her sopping hair, gripping her head and staring down at her. His eyes were the fiercest she'd ever seen them, and his heart was racing as fast as her own.

"I thought I'd lost you. I was outside talking to a trader about roads when your terror shot through me like a fucking arrow, nearly dropping me to my knees. And then you screamed."

He swallowed. "Enemies of flesh and bone I can handle. I'll cut out their hearts and lay them at your feet, but I can't fight gods damn water."

She chuckled, but the sound came out raspy, burning up her ravaged throat. "Some mate you are if you can't even do that."

He didn't crack a smile. His nails dug into the tender skin behind her ears, and his emerald gaze seared into her. The pain pulsing out of him destroyed her.

"Tell me what happened."

She frowned, pulling away from his grasp and looking around the room as she tried to remember it all. The floor was drenched, and her once-clean pile of clothes was saturated from when he'd fought to yank her out.

Oh. *Oh.*

CHAPTER 6

VERA

eyes wide, she looked down, her pulse picking up for an entirely different reason. "Um."

"Your nakedness is the least of my worries."

That made one of them. Crossing her arms over her breasts, she discreetly peeked to make sure both her nipples and shoulders were covered. Confirming her soaked, matted curls were hiding all necessary bits, she exhaled, relieved he hadn't brushed it back.

Misinterpreting her sigh, he raised his eyes to the ceiling and muttered under his breath. He pushed her off his lap, shifting onto his knees, and reached behind him to drag his tunic up over his head.

She barely had time to glimpse the definition of his torso before he slid his tunic over her, blocking her view.

"Thank you," she whispered when it settled down over her shoulders.

He nodded, straightening his legs and reaching out an arm. Her own legs shaky, she accepted his help, his tunic dropping to just below her ass as she stood, teetering as her vision blurred for a moment.

Jaren led her through the doorway, instructing her to sit before the hearth as he moved to light it. She shook her head, wanting nothing more than to curl up and not move again for the rest of the night.

She passed the sitting area to the lone bed and couldn't hold back a tired smile. Jaren had the influence to get them a large room at a reputable inn, but somehow, he'd still made sure to find a room with only one bed.

Typical.

"I had a nightmare," she began, grabbing a second tunic from their supply bag and wrapping it around her wet curls. Then she climbed up on the bed, leaning back against the pillows and tucking her feet under the blankets.

"At least, I think that's what it was. It was..." she shuddered. "It was horrible."

His motions paused for a moment before he continued stoking the fire to life. "Was it about Trey?"

She winced, her heart squeezing at the sound of her friend's name. In the grand scheme of life, she hadn't known Trey all that long, but she missed him all the same.

She'd dreamt about him often at the beginning of their trip

to Bhasura, her mind determined to torture her with the last look he'd given her before she left, breaking her heart again and again.

"No, it wasn't about him. And I honestly don't know how I could've fallen asleep. It was more like…like a vision or something. I was here one second and then gone the next."

He turned at that, giving her his full attention. "What do you mean?"

"It felt *real*, Jaren. As real as sitting here next to you."

His brow creased, and he crossed the room, climbing onto the bed to sit beside her. "Is this the first time something like this has happened?"

"Yes," she stopped, pressing her lips into a thin line. *Was* this the first time she'd had a dream like this? She'd always had vivid ones, even as a child, and there'd definitely been times she'd struggled to separate them from reality.

Back then they'd been more like flashes, but they'd been just as real. She'd lost count of how many times she'd awoken as a child with a woman's laughter in her ears, or the smell of blood in her nose.

Then there was that day on Aleron when Jaren had been injured, and Hayes held him at sword point. She'd blacked out just like today. There one minute, and then…not.

She hadn't thought much about it until now. At the time, her life had been chaos, and her mind had simply tucked it away as nothing more than a memory. Now, she wasn't so sure.

"I don't think it's the first," she finally said, "but it's the first one that held me so tightly. It was terrifying, like nothing existed anymore."

He sat quietly, listening as she described it, the sense of absolute nothingness, the terror of drowning, and the glass-covered cavern she'd caught a glimpse of.

He twisted onto his side to face her; his brows pinched together. "What were the others? The ones before today?"

"Memories, mostly. Of you. And my mother, I think." She raised her hand, gliding it over the scar at her throat, and his eyes tracked the movement.

"That day with Eithan I had a vision, or whatever it was. Of someone pinning you to the ground with a sword. You'd been just a boy, and you were reaching for me." She lowered her hand to her chest. "That's when our bond sparked to life."

As if her mentioning their bond called to him on an instinctual level, Jaren threw a leg over both of hers, and leaned down over her face. Her heart, which had only just settled, picked up with a vengeance.

With his long, dark hair falling into his eyes, his naked torso inches from pressing against her, and his full lips curling into a devilish grin, he was the most gods damn beautiful male she'd ever seen.

A flush crept into her cheeks. "What are you doing?"

Propping himself up on one arm, he caressed his other hand along her jaw and down her neck. His jaw clenched when he reached her shoulder, and she swallowed, nerves firing up.

But he continued down, trailing his fingers over the fabric between her breasts. "When I think of that moment, it becomes so hard not to claim you, little star."

His hand lifted, and a second later she felt a sharp pinch on one of her nipples. She yelped, smacking at his hand, but he only pinched harder, chuckling.

Her pulse went erratic at the sound, and she wondered if her heart was pumping faster now than it had in the water. "Then why don't you?" She breathed.

He was so hot and cold, rejecting her one minute, and then playing with her nipples and declaring he wanted her the next. It was hard to keep up.

He rolled the rest of the way over, nudging her legs apart and tucking himself between them. She instinctively bent her knees, her borrowed tunic riding up her thighs as she opened for him.

His eyes darkened, and a vibration worked up his chest when the hard length beneath his trousers pressed against her bare center. She could barely make out his words through the gravel of his voice.

"Because I promised my mate a palace." And then his lips crashed into hers.

She didn't hesitate, needing the distraction, needing the release, needing *him*. She tilted her head, opening her lips for his tongue to dive in, sweeping her mouth in a silent demand to taste every inch of it.

He teased her, gliding his tongue along her own, but as soon as she responded in kind, he pulled back, sucking her bottom lip into his mouth. Then he did it again. After a third time, a growl worked up her throat, and he smirked, biting down just enough to turn the sound into a gasp.

"So fucking needy for me, little star."

"So fucking full of yourself, green eyes."

Those eyes sparked with challenge, and he rolled his hips against her while taking the same nipple he'd pinched and rolling it between his fingers through the fabric.

She locked her spine, biting down on her tongue, and tried in vain to fight her body's response. The asshole's head didn't need to grow any larger.

But he just *tsk*ed, gripping the hem of her tunic and yanking it up. She sucked in a breath as warm air skated across her peaked tips, sending a wave of gooseflesh over her skin.

"I thought you said my body was the least of your worries," she said, clenching the blankets to keep herself from grabbing at him.

"I know when to offer comfort and when to offer pleasure, Veralie. Your body speaks to me, and I listen." He lowered his eyes to her exposed breasts. "It helps that you also look less like a drowned rat now."

"You're such a fucking assho—*oh, fuck.*"

Jaren held one of her breasts cupped in his hand and sucked her nipple deep into his mouth, his unshaved jaw abrasive against her skin, while his other hand slid between their pressed bodies.

She bucked, no longer caring about him being right. She'd had no idea his mouth on her breasts would ignite so many nerve endings, and she felt really fucking needy.

She buried her hands into his hair, fisting the thick strands and rotating her hips in an attempt to find any bit of friction against his unmoving fingers.

He raised his head, pulling on her nipple until it popped free of his mouth, then flicked it with his tongue. Once. Twice. She groaned, yanking at his roots, and ground faster. But he just pinned her hips to the bed, moving his lips to her other breast and murmuring against her skin.

"Say please, Veralie."

Snapping her eyes open, she stopped her erratic motions and dug her nails into his scalp. Bastard.

"You haven't earned me begging, green eyes."

JAREN

GODS, HE LOVED WHEN THAT FIERY TEMPER GOT THE BEST of her. She was beautiful all the time, but when her body tightened and her cheeks heated with irritation, she was fucking stunning. If she wanted to run her mouth, he certainly wouldn't stop her. It only made him harder.

"And what will you do when I earn it?" he asked, brushing his tongue over her in teasing flicks. "Will you beg me to fuck you, little star? Because if memory serves me right, you've already done that."

He could practically hear how hard she was grinding her

teeth together. "I'd rather take your beloved dagger and shove the handle right up your—"

Taking her now-swollen tip between his teeth, he bit down, grazing his canines against her skin right as he finally slid his fingers through her wet heat.

Her words cut off, a cry breaking from her lips, and he hummed. Much better. He dragged his fingers back up, gathering her arousal and rubbing it onto her clit in slow, tantalizing circles.

Fuck, she was already so ready for him. All it would take was a little play, a little stretching, and even untouched as she was, her body would swallow him in one go. He'd fit fucking perfectly when he finally slammed home inside her. The temptation was driving him mad.

"So violent," he cooed against her breast, pressing harder onto her clit and eliciting a long, husky moan from her. "Now stop lying and tell me how much you want my tongue inside you, little star."

She choked, and he knew, without even looking at her face, that she'd flushed down to her toes. Still so innocent. It was going to be so much fun eating that right out of her.

He worked his way down her delectable body, licking and kissing across her abdomen and feeling each muscle go taut under his touch. "Tell me how much you crave to have my face buried between these thighs."

He chuckled when she tensed, her frustration building from both his teasing touches and her desire to continue fighting him every step of the way.

"Yes," she snapped when he made no move to continue down. "I want that."

"Want what? Use your words."

It was an effort to get his own past his lips. *He* wanted it. This close to her sweet center, her scent was damn near suffocating. He had to almost bite a hole in his tongue just to prevent himself from stealing a taste before she spoke.

"Yes, you arrogant fucking bastard! I want your head between my thighs!"

He grinned. "So needy."

Not giving her the chance to knee him in the face, he skipped over her clit and went straight to the source, sinking his tongue in until his nose pressed flat against her body.

He groaned into her heat. *Fucking fuck.* This was where he belonged, tongue impaled in his mate while she gyrated and cried out above him. It was damn near ecstasy.

He held his weight with one arm, continuing to work his tongue in and out of her, and used his other to untie the top of his trousers and remove himself.

As much as he wanted to make this all about her, he couldn't. He wanted her too much and had waited too long. He hadn't even touched himself once since the last time he'd buried his face in her.

Whether he wanted to or not, he was going to erupt. There was no stopping it. Not with her star-fire scent shoved up his nostrils and sliding down his throat.

And he had no plans of ruining his trousers when he could paint her body with it, instead.

Clenching his fist around his shaft, he worked his hand up and down in tight, angry pumps in time to the flicks of his tongue against her clit.

Her nails carved crescent moons into his shoulders, and she ground into him harder, her words an incoherent jumble of both languages.

He felt it the moment she hovered on the edge, the arch of her back, the increase in her pulse. Tightening his grip on himself, he jerked in quick, uncoordinated pulls right as he took that bundle of nerves in his mouth and sucked, *hard*.

She broke, flinging her hands up to his hair and nearly ripping it from his head as she cried out. The sharp bite of pain mixed with the sound of his name on her lips was the last push he needed.

Cursing, he shoved up and slammed a hand near her head, aligning their bodies just in time to cover her in long, hot spurts.

His canines sliced into his lip, and he groaned, thrusting into his fist again and again, determined to coat her in every last drop. When the last wave finally ended, he dropped his hand, caging her head in with shaky arms as he admired her body beneath him.

The sight of her flushed and clammy, chest heaving, with his release stark against her skin, made him feral. Like he just might say fuck the world and everyone in it, if he could just have her like this for him every fucking day.

"I would have..." her hand fluttered to her throat as she tried to speak. "I would have touched you back."

His nostrils flared. He didn't want her to have touched him with her hand to make it happen. *He* hadn't wanted to use his hand to make it happen.

Because as hot as it was to see his release on her body, that's not where it belonged.

He pushed back until he was kneeling between her legs, his ass resting on his heels and his cock hovering inches from where he so desperately wanted it to be.

"The days are ticking down, little star."

"Until what?" she asked, her voice still shaky and hoarse.

He ran two of his fingers through the mess he'd left, circling her swollen clit once before smearing it down to her entrance. "Until I see this dripping out of you the way the gods intended it." Then he shoved his fingers in.

Her back arched at his rough intrusion, and he rotated his fingers against that hidden spot, soothing her discomfort before repeating the process again. And again.

If he had it his way, his release would stay there forever, infecting her scent until she no longer smelled like anything other than *him*.

"I will fill you over and over, until you no longer remember a day when I'm not dried between your thighs," he whispered, pushing the last of it inside her.

"Every male within eyesight will smell me upon you, and still I'll give you more," he continued, thrusting his fingers in time to his words.

She groaned, long and low, and he sensed that familiar tingle begin to build inside her. Gods, she was so gloriously fucking receptive.

"But won't that…" she said, pausing when he leaned down and sucked her nipple deep into his mouth. She cursed, and he swore even he could feel her mind splinter as she clawed at the sheets beneath her.

"Won't that lead to…to children?"

He smirked, removing his fingers and making her whine in a way that had him semi-hard again.

He gazed at his hand, admiring the delicious mess on them. "That's what *truik elixir* is for."

Before she could ask what he was doing, he lowered himself back over her body and rubbed his fingers across her lips. Her eyes widened in shock, and he couldn't stop the sinful smile from spreading across his face before he pressed his lips to hers.

Making love to Veralie's mouth was one thing, but doing so with their combined arousal on his tongue was an entirely different experience.

She moaned, wrapping her legs around him, silently begging him to finish what he'd started. He readily obliged, thrusting the same fingers back in and rocking his hips into them until he was fucking her with his hand.

She'd already been so close, it didn't take long before she broke, clenching around his fingers and crying out into his mouth. He felt like an animal as he pulled out and circled her clit once more.

Teeth bared and voice more growl than syllables, he said, "Give me one more, little star. I need it."

The look she gave him said it for her. Her entire body shook, the muscles in her thighs spasming around him. "Then I suggest you crawl back down there."

His blood heated. "Good girl."

CHAPTER 7

TREY

*D*isorientation was the first thing he felt. Then the discomfort crept in, which only furthered his confusion. He couldn't remember the last time he'd felt something as mild as *discomfort*. Mind-cleaving, throat-ravaging torment was what he'd grown accustomed to.

His fingers twitched, further proof he was, indeed, awake. Gods be damned, why was he still alive? Did the gods have no mercy? Was it some elaborate joke to tease him with death day in and day out until he lost his mind and went mad from it all?

If it was, it was working. He had the urge to laugh, confirming he was at least halfway to insanity, if not a solid three quarters of the way there.

He groaned, attempting to sit up but failing, his spine stiff and his core muscles adamantly refusing to curl. It didn't surprise him. If he had a coin for every time his body had refused to obey him in the eternity he'd been there, he'd be richer than the motherfucking demon himself.

Starting smaller, he tried to raise a hand to pick off the crust that had accumulated around his eye, but even it refused to listen. The limb only made it a few inches above him before it flopped down onto his stomach with a dull *thwap*.

This was different than his usual exhaustion and pain-addled comas. His body was laid out on something soft, his head swimming rather than pounding, and although his mouth was still dry, it was free of the lingering taste of bile.

It felt like he'd been drugged.

The broken part of his mind was thankful, wanting nothing more than to sink back under and never wake. But the other part latched onto the question of why?

Why would Eithan drug him? He wanted Trey to feel every single thing he did to him. Putting him out of his misery, however temporary, didn't make sense. And Eithan did nothing without specific, planned-out purpose.

Daring to open his eye, he had to blink like a damn insect fighting high winds before he was able to clear his vision. He furrowed his brow as he took in his surroundings. Empty cots, organized counters, and a harsh chemical smell he hadn't noticed at first.

He was in the…infirmary.

What the fuck?

He tried and failed to sit up again, but it wasn't until his third attempt that his addled brain realized the reason. A strap was secured across his chest, and another at his hips, keeping him firmly stuck to the cot.

He relaxed back, closing his eye again and wondering why now, of all times, Eithan had finally chosen to bring him in.

The last thing he remembered was a sharp-tipped tool clasping onto a toenail and feeling a deranged sense of relief. Losing a few toenails was nothing, absolutely nothing, compared to everything else he'd experienced.

Raising his head, he glanced to his feet to inspect the most recent damage. But instead of the gruesome sight of bloodied toes, he found them covered in clean, white wrappings that stood out starkly against his dark skin.

He felt the cold plunge of despair shoot through his veins at the sight. Eithan wasn't just having him checked. He was actively healing him. Which meant Trey had to have been close—so fucking close—to death.

His face burned, his tear ducts struggling to work through his dehydration. Why wouldn't his body just give up already? He didn't even care how slow his death was as long as it *just fucking came*.

There was nothing for him to live for anymore. No future to look forward to. He had no family sitting at home, no wife waiting to greet him with loving touches, and no position to work hard at and be proud of.

He didn't even have a single friend left to his name who wasn't loyal to Eithan—not on this continent, at least.

He had nothing.

Wallowing in self-pity, his soul nearly left his body when he turned his head and found a man standing next to his cot, watching him.

"Fucking Aleron," he burst, his hand sliding up his chest to where his heart beat rapidly.

But 'man' might've been the wrong term to use. The scrawny scrap of human looked more like a boy barely old enough for his balls to have dropped.

Small, swollen pores covered his pasty forehead, and he was wearing a white tunic tucked into white trousers. His sleeves were rolled up and uneven, revealing a pair of slender hands he was currently wringing like his life depended on it.

"Who are you?" Trey asked, the effort of talking making him feel like he was gurgling gravel. He hadn't seen another face other than Eithan's since he'd first been imprisoned with the Weapon's Master.

The boy's eyes darted around at his question, landing on everything except his face. "I'm in charge of your care."

"Eithan asked *you?*" He couldn't keep the disdain from his voice. If that was true, then this kid wasn't someone Trey could trust to wipe his ass, let alone heal him properly.

The boy flinched, whether at him omitting Eithan's title, or at his tone, he wasn't sure. And frankly, he didn't give a fuck.

"Healer Tilly is no longer with us. I'm his replacement. You can call me Healer Perry," he stuttered, and his blue eyes finally flicked to Trey's, shame dulling them before he glanced away again.

His pulse picked up. Perry knew. He knew why Trey was here, and he didn't like it. This was the chance he'd been waiting for. He leaned up as much as his body, and the strap around him, allowed and said, "Kill me."

Perry's wide lips fell open, and he fumbled over his reply, starting and stopping twice before getting out, "I beg your pardon?"

"Please," he choked. "Just kill me. There's no healing what he's destroyed. All that's left for me is to meet the God of Death and hope he is lenient," he said, his voice cracking on the last word. "Please."

"I—I cannot. I've been put in charge of your care by His Highness, himself. He's worried for your health."

Trey fell back, chuckling humorlessly. "You do realize he's the one who did this to me, right? You must, given I can guarantee he made you swear to secrecy." He scoffed, pushing down the mania surging toward the surface. "How can you turn a blind eye and call yourself a healer?"

Perry flinched, his hands fluttering up to his mouth as if Trey's treasonous words held a dark magic that would curse him and his entire family.

They probably would if he was ever stupid enough to repeat them. But Trey refused to give up, no matter what Perry believed. Not when this was the only chance he had.

"Just tell him I never woke up from the drug he used. He can't blame you for something he did before I was ever here."

Perry began wringing his hands again, swallowing nervously. "I'm the one who administered your sleeping aid. His Highness brought you in unconscious and requested you stay that way. I'm here to—to deliver your next dose."

Trey snapped his mouth shut, rolling his lips in and biting down until he felt the imprint of each remaining tooth. Was anyone on Aleron not a blind servant to the house of Matheris? Did anyone actually care about the quality of their leaders, or just protecting their own fucking skin?

Despair seeped into his pores as the harsh truth battered against him. No one was going to help him. If he wanted to die, he'd have to take matters into his own hands. If he could just get this gods damn strap off, maybe he could locate a scalpel or another tool of some kind.

"If you could take one mouthful of this, please."

He glanced over to see Perry's trembling hand holding out an amber-colored bottle. Sleeping aid. Trey instantly perked up, his heart rattling in his chest.

That was it. He could down the entire bottle before Perry snatched it back. He'd had plenty of practice over the years chugging pints of ale with Jensen, it'd be easy. Compared to shoving a scalpel in an artery, death by sleep seemed like a pretty nice fucking way to go.

He raised his hand to accept the bottle, but like an idiot, his eagerness gave him away. Perry's eyes narrowed, and he pulled his hand back, holding the bottle to his chest. "I'll get you a cup."

Apparently, the kid wasn't as naïve as he looked. How

fucking convenient.

When he returned, Trey took the proffered cup without a fight. He no longer had one. What other choice did he have? To stare at the ceiling with a stomach caving in on itself, awaiting Eithan's grand return? No, thank you.

With the amount of weight and muscle mass he'd lost over the last few weeks, it didn't take long before the effects of the drug began to pull at his consciousness, and his arms flopped to the cot, his body somehow feeling both boneless and heavy at the same time.

His head lulled to the side, and Perry's furrowed brow and hollowed cheeks were the last thing he saw before sleep finally took him.

Fuck this entire continent.

JAREN

HE'D ALREADY BEEN STRUGGLING WITH THE TEMPTATION TO cut out his father's tongue and shove it down his throat, but now he'd added breaking all his knuckles to his to-do list as well.

The knocking that had yanked him from sleep came again. Harder this time.

"I know you're in there, Jaren Barilias. I'm well acquainted with the smell of arousal permeating from your room. Don't make me break this lock, I have no desire to see whatever it is that's going on in there."

"Who is that?" Veralie's muffled voice came from beneath him, pulling him from his dark thoughts.

He cracked open an eye, peering down at her groggy face. Her squinted, silver eyes clashed with his through the nest of frizzed curls between them.

"Did he just say something about arousal?"

A smile pulled at his lips as he batted her hair away to uncover the entirety of her face. Like usual, he'd gravitated to her during the night and woken sprawled across her.

She didn't exactly look comfortable smashed under his body weight, but at least she hadn't immediately launched him off the bed this time.

Probably because she was half-naked. Still, it was progress.

"He didn't say anything about arousal. Sex on the mind, my *aitanta*?" A laugh tickled his throat, threatening to slip past when her brows creased in confusion, second guessing what she'd heard.

"Maybe we should start using Thyabathi in private as well, to help you learn faster. I can think of a few enjoyable ways to reward you when you do well."

She glared up at him, and his pulse quickened. Gods, he loved her fire. But knocking came again, rattling the door and cutting off whatever string of expletives she was about to spew.

"I can hear you, you *nlamb jekhna!*" Jaeros yelled, loud enough to wake any patrons unlucky enough to still be in their rooms.

His good mood at waking up pressed to Veralie vanished at

being called the equivalent of a "horny idiot." He glanced to the nightstand, contemplating snatching a dagger and flinging it at the door.

Veralie poked him in the side. "Is that Jaeros?" He didn't reply, but she nodded, his silence answering for him. "Maybe we should just see what he wants."

"No."

His fathers had left his mate to survive on her own, not knowing if she was safe or taken care of, or even alive. They didn't deserve a second of her gods damn time. No flimsy excuse they gave would ever be good enough.

She sighed, shoving against his chest until he shifted back. He let her roll out of bed, the sight of her in nothing but his tunic eliciting a rumble from his chest, reminding him of the previous night.

As much as he didn't want to see his father, the idea of Veralie opening the door and pouring their interwoven scents into the hallway gave him immense pleasure.

Maybe he'd go one step farther and repeat last night, right up against the door his father wouldn't stop fucking touching. If Jaren ignoring him wasn't sending a clear message, that sure as fuck would. And it'd be even sweeter since he'd finally shaved the night before and would be able to feel her heat directly against his skin.

She glanced at him over her shoulder, dropping her eyes to his suddenly too-tight undershorts before shaking her head and walking toward the wash basin in the corner of their room.

He shifted to follow, intent on following through on his plan, but froze when she leaned over the basin. His heart picked up as he watched her splash water across her face, his eyes zeroing in on the droplets as they traveled down her skin.

He might have made a full-course meal out of her last night, lapping at her until tears poured down her face and she begged for mercy, but it was the reminder of *why* that stopped him in his tracks.

Why she'd needed the distraction. Why he'd so desperately needed to touch her and taste her. Why she'd been naked in the first place.

Frozen in the center of the room, he glared back and forth between her and the door, which was, yet again, being hit with a fist from the other side. If only he could rid himself of the image of her drowning as easily as he was about to dispel of his father.

Veralie turned back toward him, snatching up the new leggings he'd purchased for her. She worked her legs in, scowling down at the unfamiliar snug clothing before moving on to her socks and glancing sidelong at him.

"I can't make you do anything, Jaren, but I, for one, want to hear what he has to say."

"Thank you, Veralie," came from the other side of the door. Jaren crossed his arms. "No."

"Suit yourself," she said, hastily tucking the front hem of his tunic into her leggings, leaving the back still hanging past the curve of her ass.

He lunged when she reached for her boots, blocking her path to the door. "You're not going anywhere with him."

She shoved her feet into them, not bothering to lace them up. "I'll make my own choices, thank you."

He snarled but didn't stop her as she threw her cloak on and began quickly braiding her hair down one shoulder. "He threw you away like garbage, Veralie. If memory serves me well, you've never let any male get away with treating you as such."

"You don't know what the fuck he did, and you never will if you can't find the balls to ask," she snapped back.

He seethed, hating that she was right. He *did* want to know the truth of what happened before he'd regained consciousness that night. He just also knew no answer would ever be good enough.

"I won't forgive him."

"I'm not asking you to, and neither is he. I know you're hurt and upset—okay, pissed off, but I was the one carted off, not you. I deserve to know."

His lip curled. "You'd forgive him, just like that?"

"No," she said, resting her hand on the door. "But I'm going to give him the chance to earn it."

CHAPTER 8

VERA

Not wanting to draw further attention from the patrons at the inn, they'd all agreed to leave, opting to walk a few blocks to a day-and-night tavern Jaeros knew the owner of.

Hungry and desperate for a hot meal, it'd taken everything in her not to demand they run there. But her excitement had died a sad, quick death when the tavern finally came into view. Rough was an understatement.

The awning was broken, the ripped pieces swinging in the breeze, it had planks nailed over one window, and its sign hung by a single corner, bumping against the wall.

She'd openly balked, but Jaeros had been adamant, claiming it was the only place they could safely talk. Jaren had scoffed, and she'd echoed his sentiment, unsure how a place falling apart could possibly be trusted.

But Jaeros had walked straight up to the owner and only had to whisper a request for privacy for the older male to immediately begin shouting at patrons, ordering them to "get the fuck out" in heavy Thyabathi.

Given the time of morning, there hadn't been many inside, but the few who'd been there jumped to their feet and complied like a plague was sweeping in. They'd either been genuinely terrified of the lumbering, white-haired owner, or they were just clearly used to his demands.

But even so, not one patron slipped out without first shooting them a curious glance, lingering on her hooded face. She'd pulled it lower, more than glad that she'd listened to Jaren and worn it.

Now here she was, sitting at a sticky, circular table with two males more interested in glaring at one another and avoiding conversation than actually having one.

She bit back a groan of frustration and looked to the least infuriating of the two, allowing herself to take in the details she hadn't been able to see the day before.

Jaeros's peppered hair hung loose around his shoulders, accentuating his pale blue eyes, and his thick beard covered most of his face, making Jaren's freshly shaved one seem sharper than usual.

He wore a plum-colored tunic with silver embroidery on the collar, untucked over wrinkle-free, gray trousers. And if all that didn't give away his capital origin, his scruff-free, pristine boots certainly did.

"You don't remember me, do you?"

The question had her eyes snapping up from his clothing, surprised he'd used the common tongue. She flushed, embarrassed to be caught staring.

"Um," she started, but then paused. How did you politely tell someone you had no memory of them at all? "No," she finally admitted, flushing a deeper shade of red. "I'm sorry." But he just nodded, as if he'd already assumed as much.

"It's not just you," she continued, wanting to ease the sting of her words, even though she didn't know why. It wasn't like it was *her* fault. "I don't remember anything apart from a few pieces. It's taken me weeks just to get comfortable with Thyabathi again."

He sat up straighter, setting the mug of tea he'd been sipping on the table. "Wait, you don't remember *anything*?"

"No."

"Not even him?" he asked incredulously, pointing a finger in Jaren's direction.

She shook her head.

"Her soul recognized my own just fine. She just didn't understand what it meant because my *mate* has been raised with fucking humans," Jaren bit out beside her.

Jaeros's expression tightened. "I'm sorry, Veralie. I don't know why—"

"Unless you want to lose that tongue, I suggest you use her proper title when speaking to her."

Puffing her cheeks out in a heavy sigh, she tipped her face up and rolled her eyes as father and son had yet another stare off. She could probably walk to the inn, nap, and walk back, and they'd still be staring at each other.

She grumbled, leaning forward to rest her elbows on the table, and released a small yelp when it tilted under her weight, rustling their dishes.

Both males twisted toward her, and she launched back, tucking her hands in her lap, and cleared her throat. At least she had their attention.

"Don't you think kicking everyone out will only give them more reason to gossip?" she asked, hoping to steer the conversation away from titles and torture.

Jaren grunted his agreement, but Jaeros was already shaking his head before the last word had passed her lips. "Not any more than your face will already cause on its own. By night, every Magyki here will have heard about the *daż* of the queen."

"*Daż?*"

"It doesn't translate well, but think along the lines of 'remnant'," Jaren said, his expression softening slightly when she met his eyes.

A remnant of the queen? "As in...like a spirit of her or something?" she asked.

"More or less. *He*," Jaren said, curling his lip, "means they will think you are the queen and take it as an omen."

"A good or bad one?" she asked, feeling a wave of nerves bubble under her skin.

"Either."

She clenched her fists over her thighs. She'd lived her whole life in the shadows, wishing and begging for things to be different, but now she wasn't so sure that's what she wanted.

"But why will they think I'm this *daż?*"

"Because you look just like your mother," Jaeros said, sitting back and rubbing his hand down his beard.

Her eyes widened, and her voice came out higher than usual. "I do?"

"Eerily so, yes. So, you might as well get used to the idea of being stared at because it's only going to get worse."

"Don't tell her what to do," Jaren snapped, fingers twitching on the table.

Vera rolled her eyes, but even the bite of his temper couldn't keep away the small smile that tugged at her lips. She looked like her mother.

Focusing her attention back on Jaeros, she asked, "Will you answer any questions I have? Even if you don't think I'll like the answer?"

Jaeros cringed, pushing stray strands of hair out of his face. "No, my dear, I won't. At least, not the questions I know you want to ask."

Jaren tensed like an arrow seconds from exploding from its bow, but part of her was thankful for Jaeros's blunt honesty. She'd take that over quick-tongued, empty promises any day.

"I will happily tell you about the years you lived with us," he continued, "but for any questions about that night, or your mother, I will not discuss without Dedryn present."

He narrowed his eyes at the furious male next to her. "Don't give me that look unless you want me to smack it off your face, boy. He deserves to be heard as well before you damn us for eternity."

"Too late."

Jaeros flinched, but hid it quickly, picking up his mug and taking a sip. "Dedryn will be expecting my return by tomorrow night if you wish to meet him then. Last night, I instructed the stable north of here to have three horses ready in case you chose to leave with me."

"Thank you," she said, sincerely meaning it even though the thought of traveling again so soon after they'd arrived sounded horrendous. "That's very—"

"We will do no such thing," Jaren barked, smacking his palms on the table. "In case you've forgotten, I've done this trip more than you and know the damn way. We do not need, nor desire, your assistance."

Vera's blood boiled. Fuck that. Mate or not, if he thought he was going to keep talking over her, he had another thing coming. Reaching across his lap, she grabbed the soft underside of his arm and pinched as hard as she could.

He lurched away, barking out a curse and snatching her hand faster than she could avoid. Her chair legs screeched against the floor as he dragged her right up against him.

"Something you want to say?" he asked, a threat lacing each word as he gripped her arm tighter and loomed over her.

She felt, more than saw, Jaeros freeze across from them, but she ignored him, focusing on her anger and hoping Jaren felt every gods damn stab of it.

"You do not speak for me, Jaren Barilias. I said I wanted to hear what he has to say, and I meant it. So, either get your shit together or shut the fuck up."

The bite of his nails on her wrist was her only warning before he yanked hard on her arm, pulling her completely out of her chair and onto his lap. Using his other hand to wrap around the back of her knee, he spread her legs, his scent spiking as he straddled her over his thighs.

His eyes latched on to her shoulder before flicking up, and she raised her brows in challenge. If he thought a claiming mark gave him the right to talk for her, she was going to show him its absence right before ripping his fucking teeth out.

But he just leaned down, brushing his nose along hers. "Are you speaking as my *aitanta* or ordering me as my *Nlem Snadzend?*"

She opened her mouth, but he beat her to it, nipping sharply at her lip. "Choose your answer carefully."

"Neither," she said, lifting her chin. "I speak as a female who has her own gods damn voice."

He wrapped a hand around the back of her neck, his answering smile as sinful as it was cruel. She felt the sting of snagged hairs along her nape as he fisted the base of her plait and pulled, smashing his lips to hers.

The fingers of his other hand dug into her thigh, and his

thumb inched dangerously high as he growled into her mouth. He kissed her with a frenzy, his tongue sweeping in and demanding everything she had.

It wasn't until she was out of breath, and Jaeros was grumbling about horny idiots, that Jaren finally pulled away, his eyes clearer than they'd been all morning.

She blinked, fighting her way up from the haze his taste always put her in. She'd expected him to be angry at her lashing out, not kiss her senseless.

Reading the confusion in her gaze, his lips quirked. "You're fucking beautiful when you burn, little star." He leaned closer, hovering his lips over her ear. "But just because I like it, don't think I won't punish this wicked mouth."

His thumb inched even higher, brushing her center, and her face flooded with heat. She tried to scramble back, but he held on, the green of his eyes searing into her soul.

"Your lead, Veralie."

THERE HAD TO be a hole somewhere on this island to tuck herself into. A nice deep one, where no one would find her. Her anxiety was already frayed from the tension between Jaren and his father, but the walk to the stable had only made it worse.

If them kicking everyone out of the tavern hadn't been enough, walking through the city with a male clearly from Naris and a bodyguard with no respect for personal space was practically screaming she was someone of importance.

After catching yet another stranger pointing and whispering, she gave up her attempt at hiding beneath her hood and sprinted toward the cover of the stable.

Why were they all whispering, and about *what?* Did anyone guess at who she was, or did they all really think she was some type of omen? She'd give anything to be able to tap easily into her hearing the way everyone around her could.

The main question scraping against her composure was how many would be happy to learn who she was, and how many had secretly supported the rebellion against her family?

Her family. Gods, it still didn't seem real that she had one. She'd obviously known she did, but to know she was about to meet one of them? Her father, no less? It was overwhelming.

She was leaned up against a wood pillar, catching her breath, when her companions caught up and entered. They each wore differing expressions of concern, but neither pressed her about running off.

They'd left the tavern soon after Jaren agreed to follow her lead and travel with Jaeros, all of them eager to get out of Ocridal and head to Naris as quickly as possible.

"It's hard to have secrets when even whispers can be heard through the walls," Jaeros had said, and even Jaren nodded.

A stable hand, who hadn't bothered to approach her when she was alone, hurried their way as soon as Jaeros entered. He gestured for them to follow, talking too quickly for her to understand, and pointed to the three horses they'd be taking on their two-day trip to the capital.

Although her body was glad she only had to ride for a couple days, her mind wished it was longer. Two days. That's all she had left before the stares and attention got so much worse.

"We don't need this one."

Lost in her thoughts, she startled, dropping her hand from the brown mare she'd been quietly petting. "Why? There's nothing wrong with her," she said, glancing over her shoulder to raise a brow at him.

"She's not big enough to hold our weight. We'll take the other," he said, referring to the stallion she'd passed.

"There are three horses, Jaren," Jaeros called from another stall. "I know how to count. That mare will do a fine job for her."

Jaren didn't even flinch, refusing to take his eyes off her. His expression was neutral, but what brewed on the inside was anything but. "What have I told you? You ride with me. Always."

"Don't you think you'd be more comfortable if we—"

"*Always.*"

She stared at him a second longer before accepting he wasn't going to change his mind. In truth, she didn't mind riding with him, she liked the comfort of his warmth, but she also didn't want to look weak after *just* telling him she'd make her own choices.

Reading all of that across her face, and more, he smirked, knowing he'd won. "Oh, my sweet Veralie, I promise you'll prefer to ride with me."

He placed his hand at the small of her back, pulling her away from the stall, and leaned down to nip at her ear. "Or do you not remember our last trip?"

Memories of his hand working her from behind trickled in, but she shoved them down, ignoring the way her body practically throbbed in answer. Bastard.

Sensing her reaction, he hummed and moved to nip at her again, but she dropped her weight, taking him by surprise. She sank into a squat, twisting, and slammed her elbow straight into his gut. He bowed forward, pressing a hand to his stomach as she darted out of his reach and stood.

"I could get used to the sight of you bowing, green eyes."

His head snapped up, but it wasn't anger she saw swirling in his eyes. Adrenaline filled her veins, and she flashed him a full tooth smile before dashing out of the stall.

CHAPTER 9

EITHAN

He walked around the small cot, eyeing the bandages adorning Gibson's limbs and torso. They were stained a light pink, but nothing warranting concern.

"When was he last cleaned up?"

"This morning, Your Highness," Percy stuttered out. No, not Percy. Perrin? Something like that. At barely eighteen years old, the kid had been working under the head healer, Tilly, for only a year when the older man unexpectedly passed.

Eithan still wasn't sure if promoting the skittish kid to take Tilly's place was the best idea, but he'd needed someone fast, specifically, someone he could use. Perrin, or whatever his name was, had been the perfect candidate.

"How is his fever?"

"Broken just last night, Your Highness. I gave him another

dose of sleeping aid when he awoke because he was quite distraught. But that was hours ago, so he should be waking again soon."

Eithan gave the kid an appreciative look. Maybe he'd be a decent replacement after all. At least he was semi-competent. "Good. Did he say anything of interest?"

He watched Perrin closely, noting the way his eyes widened, and his fingers pressed in on the vial he was holding. "No, Your Highness. I mean, yes, he spoke, but no, it wasn't interesting. He ran—ranted incoherently mostly. But...th–that's not uncommon with people coming out of forced sleep. He—"

Eithan raised a hand, stopping him mid-ramble. "Thank you, Perrin, that'll be all."

The kid's brows pinched ever so slightly before he jutted forward and gave a deep bow, shuffling back until his ass bumped the door. Then he spun and darted out, the empty vial still clutched in his hand.

Eithan rolled his neck, trying to ignore the hair sticking to his skin and soothe his stiff muscles, before turning his attention to the restrained guard. "I know you're already awake, Gibson. The rapid movement of your chest when I entered gave you away."

Gibson's jaw clenched, and Eithan watched the tendons in his hands twitch as he clamped them in tight fists on top of the thin mattress.

"No hello? Or even a thank you?" he asked, clicking his tongue in reprimand. "And after I had you cleaned up and your

117

wounds tended to. I'm disappointed."

Gibson's head slowly turned his way, his remaining eye a dull, dead thing in his face. It dipped for just a moment, taking in Eithan's own disheveled state, before flicking back up.

His throat bobbed once before he parted his lips, his tongue making a thick, sticky sound as he pried it from the roof of his mouth. "You're going to kill him, aren't you?" he croaked.

"Who?"

"Healer Perry."

"Perry! That's it!" Eithan said, snapping his fingers and pointing at him. "Damn, I was close. Oh, don't look at me like that, I'm not going to kill him." Not as long as he kept his blubbering lips closed, at least.

At Gibson's scoff, he sighed. "No matter how much you might contest it, I don't just go around murdering people for fun," he said, tilting his head. "Do you actually think I enjoy seeing people the way you were down there? Broken and useless?"

The tightening of Gibson's lips was his only reply.

Eithan took a single step toward the cot, delighting in the way the guard's body tensed. Looked like there was still some life left to be snuffed out.

"In case you're unsure, my question wasn't rhetorical."

Gibson cleared his throat, trying to hide his wince before spitting out, "The ecstasy that's always plastered to your face would suggest that you do."

Eithan chuckled, taking the last few steps and reaching over to grab the healer's chair. He pulled it closer and lowered himself onto it, careful to avoid angering his own wounds that had finally stopped seeping blood onto his clothing.

"True. But I should clarify my meaning." He leaned back, crossing one leg over the other, his mask remaining smooth and unperturbed even as his split skin pulled and burned.

"You're right, I enjoy what I do. Probably more than anything else in this world and whatever world awaits us after. But do you think I'm proud of that truth?

"Do you truly believe I thrive on the knowledge that I'm a monster with no soul? That I enjoy having no heart left to pump blood throughout this shell of a body?"

"Yes."

Eithan dipped his head. He didn't fault him for his answer. Gibson might've grown up a commoner, but he'd been free of a father and fiercely loved by his mother. He couldn't understand.

People were not capable of understanding what they, themselves, had not experienced. Pity existed, but real empathy was little more than a myth created by those who sought to better their own image.

No one was capable of empathizing with Sulian holding his hand over a flame when he'd dropped his sword one too many times as a child. They weren't capable of understanding the mental and physical black hole he'd had to crawl out of on his own. Not unless they'd experienced the same. And he highly doubted a soul in Matherin had.

"I used to fight it, you know. This innate urge that Sulian

awoke in me." He inspected his hands, picking out dried blood from under his fingernails.

"As a boy, I tried to hide from him like a coward. I'd beg and cry and break my body in training to be the best. I even went so far as to make him gifts, all in an effort to please him."

He huffed a breath, lowering his hands to his lap and forcing them to lie flat when all he wanted was to wrap them around Sulian's neck and twist.

"As a teen, I stooped to the level of a commoner, teaching myself to paint and sew. I exercised and ran, wrote poetic nonsense, read entire libraries, and had so much sex I'm not sure how my cock didn't fall off my body."

He laughed at the thought, then laughed harder at the incredulous look on Gibson's face—a feat given its condition. But his laughter quickly died out as he continued flipping through his memories.

"Nothing worked. Nothing. I could feel my mind fracturing more and more each year, and I just wanted the constant agony to stop. The voices, the pit, the complete and utter misery that ripped at my chest with every breath."

He exhaled, the only show of emotion he allowed himself to have, and for a split second, he could've sworn he saw a flicker of pity in Gibson's gaze. Just further proof that the guard would never understand.

Eithan shot forward, resting his elbows on his thighs, and hovered over Gibson's face. He thrashed against his restraints, a choked grunt slipping past his cracked lips.

Too lost in his own head to soak up his fear as he usually would, Eithan ignored his panic and continued. "Then one day, an elderly servant bumped into a vase in my room. A vase I'd made as a boy in memory of my mother. I watched it shatter at my feet, feeling as empty and worthless as each broken piece.

"When he returned with a broom and a half-assed apology, I didn't think it through. I just picked up one of the broken shards and buried it in his pale throat, watching his blood gush out over the pieces. He looked so shocked as he fell, grasping at the flayed skin like he could somehow hold back the flow."

He remembered the way his heart had sped up, watching the man struggle that day. Each gurgled plea had slithered through his veins like an antidote, bringing him back to life as the man beneath him lost his.

"It was like I could breathe again, Gibson. After that day, I began visiting the dungeon, and found the more bodies I infected with this poison, the less of it lived within me. For the first time since my mother died, I felt *alive*."

Gibson swallowed, shaking his head minutely. "What your father did to you doesn't make any of that okay. It just makes you as bad as he is."

Eithan shrugged. "I am what I am."

"Fucked in the head is what you are," he said, his lip curling as hatred flickered back into his gaze.

Eithan just sat back, running his tongue over his teeth. "Fucked I may be, but you did this to yourself. First by breaking my trust, then by forging a connection with my bride."

"I don't have a—"

He waved a hand flippantly, stopping his denial. "I don't mean romantically, of course. But she values you and would happily sacrifice her life to save yours. Which is exactly what I'm betting on."

Gibson's eye widened, and he lurched up only to hiss in pain when his body dug into the straps holding him down. "What the fuck did you do?"

Eithan grinned. "I simply wrote a letter. Nothing important. Just that you were imprisoned for aiding in her kidnapping and are awaiting execution." He winked. "I may have alluded to Emperor Sulian being behind it."

Gibson seethed, spittle flicking out onto his chin. "If tricking her was your goal, you could have already executed me and lied."

"No," Eithan said, the chair legs scraping across the floor as he pushed to stand. "From what I saw, Vera's power didn't come out until she got angry."

He walked to the door, more than ready to wash the dried blood from his body. He wrapped his hand around the handle, watching Gibson's thoughts play out across his face as loudly as if he'd screamed them.

"You see, Gibson, I need your body tortured, yet discernable, when she comes running back. I need her to see your mangled body and know she was so close to saving you."

"I don't need her angry," he said, tightening his grip until the etchings of the handle cut into his palm. "I need her to *rage*."

CHAPTER 10

VERA

Naris loomed before her, and her entire body seemed to tense in an equal measure of anticipation and nerves. Size wise, the Bhasurian capital didn't seem all that different than Matherin, but where Matherin was busy with the daily bustle of people going about their lives, Naris exploded with it.

The main street they led their horses down was crowded beyond anything she'd ever seen before. If it wasn't for the obvious lack of decorations and zeal, she'd have thought some form of festival was taking place.

Squeezed between two rows of what she could assume were general shops and taverns, were rows of vendor tents, other travelers on horses, and countless Magyki ambling about. Not to mention the overwhelming noise of voices all shouting over each other.

She stared bug-eyed, watching yet another group dash in front of Jaeros's horse, when a memory flickered in the back of her mind. Something Emperor Sulian had said about Bhasura being overpopulated.

He'd mentioned during their dinner that he was willing to offer land to the Magyki in return for fair trade with the island. She hadn't thought much about it then, the idea seeming foreign and unrelated to her at the time, but if all Bhasura's cities were this crammed, she didn't understand how King Vesstan could say no. Was his desire not to intermix their people that strong?

When you had a population who could heal most injuries and sickness, and who lived twice the lifespan of what was considered normal, overpopulation was an obvious outcome. Then again, with what Jaren had said about the taint hindering their abilities, maybe that wouldn't always be the case.

Pulling her eyes from the Magyki lining the street, she took in the scenery around her—or what one would call scenery in the midst of a busy city. Like Ocridal, there were pops of color everywhere, but it wasn't just in the clothing of its occupants.

Everywhere she looked had some form of color that added just a little something more to what would normally be a dull, drab building. Bright banners hung from doorway awnings, bringing attention to what each shop sold, window ledges had boxes of flowers, and deep green vines grew between doorways and up alley walls.

And somewhere within the chaotic beauty of the city, her

father was casually living his life, completely and utterly unaware of her existence. What was he going to think when he saw her? After all these years thinking she was dead, would he believe she was who she said she was?

And what if he'd never even thought that? What if he'd been in on the plan to ship her off all along? Would she have to find some way to prove who she was? According to Jaeros, she could assume her appearance alone would be enough, but still, it was a huge claim.

She wanted to ask him, but without Dedryn present, he was adamant about not discussing her parents or why she hadn't lived with them. She tried not to let the unknown get to her. It wasn't like she could change the past anyway. She could only hope they'd had a good reason. It hurt too much to think otherwise.

Other than that, Jaeros had talked openly with her during their first day of travel, telling her story after story about how spoiled and ornery she was as a child. How she'd hidden in dark corners to scare the shit out of Jaren, or how she used to hang on Jaeros's clothes, trailing behind him crying until she got what she wanted.

It was hard to wrap her mind around his descriptions of her, and she might not have believed it, if Jaren hadn't confirmed them with quiet grunts of amusement. She couldn't remember ever being carefree and ornery. Elric had said she'd refused to talk for weeks, and even then, it'd only been when prompted.

What had happened that night to change her entire personality into the quiet mouse she'd become? And what had made her forget it? When she'd voiced her frustration over her inability to remember any of his stories, Jaeros had waved her off, certain the memories would return in time. He said trauma was a tricky beast that followed no rules but its own, and only time and patience could tame it.

She glanced at the male in question. Unlike their first day, he hadn't said much during the second. She'd noticed the change in his mood and had backed off her questions, assuming he was simply exhausted and missing his mate. But the closer they'd gotten to Naris, the quieter he'd become, and she'd begun to wonder if maybe it was more than exhaustion.

What would King Vesstan do to Jaren's fathers for lying to him all this time? And if they hadn't lied, if he'd been in on the entire plan, would he blame them for her coming back? She had a feeling she knew what Emperor Sulian would do, but she had no idea how King Vesstan ruled.

Her stomach roiled at the thought of Jaeros being punished because of her. Even knowing he had secrets, ones she probably wouldn't like, she couldn't help but feel a connection with him. He reminded her of Trey—or what Trey might be like at his age.

If it wasn't for the tension and stress her appearance had caused, she was sure Jaeros would have the same bubbly personality as her friend. His humor hadn't slipped out often, but the few times it had, it'd been just as ridiculous as Trey's.

She closed her eyes, remembering how she'd felt the first time she'd seen her friend's full face. How bright and welcoming his smile had been. Gods, she missed him. His infectious laugh, his taunts, even the way he poked fun at her and drove her nuts.

What would he be doing right now? He never talked about what he did when Eithan wasn't traveling, and she'd never really thought to ask. She couldn't imagine Eithan required all twelve of his guards to follow him around his own home. Right?

She smiled, picturing Trey having to stand outside random doorways staring at a wall while Eithan did basic things like bathing or reading a book. His fingers would be tapping away at his leg, his mind a chaotic mess of random thoughts as he counted down the minutes until he could rip the mask off and relax.

She startled when she felt the light touch of Jaren's lips against her temple, and his arms immediately released the reins to circle her waist and steady her.

"You're warm," he murmured.

She frowned, touching her forehead with the back of her hand. She didn't feel warm. The sun had begun to set, and it was nice out, the breeze occasionally rustling her hair about her ears, cooling her face and neck. "I am?"

He chuckled, lowering his head and placing a hand over her chest. "I meant, in here."

Oh. "Is that a good thing?" she asked, trying to ignore the fact that his hand was dangerously close to brushing her nipple.

He smiled against her ear, reading her thoughts, and his fingers began to trail down as his breath sent gooseflesh down both arms. "Depends on what you're thinking about."

"It's beautiful, isn't it?" The voice cut through their hushed conversation, and she nearly leapt off the saddle, heart in her throat. In the span of seconds, she'd already forgotten they weren't alone. Jaren's touch had a way of instantly blocking out the rest of the world. None of it seemed to matter when his hands were on her.

She pulled away from him, flushing when she met Jaeros's glance. Mistaking her expression for nerves, he gave her an encouraging smile. "Don't worry, dear, there's nothing to be nervous about for tonight."

"We're not seeing the king?" she asked, hoping the hitch in her voice wasn't as obvious to them as it was to her. Jaeros's faltering smile told her she was not so lucky.

"I assumed both of you would want to wash up and rest before meeting anyone, Dedryn included. Tomorrow is as good a day as any."

She nearly sagged in Jaren's arms with relief. She didn't want to think about any of that yet. The thought of meeting her father, and everything it would entail, was just too much right now. After two days on a horse, a hot, soothing bath sounded way better. Although, with what happened the last time she'd taken one, maybe not.

"We're not staying under your roof."

She twisted at Jaren's clipped words, about to lash out about him speaking for her again, but he squeezed her hip, staring at her unapologetically. "That's a hard line for me, Veralie. I won't stay there."

She snapped her mouth shut, reading the emotion in his gaze and the way his heart beat steadily with hers. She didn't want to stay at another grimy inn, but it wasn't just about her. "Okay," she said, turning to settle back against his chest.

"Good thing I didn't invite you," Jaeros huffed. "I'm accompanying you to the guest wing of the palace. It's used for Magyki who've been approved an audience with the king."

That news surprised her. The palace had guest rooms specifically to house citizens who wished to speak to their king? "They allow anyone who requests an audience to stay there?"

Jaeros cleared his throat, shooting her a quick glance. "Well, no, not just anyone." He didn't say more, and he didn't need to. *Nobility* could stay comfortably and request an audience with the king. All while the rest of their people fought for space out on the streets. Figures.

Why was it that people in power were only ever willing to listen to the voices of those who didn't need their help? Apparently Sulian and Vesstan were more alike than either wanted to admit. Both doing the bare minimum to keep their citizens' mouths above water, while the wealthy stood on stable bridges ten feet above the surface. But hey, as long as no one was actually drowning, it was fine, right?

"We don't exactly look like nobility," she said, gesturing to herself and Jaren. She was still wearing his two-day old, oversized tunic over travel leggings, while he looked like an alley dweller with his unkempt scruff and shaggy hair. "Something tells me we won't be welcome."

But Jaeros waved her off, leading his mare ahead of them as they continued their trek through the city. "The guards and staff will take my word for it, and Dedryn and I will meet you in the morning before anyone else sees you."

"Is that okay?" she whispered, tilting her head to the side and tapping her fingers over Jaren's. She expected him to argue, but he just buried his nose in her hair and grunted, like he had no more shits to give at that point. She'd take that as a yes.

BY THE TIME they'd made it to the stable and found someone to care for their beasts, it was dark out, forcing them to trudge the rest of the way with nothing but vendor lights and moonlight to guide them.

She craned her neck back as they finally approached the palace gate, taking in what little she could see—which wasn't much other than the fact it was fucking huge. She knew her eyes were probably taking up her entire face, but she couldn't help but gawk. This was the home she should've grown up in.

It was a shame her enhanced sight couldn't help her see in the dark—not that she could've focused her power well enough regardless. But exploring the grounds would apparently be yet another thing she'd have to push off until tomorrow.

Two male guards, sporting light leather armor and sheathed swords, monitored their approach. Their eyes flicked quickly past Jaeros, clearly used to his face, but hesitated on her hooded frame. Their lingering attention made Jaren pull her closer, resting his hand on his dagger as he stared back.

But they said nothing as Jaeros spoke quietly to them, before glancing away from her and nodding. Vera's nerves shot in every direction, wondering who he'd said they were in order to get them past the gate. They hadn't discussed whether he'd introduce her as herself or not, and she wasn't sure how she felt about it. But Jaren seemed unworried as he gently caressed a thumb along her waist.

After another minute and a gruff nod, the guards stepped aside without a word, letting Jaeros through and aggressively gesturing for them to follow.

She swiveled her head side to side, squinting and trying to absorb every bit she could of the courtyard they walked through. They continued following Jaeros around the side, wandering off the main pathway onto a much skinnier, well-worn path. She wasn't sure what she'd expected, but a nondescript door nearly hidden in the dark wasn't it.

"The cook's entry," Jaeros said as way of explanation, and pushed open the door to reveal a long, dim hallway leading to a narrow set of stairs, empty apart from the lit torches on the walls.

She moved to follow, but Jaren laced his fingers with hers, pulling her back and pausing at the entrance. "You're sneaking us in? I thought you said they'd take your word for it?" His tone was saturated with clear, unveiled disdain.

Jaeros turned from where he'd been about to ascend the staircase. "What, you thought you'd just waltz her through the palace unnoticed? A palace lined with multiple large portraits of previous queens, including her mother, I might add." At Jaren's silence, he scoffed. "That's what I thought. Let's go."

He led them up the stairs and down several hallways, all just as plain and dim as the first, only stopping to talk to one young female who nodded at his question and smiled warmly.

It wasn't until they'd topped the third staircase that their surroundings changed. The sconces were more gaudy and detailed, and the walls were decorated with a plethora of paintings and plants, indicating they were no longer in a servant corridor.

Stopping beside a large oak door, Jaeros raised his hand in its direction before tipping his head down the hall toward another one just to the left.

"She told me both of these rooms are empty," he said, referring to the female he'd spoken to on their way up, "and I requested she inform the staff that you are not to be disturbed. But even still, take care of how you speak."

She nodded, ready to burst through the door and fling herself on the bed, but Jaren just crossed his arms and planted his feet, looking every bit the raging asshole. "We don't need a fucking babysitter. You did what you needed to do. Go home. I'm sure your *mate* is just dying to hear this story."

Vera wasn't sure how the male didn't wither under the pure hate pouring from his son, but he just met his stare, his expression blank, and said, "The other room is for you, not me."

She jumped when a deep laugh exploded from Jaren's chest,

filling her own and vibrating down her spine. Both of his canines peeked out as he smiled at his father, the expression was anything but sincere, before he grasped the handle to the first room and flung it open.

"Holy Aleron."

She'd obviously known any room for palace guests would be nice, but seeing it was something else entirely. Her and Elric's entire home could've fit inside the single room. The ceiling went straight up like a mountain peak, the torches at their level causing eerie shadows to dance up above them.

On the left was one of the largest beds she'd ever seen, easily big enough for three adults to comfortably fit, and covered in maroon blankets and stiff-looking, cream pillows. Against the far wall was a large window she couldn't yet see out of, and next to it was a long desk and a shelf lined with books.

Her legs itched to run over and look at them, curious what the Magyki nobility enjoyed reading, but considering she'd never learned to read Thyabathi, it wasn't like she'd understand it anyway.

On the right was a doorway she could only assume went to a bathing room, and next to it a hearth that took up the rest of the wall with several large, bucket-like chairs before it.

It was absolutely gorgeous, easily the nicest room she'd ever been given. Yet it somehow felt cold and uninviting, and she found herself homesick for the comfort of her old room.

"Dedryn and I will see you in the morning."

She drew her gaze from the room to look back at Jaeros,

who lingered just inside the doorway. The circles under his eyes were more pronounced and, she again wondered how old he really was.

He turned to leave, and she knew she needed to let him get some rest. They all needed it. But she had one question she desperately wanted the answer to. One she needed to know before she met King Vesstan.

"Jaeros?"

He turned back, his brows raised. "Yes?"

"Did my fa—did King Vesstan know? That I wasn't dead, I mean. Was he the one who asked you to send me away? Did he make you lie?"

She felt Jaren's hand lock around hers as his father stared hard at her. It was an unfair question to ask him in front of Jaren, but they both deserved to know before tomorrow. She needed to know if her father had ordered them to make the choice, or if they'd chosen on their own to lie to everyone. She squeezed Jaren's hand back, hoping for his sake, it was the first.

Jaeros's lips tightened, and for a second she thought he'd refuse to answer, but then he closed his eyes and shook his head. "No, Veralie, he didn't know."

The pain that shot through Jaren nearly sent her to her knees. She sucked in a shaky breath, wondering how he was standing so stoic when his insides were anything but.

None of it made sense. Why would they have done that to their son? She could see Jaeros's love for his son clear as day in his eyes. There had to have been a reason. But Jaeros said nothing else. He just looked at Jaren with an almost crippling sadness before walking out and shutting the door behind him.

JAREN

THEY'D NEVER TOLD HIM.

All these years, all this time, he'd believed King Vesstan had personally assigned him scouting duties on Aleron as a form of penance for his part in Veralie's death. His fathers might not have ever said it, but they had to have known it's what he assumed. Just more deceit to add to their ever-growing pile.

The hatred he felt was heavy and bitter, and if it weren't for the warmth of Veralie's presence, he wasn't sure what he might be capable of, to them or anyone else. Their betrayal cut all the way to his soul, slashing his ability to trust and ripping it out with apparent fucking glee.

He thought he had a handle on it, thought he could lock it all away like he'd always done, so Veralie would have the opportunity to find out what she needed. But for the first time in his life, he wasn't sure how much more he could take. Tomorrow would be the most important day of Veralie's life, but he feared, for him, it might be the one to break him completely.

"Why don't you check out the other room? I'll be all right."

He froze, his muddled brain taking a moment to realize what Veralie had just said. Slowly turning to face her, he narrowed his eyes and stalked toward her, giving her every chance to take it back. But she didn't.

Inhaling deeply, he fought against his limbs, forcing them to stop just shy of touching her. As much as he craved and needed her skin against his, he didn't trust himself to touch her. Didn't trust the thin layer of control that was barely holding back his violence and anger.

He wasn't afraid of maliciously hurting her—he could never do that—but his visceral need for her, for the reminder that she was here regardless of what his fathers did, was almost beyond his control. Their bond lashed and pulled at him, hardening his dick and demanding he claim her with more than just his teeth.

And he could. After weeks of waiting, they were finally in a palace, and he'd made her a promise. There was nothing stopping him from taking her and completing their bond. It screamed and begged for it.

But he knew, without a shadow of a doubt, he wouldn't be capable of gentle. Not today, nor any time soon. He'd take her hard and fast, pouring everything he felt into her with each thrust, needing to make her scream, to drown out the old screams that still tainted his memories.

He wanted to imprint himself on her body and prove to his mess of a mind she was *here*, and she was *his*.

"Jaren? Did you hear me?"

He blinked, snapping out of his internal spiral to focus on her concerned, silver eyes. "I was giving you the chance to realize on your own how fucking stupid your question was," he said, tilting his head to the side. "Because I know you didn't just tell me to stay in another room, little star."

Her worry disintegrated as molten fire took its place, and his chest rumbled, imagining that fierce gaze on him while he sank inside her. When would she learn that her anger only enticed him further?

"I didn't tell you to stay there, you sensitive ass. I just meant, there's an entire other bathing room down the hall." He didn't bother responding, and she rolled her eyes, gesturing to his body.

"I was trying to be nice, although now I'm not sure why. I just thought maybe you'd appreciate a silent bath. You certainly need it. Only one of us bathed in Ocridal, and it wasn't you," she said, wrinkling her nose.

His dick twitched at the thought of her bathing, and he fisted his hands, digging crescent moons into his palms to prevent himself from wrapping one around her throat and stealing her mouth. Her neck always arched so fucking pretty for him.

Gods damnit. He closed his eyes, expanding his lungs to calm himself only to unintentionally pull in even more of her scent. He snarled, launching himself backward and running for the door, ignoring her shocked expression as he almost ripped the door off its hinges.

He wasn't a fucking animal. He repeated it over and over as he barreled down the hall and into the other room, slamming the door behind him.

But an hour later, even after pouring an entire basin of cold water over himself, he was still repeating it. Ignoring his painfully hard erection, he scrubbed his skin raw for the third time, desperately trying to dig out the knowledge that his mate was naked and wet just across the hall.

"Gods dammit," he groaned, scrubbing harder.

He wasn't a fucking animal.

CHAPTER 11

VERA

Skin pink and hair dripping down her back from her last-minute decision to dunk her frizzed curls into the basin, she finally felt clean enough for bed.

She would much rather have been able to soak in a scalding tub for an hour, but she'd accepted that wandering the halls to find a servant wasn't exactly the best idea. Especially given the way Jaren would respond if he found out.

She worried her lip at the thought. He'd always been an overbearing asshole, even before he knew who she was, but the last few days had been so much worse. It was easy to understand why, but she had no idea how to help him.

She pulled her hair over her shoulder, wringing the excess water out as she contemplated what to do, if anything. Jaren would rather fall on a sword than willingly talk about his feelings, but maybe they could spend the morning beating the shit out of each other instead? Or…maybe do something else entirely.

She glanced at the door for the fiftieth time, her face flushing at what she could still feel pulsing from him down the hall. She'd been worried she'd truly pissed him off when he'd thrown himself from her and stormed out, but her worry hadn't lasted long.

He'd been gone less than five minutes before his pulse raced like he was fighting for his life, and then her chest exploded with a thick, heady feeling that made it quite clear washing was not what he was doing.

Jealousy and a tinge of hurt flickered through her, but she stomped them down, burying them as far as they'd go. She had no right to feel either when she'd been the one to send him off and tell him to enjoy some peace and quiet. Who was she to judge how he used his alone time?

It wasn't like she'd offered anything anyway, even though he'd clearly been thinking about it. Between the rhythm of his pulse and the way his scent had swirled around her, she'd fully expected him to snatch her up and throw her on the bed. But just as his tunic had brushed against her, he'd whipped around and rushed out like she'd set the room on fire.

His mood changes were going to give her whiplash one of these days.

She grabbed the last clean rag folded next to the basin and began squeezing her hair, determined not to let his ever-changing moods bother her. There were more important things to stress about than what Jaren did alone.

She'd just yanked up her annoyingly snug leggings and was glaring down at them, missing her loose trousers, when she heard the bathing room door slam open behind her.

She spun around, heart in her throat, only to be ensnared by a pair of hooded, emerald eyes. Voice higher pitched than she'd like, she flung her arms over her naked chest on instinct. "Gods, don't you knock? What are you doing?"

He didn't move from the doorway. He just stared at her, his skin reddened and his long hair damp across his clean-shaven face. His gaze moved hungrily over her body, taking in the skin peeking out from beneath her arms, and his eyes heated. They trailed up, devouring every inch of her exposed collar and shoulders like he could consume her from across the room.

He made no effort to hide his erection, and his scent assaulted her senses, causing her to squeeze her thighs together. Fuck, was she ever going to get used to feeling his desire tunnel through her without her own immediately responding?

As if he could hear her thoughts, his lips curled at the corner, warning her he was about to say something irritating, when he suddenly stiffened. His grin fell and his brow furrowed for just a moment before his entire body went unbelievably, unnaturally still.

What was he—but then she noticed where his eyes had zeroed in on. *What* his eyes had zeroed in on.

Shit.

141

"Where is it?"

She squeezed her arms harder against her chest, feeling like she was going to choke on the sudden lump in her throat. In her surprise, she'd been careless, not realizing her hair had fallen off her shoulder when she'd turned. "Where is what?" she asked stupidly, like they both weren't painfully aware of what he was looking at.

He took a single step toward her, biting out, "You know what."

Her fingers twitched, but she fought the temptation to drag them over the spot he was glaring a hole into. She'd known he'd find out eventually, she just hadn't planned on it happening before she'd prepared what to say.

"I, um…I healed it."

Another step. "You would've had to have done that soon after and hid it this entire time."

She winced. If words could cut, she'd be bleeding out on the floor. Swallowing hard, she lifted her chin, trying to look as confident as she could while half-naked. "Yes."

His nostrils flared and his hands fisted at his sides like it was taking everything in him not to throttle her. "Why?" he demanded. "You enjoyed it. Quite vocally, if I recall."

She blushed, remembering how she'd screamed his name, writhing against his hand. "Yes, but that doesn't mean I wanted to flaunt the details of our relationship to everyone around," she said, hoping he'd understand that her choice didn't mean she hadn't enjoyed it.

But it was the wrong thing to say.

He snarled, taking two more steps. "It's my mark, it's *meant* to be seen so your status of a mated female is known."

"It doesn't need to be known, Jaren. You don't own me, and my mated status is no one's damn business."

She sensed his heart rate spike as he dipped into his power, but with her arms wrapped so tightly around herself, she could do nothing as he lunged, closing the remaining distance and slamming into her.

The air whooshed out of her chest from the force, only to get caught in her throat when he wrapped a hand around it. He pressed a thumb under her jaw, forcing her head to tilt back sharply, while his other arm wrapped around her torso, his fingers hot against the base of her spine.

"Wrong," he said. "We are mates, Veralie. That means you are mine. Marking each other is done for pleasure, but *that* one had been for protection."

Her eyes narrowed, and she swallowed, having to push her words past the firm pressure on her throat. "I can protect myself."

"I didn't say it was to protect *you*."

He leaned down, grazing his lips over the crease that had appeared between her brows. "It protected everyone else from trying to take you from me. Because if anyone even considers it, I will kill them without hesitation."

Indignation flared. "I'm not some treasure you found, Jaren. I can't be taken."

"I know you can't," he whispered, releasing his grip to slide his hand to the back of her neck. "And I'm going to make sure of it." Taking a fistful of her hair, he jerked her head to the side and struck, sinking his teeth into the same spot he'd marked before.

She cried out even as arousal soared inside her, responding to his touch like a fucking puppet. But unluckily for him, her anger was stronger. She pulled her arms out from where they'd been pinned between them, no longer caring about covering herself. He wouldn't be able to see her breasts from the grave anyway.

Reaching up, she took two large handfuls of his hair and yanked at the roots as hard as she could, glad he hadn't cut it yet. She was going to rip out every gods damn strand.

He unlocked his jaw from her shoulder, pulling back only far enough to run his tongue over the new mark, and a soft moan slipped past her lips. Fuck, she'd felt that caress all the way down to her core.

He smiled against her, his self-satisfied, male ego flaring in her chest. Rolling his hips into her center, he repeated the gesture, giving each puncture quick flicks of his tongue.

She shuddered, the two sides of her heart and mind warring with one another. The human she'd been raised to be was enraged he'd so blatantly mark her against her wishes, but the Magyki in her blood reveled in his need to claim her. Their bond practically purred at the notion.

He ground his hard length into her again, purposefully

using her desire to his advantage. It only infuriated her more. She hated that she couldn't block his front row seat to every feeling she experienced. The ass didn't deserve to know how strongly he affected her.

His eyes sparked at whatever he felt pulsating through their bond. "Stop fighting your nature, Veralie. You're not human. You're Magyki, and you're mine."

Lowering her hands from his hair, she placed both on his chest and shoved him back, knowing she only succeeded because he let her. He smirked, and the arrogance dripping from his expression had her rearing back and punching him in the face.

His head snapped to the side, and a string of expletives graced the air as he stumbled, blood dripping from his now split lip. His gaze snapped to hers, and he worked his jaw, not bothering to wipe his face. Eyes dipping to her uncovered breasts, he smiled savagely, the white of his teeth smeared with red. "I suggest you run, little star."

So, she did. Launching herself forward, she smashed into him, catching him off guard and sending them both flying through the open door. They hit the bedroom floor hard, Jaren's head bouncing off the wood as he took the brunt of the fall.

Taking advantage and hoping the whack to his head had knocked some gods damn sense into him, she straddled his torso, landing two more hits to his face. He wanted to mark her? Fine. She'd mark him right fucking back.

His hands came up to grip her hips even as his head whipped to the side from another blow and blood coated his chin. He bucked his hips while gripping and pulling on her own, trying to throw her over him.

Fucking asshole. She squeezed her thighs tighter, refusing to be dislodged, and fisted his tunic as she leaned down into his gloriously busted face.

Staring directly into his eyes, she searched for that well of power, coaxing it and hoping it listened. She smiled when she felt the burn of her skin stitching together.

His answering look was nothing short of feral. Their bond hummed, and he bared his canines, looking seconds away from ripping out her throat.

Unlike her, he didn't coax his power. He tore it open and rammed a fist in, striking her chest and launching her backward into the air. Her stomach flipped, and she had a split second of shocked fury before her back smacked the cold floor and her hands were pinned above her head.

The bulk of his weight pressed into her as he wrapped his hand around her throat and snarled. "We can keep at this all day. You have zero control and will only succeed in draining yourself. So, go ahead, fight me. When will you learn I fucking love it."

He struck again, biting the same spot deeper. She screamed, thrashing and kicking, trying to ignore the answering warmth that trickled through her body.

"Gods dammit, stop biting me!"

"No." He switched hands and moved to her other shoulder, sinking his teeth in again.

She cursed his name, bucking beneath him even as wetness

pooled between her legs. Gods damn her body and the way it responded to him. How could she want to fight and give in all at the same time?

He inhaled, growling into her neck, and glided his tongue over her heated skin before pulling back. "Your fury only heightens the taste. It's fucking divine."

She glared, ready to head butt him in the nose, but he anticipated it. Tightening his grip on her wrists, he smirked and dropped his head to her chest, wrapping his lips around one of her nipples.

Blinded by her clashing emotions, she'd completely forgotten she was topless, and the sensation of him sucking her nipple deep into his mouth had her mind emptying. She whimpered when he sucked harder, punishing her, before releasing her tip to run his tongue over it.

She shuddered as he did it again before trailing that gods damn mouth up her breast. He pressed a single, soft kiss to her skin before sinking his teeth into the top of her breast.

"What in Aleron is wrong with you?" She screeched.

Raising his head at her tone, he rolled his hips sharply into her, eliciting an uncontrolled groan from her throat. "I'll stop when you say it."

Her pulse rocketed out of her veins and her breathing became labored. She wanted to give in. Gods, did she want to. The Magyki in her wanted to scream, "I'm yours!" at the top of her lungs and lie there submissively while her mate used and pleasured her body.

But the human in her, the human who'd been raised by Elric to defend herself against anyone, resisted. She wanted him. She wasn't ashamed of it and couldn't deny it even if she wanted to, not when he could feel it. But that didn't mean she had to make it easy on him.

Giving free reign to her lust, she allowed it to flow through her body, lighting her on fire and drenching her, hoping it would distract him. By the darkening of his eyes, she was right. He released her wrists, resting his hand next to her head while his other moved to her breast, and captured her mouth in a vicious kiss.

She accepted it, kissing him back with all the hunger and aggression he'd awoken in her. The metallic taste of his blood filled her mouth, and she pulled harder on his lip, his answering groan shooting straight to her core.

She ignored it. The weight of his body on hers, the way his fingers worked her nipple, and the orgasm slowly building between her legs. She ignored every single desire she so desperately wanted to give in to, and slammed her head up into his nose.

He roared as his head snapped back, and she wasted no time. Pushing against his chest as hard as she could, she twisted onto her stomach to crawl out from under him. There was nowhere for her to go, but at least she wouldn't be pinned beneath him.

She pushed to her feet, but only made it about a foot before his hand snatched her ankle. Unprepared for him to have recovered already, she slammed back down, face first.

The crack of her head hitting the wood echoed in her ears, and she blinked dots out of her vision, feeling the spread of warmth as blood smeared across her forehead.

She cursed, calling him every horrible name in both languages to hide the way her body sang at the pain. As if there was any way to hide what she felt from him. And she didn't really want to anymore. Whatever this was? His body sang for it too.

Ignoring her foul mouth, Jaren grabbed her hips, pressing his nails in painfully as he flipped her onto her back. But instead of pinning her beneath his weight like she expected, he dipped both hands under the band of her new leggings and ripped them down the front.

The snug fabric dug into her sides from his brutal treatment, and she inhaled sharply, choking when his scent poured down her throat. Whatever minimal restraint he'd been using was gone, and nothing but unquenchable, feral lust remained as he tore the rest of her clothes from her body.

She couldn't fight against the pull of it—of *him*—and she no longer wanted to. Not as their bond pulsed, and he flung her thighs open and dove down, gliding his tongue straight through her center. Her head fell back in bliss, the firm pressure of his tongue drawing a hoarse groan up her throat.

He growled in answer, the vibration doing unimaginable things to her as he frantically lapped at her wetness like it was the nectar to life.

"You taste like you enjoy my marks, *aitanta*," he murmured

into her heat. "Tell me, am I going to have to leave one on every visible inch of your skin, or are you going to behave?"

She cursed, digging her nails into his scalp, even as her back arched and her thighs clamped his head in place. "Please."

"Or maybe misbehaving is exactly what you want." He thrust his tongue inside her, swirling and caressing before pulling out and working it over her clit in a way that nearly had her in tears.

"I do not own you, Veralie, just as I do not own any star in the sky," he said in between hard flicks. "But you are mine, nonetheless."

Her breaths came harsher and quicker as he pushed his thumb inside her, that tingle working higher up her spine and threatening to tip her over the edge. "Okay."

"I want to hear you say it." He pulled his thumb out only to quickly replace it with a sharp thrust of two fingers. He buried them as deep as they'd go, sucking hard on her clit as he did.

She arched off the floor, holding onto his hair for dear life while she ground against his face. "Oh gods, I'm yours."

"*Mine*. Mine to use, mine to pleasure, mine to hurt. And I will mark you until every Magyki on Bhasura knows it."

"Please, Jaren." She didn't care anymore. He could cover her arms in them, and she wouldn't say a word against it, just as long as he stopped talking and put his mouth back on her. But he didn't. He just kept thrusting his fingers as he raised his head and met her gaze.

"I wanted to wait. I wanted to go slow with you and bind

our souls together gently. But I can't. I need you too badly, little star."

His body shuddered, and she could sense he was struggling to hold himself back, needing this—needing her—to repair the wound in his soul. But even still, he waited, giving her the chance to say no.

The bite marks on her body throbbed in time with the fingers pumping in and out of her. Forcing his marks on her had been a bastard move, but there was no doubt in her mind, if she said no to this, he'd accept it.

She placed a hand on his cheek, rotating her hips to give him better access. "I need you, too, Jaren."

He closed his eyes, his fingers thrusting in deep. "I won't be gentle," he warned, a low growl in his voice as he added a third finger.

She winced, her body unprepared for the fullness, but the discomfort quickly faded when he curled his fingers to press on that blessed, gods damn spot. "I told you before, I can take it."

His chest rumbled, and he removed his fingers to undo his trousers, chuckling darkly when she whined. His rock-hard length sprang free, and he wasted no time reaching down and pressing his tip on her throbbing clit.

Pleasure rippled off him, and he cursed when he rubbed himself down her center, sliding easily through her arousal. "You fought me so hard, *aitanta*, yet feel how wet you are for me." He hummed, circling her clit with his free hand. "Your body craves my marks."

"Actually, it craves tearing your teeth out and shoving them in your own gods damn neck," she said, her body tensing when he finally aligned with her entrance.

His entire body shook when he pressed in just slightly, the last thread of his control seconds from snapping. "You could always shove in yours."

She blinked, his comment distracting her from the thick head pressing into her. He wanted her to bite him *back?* She blanched, shaking her head. "That's not going to happen."

He flashed her a canine. "We'll see." Rolling his hips, he pushed in slowly, watching her face with unnerving focus.

He'd barely moved at all when she bit back a hiss, the stretch already stinging. "You're not going to fit, Jaren."

He pressed on the inside of her thighs, spreading them as far as she could handle before wrapping his hands around her hips. "The gods made you to take me. It'll fucking fit."

Dropping his gaze to where they were connected, he bared his teeth and thrust up sharply, shattering her entire sense of self.

She cried out, closing her eyes, and grasped at his arms as her center clenched and burned. "Gods, I think you tore me in half," she croaked, breathing through the discomfort.

He chuckled. "Oh, little star, that wasn't even all of me." Her eyes flew open just before he smashed his lips to hers, tasting her cry, and slammed the rest of the way in.

CHAPTER 12

JAREN

Even drenched in freezing water, he'd been a raging inferno. Blood boiling, cock hard, and skin throbbing from his violent scrubbing, he'd felt ready to combust.

In his desperation to ease the frantic need burning him alive, he'd leaned against the wash basin, throwing his head back and fisting his shaft, working himself in a painful, punishing rhythm.

He'd just needed to get it out of his system so he could return to her feeling slightly less aggressive and crawl in bed without ravaging her. But no matter how hard he gripped himself or how fast he moved, it wasn't enough.

Not when he knew what else he could have.

After gods only knew how long of fighting it, he'd broke, deciding if he couldn't take her the way he wanted, he could at least feast between her thighs until they both came.

Her scent was still scorching his senses, but it wasn't enough to satiate him. He needed to bury his nose in her heat and drown out every thought in his head while her taste slid down his throat.

He hadn't even bothered to put his undershorts on before flinging his trousers up and stalking back toward their room with a single-minded focus.

When he'd knocked the bathing room door open and saw her topless, the shadowed curves of her breasts peeking out from under her arms, the beast he'd been holding back had rattled at its cage, demanding to be released at her.

Fuck. He'd already been on edge from the shit with his father forcing him to relive that horrifying night again and again. All he'd needed was to touch her and remind himself that she was there. Alive. That his fathers' actions hadn't taken her from him permanently.

But then he'd seen her shoulder, and the world seemed to freeze in time around him just before the cage exploded into a million pieces. He wasn't proud of what he'd done in response, but he sure as fuck didn't regret it either.

If he thought he'd desired her before, it was nothing compared to what he felt when she'd launched at him half-naked, snarling and marking him in her own way. He loved not being able to anticipate what she'd do next. She was a fucking goddess.

Being inside her was ecstasy. Pure fucking ecstasy. As life

changing as he knew it would be. She was so tight he deserved a gods damn prize for not immediately coming undone and filling her. Her body squeezed and spasmed around him like it was begging him for it. And fuck, if he didn't want to give it to her.

She cried out against his lips, instinctually shifting her hips away from the harsh, sudden intrusion, but he tightened his grip, pinning her in place. He stroked the pad of his thumb along her skin when she winced.

He knew the first time would sting no matter how gentle or rough he was, but he also knew it wouldn't last long before her body relaxed and stretched around him. Just like it was made to. "Breathe, Veralie. That's it."

Seated all the way, he didn't move for several seconds—the act its own form of agony—giving her a moment to adjust to his size. She bit her lip and inhaled sharply through her nose, her nails digging into his biceps. The sight of her stiff and breathless beneath him should've made him feel guilty, but gods damn him, it didn't. He reveled in it.

He'd never purposefully seek to cause her any real pain, but *this* pain? This pain he liked. Each heavy breath and wince was proof it was really happening. Proof that she'd feel him with every step she took tomorrow.

When she met the King, when she was announced to the court, and whatever else they required of her tomorrow, she'd do it while simultaneously thinking about what it'd felt like to have him inside her.

He gave her one last second, and then, convinced he might

actually die if he didn't move, he twitched his hips forward to test her reaction. She squeezed her eyes shut, her body tensing as her knees tightened their hold around his hips. "Holy gods."

Trailing his lips up the smooth skin of her jaw, he whispered, "Did I hurt you?"

She sucked in a short breath. "A little, yeah."

"Good."

Her eyes snapped open, and when he didn't retract his response, they narrowed. "Wanting to cause me pain is a character flaw you should reflect on during meditation," she said, repeating back to him the taunt he'd used.

He grinned, pulling out agonizingly slow only to slam back in, his arms stinging as her nails finally broke skin. "Then I suppose I'll have to spend the entire rest of the night meditating after what I plan to do to you."

"You're insane," she whispered, even as her shoulders relaxed, and her hips shifted toward him. Hesitantly, exploring and testing the feel of him.

He ran the tip of his tongue over the split in his lip, the area sticky and beginning to swell since he had no intentions of healing it. There was something about knowing she'd never be afraid to fight back that filled him with a dark sense of excitement, and he swore his dick hardened even more.

"Don't act like you don't get off hurting me, too, little star."

"I don't."

He stayed buried to the hilt, rolling his hips up into her in a steady rhythm, keeping excess friction at bay while hitting that

156

spot inside her. The one that made her hands slide up to his neck and her eyes nearly roll back. "Your possessiveness and need to mark me back disagrees."

"I didn't—"

"You may not have used your teeth, but you marked me all the same." He continued at the same steady pace, easing farther back with each roll of his hips until, eventually, he was fully thrusting in and out of her.

He watched her face for any sign he should stop, but she only groaned and arched into him, wrapping her legs around his waist. Thank fuck. He increased his speed, and her hands shot to his back as he began to move, clawing at his shoulder blades as she tried in vain to stay quiet.

"Don't hold back, *aitanta*," he said, pulling out and shoving in to the hilt, again and again. "I want to hear every sound your body sings for me."

With that, he let go, releasing the vise-like grip he'd had around his control, and letting it crumble to ash where their bodies connected. Clenching his jaw, he let his nature take over, bucking into her like a feral animal. He certainly felt like one. He couldn't get enough, feel enough, taste enough.

His knees were screaming at him, the movements and weight of his body grinding his bones into the wood, but he didn't stop. He couldn't even if he tried. He just continued rutting into her, one hand leaving finger-sized bruises on her hip while the other met back at her clit, moving in small, quick circles that he knew would break her.

As if on cue, her back lurched off the ground, and she cried out his name, carving bloody lines along his ribs. He snarled, satisfaction flaring so hot, spots danced across his vision.

"That's it. Let them fucking hear you. I want everyone in this gods damn palace to know how deep I am inside you. To know you're mine without even laying eyes on you."

Sensing she was close, he thrust deep and rocked his hips up, grinding against that blessed spot. Then he pinched her clit, right as he flicked his tongue over his first mark on her shoulder, and she exploded.

Her body shuddered and convulsed around him, milking him until he had to clench his jaw and moan into her shoulder to keep from losing his load right along with her. She cried out, her words jumbled and incoherent until it sounded more like a new language than any he knew.

Her orgasm was like nothing he'd ever felt before, flowing through him until he couldn't tell whether it was hers or his. And as the last wave washed through them, and her body slumped to the floor, something sparked to life in his chest.

Their bond.

It vibrated inside him so strong; he swore he could hear it humming in his ears, making its existence known and demanding he listen. As if he could ever forget.

Chest heaving, he stared down at the wide, silver eyes of the female beneath him, and for the first time in over fifteen years, he was whole. It was like he'd been living his entire life buried alive, ten feet underground, and had finally clawed his way out.

To her.

He slowed his movements, continuing to move into her in deep, measured thrusts, treasuring the feel of her hands caressing his skin. She was finally his in every way.

It didn't matter what happened. With his fathers, with Aleron, with the expectations of her title and what being her mate would mean for him as well. It didn't matter that they'd spent more years apart than together, nor that she'd grown up human and, he, Magyki. None of it mattered.

She was his, and only his, until the God of Death took them. And he'd chase her even then.

"Jaren," she said, his name a mere whisper on her lips. Her eyes were wide and glassy as their bond tightened and thrummed between them.

"I know," he said, pressing his lips to hers and sinking deeper, all while tugging on that thread between them. She groaned into his mouth, squeezing her thighs around his waist and placing both hands on his ass, urging him on.

He felt wild and unhinged as he thrust harder, pouring everything he was into her. The good, the bad, the blinding pleasure, and the soul-crushing pain. He wanted her to feel it all, to understand exactly who he was and how he felt about her. How he would *always* feel.

Knowing she accepted all of that and still ground into him, seeking more, had his orgasm crashing into him. He yanked her up, her legs still wrapped around his waist, and pressed her chest flush against him as he slammed balls deep inside her, finally—

fucking finally—claiming her completely.

He held her there until the last shudder worked through his body, draining him of the last of his energy. He lowered her back to the ground, careful to stay seated inside her, that animalistic hunger that seemed to grow within him the longer they were together, liking the idea of his release being unable to drip out.

He said nothing as he pressed his lips to hers again. There was nothing to say. Nothing to do but soak in the feel and taste of her and the sensation of her tongue gliding against his.

A flash of anxiety suddenly lashed through him, but it wasn't his, and then she was breaking their kiss, pushing him back and glancing down between them. "You didn't—Oh gods, you said…there's an elixir I can take, right? Do I need to take it right now? Is it too late?"

Chuckling at her panic, he forced himself to pull out and roll off her, laying his back flat on the floor. "*Truik elixir.* It's very effective, and no, it's not too late," he said, pulling her into his arms until she was perfectly nestled into his side. "This time, you'll have to take it, but starting tomorrow, I'll take a daily dose myself, so you won't have to worry about it."

The tension in her body eased, and she placed a single kiss on his chest that he felt soar through his entire body. "So," she said, pausing to glance down at the mark on her breast, "now that you've had your tantrum, does this mean you'll back off a little?"

"I'll give you one guess."

She rolled her eyes, but there was no heat in the expression, only amusement flickering between them. "We're fully bonded, Jaren. That literally means I can't be taken."

Gripping her jaw, he tilted her face up to his. "The fifteen years I went without you say otherwise."

Her eyes softened. "That won't happen again," she said. Then she smirked. "Besides, how many more ways could you possibly mark me? You were quite thorough." She trailed off, rolling her lips in as her amusement quickly turned to regret at the look he gave her.

"You should know by now, I have no limits when it comes to you, Veralie. I'll fill every hole on your body and bite every inch of skin, and it still wouldn't be enough."

Her eyes widened in horror, and he chuckled again, slowly running his hand across her shoulder and down her side, his nostrils flaring as he took in her scent.

"Mm, you always smell delicious," he murmured, caressing his fingers over her hip and continuing down until they met up with her clit. "But you smell even better when you smell like me."

She groaned, flinging a leg over his and curling farther into him to give him better access. Her breath stuttered when he added pressure and began to circle the swollen bud, their combined releases dripping out of her to coat his thigh.

"I'm sorry, you know," she said between pants. Gods, he'd never get over the sound of her pleasure. It was so fucking sweet.

He brushed his lips over her forehead, humming as he quickened his pace to what he knew she loved, reveling in his mate rolling against his hand. Even the unforgiving floor beneath him couldn't take away from his contentment. "I forgive you, little star. I like these new ones better anyway." It was true. They were deeper and would scar far better.

Her hips immediately froze, and she let out an irritated huff. "I'm not sorry I healed your mark, Jaren."

His lips paused over her skin, and he inhaled sharply, lowering his hand to cup her entirely. If she thought she was going to heal these ones, they were going to have a long ass fucking night. He'd start over as many times as he needed to.

Likely sensing his spike of frustration, she pushed up onto her elbow and leaned over him, the silver in her eyes still swirling with the lust he'd been stroking back to life.

"I won't apologize for how I felt. And expecting me to regret or second guess my emotions just because you didn't agree with them would make you a shitty ass mate."

She paused, taking a deep breath and placing her palm over his heart. "But I *am* sorry I hid it from you. That wasn't fair. Especially when I knew what it meant to you."

He stared at her for a long moment, thinking over her words. She was right. Gently pushing her off, he stood, trying to ignore how close her face was to his cock as he held out a hand and helped her to her feet.

He couldn't fight his smile. She was a mess. Her hair was only partially dry, her curls were sticking out every which way, and there were bloody streaks covering her shoulders and breast. She had a pink hue to her cheeks, and already small, finger-sized bruises blossomed over her hips and thighs.

"You're so gods damn beautiful," he said, unable to stop the awe from appearing in his voice.

She blinked, and her lips popped open in surprise, but he just squeezed her hand, guiding her to their bed. They could talk more tomorrow. For now, he needed to finish what he'd started.

Another orgasm and one hour later, Jaren lay half-asleep, the steady rise and fall of her chest lulling him to join her in sleep. He tucked her in closer, burying his nose in her hair as he finally closed his eyes.

"I can't lose you again, little star. I wouldn't survive it."

CHAPTER 13

TREY

I need her to rage. Those five words banged through his head in time with his constant headache, mercilessly repeating on an endless loop, even in his sleep, making him agitated and restless.

I need her to rage.

It'd been days since Eithan had visited him. Or, at least, that's what it felt like. It was impossible to know given he hadn't seen the sky or a window since he'd first been arrested. The only thing he had to go off of was the almost clockwork arrival of Healer Perry.

From what Trey could gather, he checked on him twice a day, removing his restraints long enough for him to use a chamber pot, change his sheets, and bring him a small amount of food.

He didn't bother trying to speak to him again. It hadn't worked the first time, and he sure as fuck wasn't going to thank him for keeping him alive.

Because of that, part of him thought he might actually hate the young healer more than he hated Eithan. To the point that if just sitting over a bucket to shit didn't wipe him out, he'd have strangled the motherfucker the first time he removed his bindings.

But in the hours between his visits, Trey's mind always seemed to wander back to Eithan's taunt. Back to Vera and what that psycho was going to do to her when she finally returned.

There was no *if* she returned. He wanted it to be possible she wouldn't; gods, did he. But he knew his friend, and as much as it should've warmed his heart to know what lengths she'd go to for him, it didn't.

The thought stalled his heart and rattled his mind, making him feel like he was going even more mad than he'd been before.

Not only had he failed in every aspect he already hated himself for, but now he'd also be at fault for whatever future awaited her when that bastard got his hands on her. His nausea swelled, and he gagged, unable to rid himself of the lump that seemed to permanently sit in his throat these days.

He knew Eithan wouldn't hurt her at first, not when he clearly needed to use her. But her usefulness wouldn't last forever, especially when she discovered he wasn't the charming prince he pretended to be.

Vera was strong in a way neither he nor Eithan could ever

be, but even her abilities couldn't protect her in a city full of loyal Matherin guards.

He startled out of his thoughts when heavy footsteps echoed outside the infirmary door, and he tensed despite himself, adrenaline filling his limbs and pissing him off. Why did he still fear the gods damn bastard? Why did just the thought of being taken back to the dungeon send a cold sweat down his spine?

Trying to wipe the fear off his face so the bastard wouldn't get the satisfaction of seeing it, he listened to the lock click and watched as the door slowly creaked open. For a moment, there was nothing, and then a thick-fingered hand curled around it, pushing it open just wide enough for a huge, bulk of a body to squeeze through.

Trey blinked, trying to understand what the fuck he was seeing as the broad-shouldered man eased it back shut, careful not to make too much noise. As if a man of his size had any hope of being quiet.

"Jen...sen?"

The visitor whipped around, his elbow smacking against the door with a loud *thud*. Cringing, he rubbed his elbow as his long-ass strides quickly ate the distance across the room.

"I don't have long," he said, coming to a stop at the foot of Trey's cot. Fuck, it really was him. His voice was the same deep, raspy tone, laced with a lilt that always reminded Trey of home.

Although they'd both grown up in Southterres, Trey had never had much of an accent, but Brex Jensen's was thick with a deep roll to it that had immediately made him the bullseye of many barrack taunts when they'd joined the guard.

When you constantly had to dress and act like one another, things like voices and hair were the only things left to talk shit on. It was why Jensen had learned to keep quiet around most, and why Vera had humorously assumed he didn't speak at all.

What the fuck was he doing there? It should've filled him with hope, but all he felt was gut-wrenching panic as Jensen stood there, eyes dark, taking in his condition. Gods, Eithan would fucking kill him if he found him there. Or worse.

The very real possibility of hearing his childhood friend's agonizing screams in a neighboring cell while their soulless prince did whatever sick shit he got off on had acid climbing up his throat. He squeezed his eye shut, blocking out Jensen's tan, weathered face to avoid having a complete panic attack. He couldn't let that happen.

Seconds ticked by, the room silent, and his body relaxed ever so slightly. Maybe he'd just imagined him. It wouldn't be the first time his broken mind had conjured up something that wasn't real. Maybe—

"You look like shit."

His eye snapped open to find Jensen lumbering over him, arms crossed and eyes narrowed, clearly pissed at being ignored. Gods damnit.

He ran his tongue over his lips, trying to wet the dry and cracked flesh, but he might as well have run sandpaper over them. "You need to leave."

His friend didn't bat an eye. "And you need to stop being a pussy."

The *fuck?* The air grew heavy as Trey waited for him to say something else. Something to explain what on all of Aleron he was doing there. But Jensen said nothing, glaring daggers at him.

Did Jensen truly hear about him being in the infirmary with no knowledge of why or the danger he would be in for coming? It didn't make sense, and there was certainly no way he'd found him on accident.

"I'm serious, Brex. I don't know what you're doing, but you need to fuck off."

His friend raised a bushy eyebrow, audibly sucking on his front teeth. "If I wanted someone to nag at me, I'd find me a wife."

May the God of Death take him already. "Eat shit. I'm trying to save your stupid ass. If you're caught in here, you'll never so much as even see another woman again, let alone find one desperate enough to marry you."

Jensen ignored the taunt, unfurling his arms to pick at a hangnail, looking completely at home and unconcerned. "It's a shame His Highness didn't remove your tongue instead. You're even more annoying with one eye than you were with two."

"Guess he's not ready to add to his collection yet. He's probably saving that for our anniversary."

Jensen's gaze flicked up to the patch Perry had recently secured over his empty eye socket and grunted, the corner of his lips twitching. "Wouldn't surprise me if the fucker carried it in his pocket like a good luck charm."

Trey released a dark chuckle, the act feeling foreign and wrong. "He does seem like the kind to keep his trophies close to him."

Another grunt. "His obsession with possessing Veralie Arenaris supports that assumption. It wouldn't surprise me if he chained her to him to prevent her from leaving again."

Trey jolted, his body screaming in pain when his muscles all seemed to tighten at once. "Tell me she's not here, Brex." Fear consumed him all over again as images of Eithan touching her flooded his mind.

Jensen just sniffed, tilting his head and staring at him with a disappointed expression, like he was impatiently waiting for something to happen.

Trey's anger flared hot. *"Tell me!"* he demanded, his voice cracking.

Jensen pushed his tongue under his upper lip, shifting his weight back and considering him before he answered. "No, he doesn't have her yet. At least, not that we know of. But if the fucker keeps sending letters, Lesta says it's only a matter of time before she shows up."

His immediate relief at her still being on Bhasura was short lived when the rest of Jensen's comment landed. Clarity slapped him across the face, and he scoffed. "I should've known Lesta was the one to send you."

A nod.

He rolled his head to stare up at the ceiling. He was so fucking tired. "Why would he even bother? To fucking punish me more?" How did he even know where he was? Eithan trusted no one. There was no way he'd told anyone other than Healer Perry. Trey would bet his life on it.

"Lesta has his fingers in more pots than even that fucker knows. The Matheris family isn't as loved as they like to think," Jensen said, glancing down Trey's body and stopping on the cot's straps, lips pursed in thought.

"I don't care how loved they are or aren't. No amount of Lesta's gods damn pots is going to get me out of here. And I don't fucking want it to. I'm done. Whatever Lesta has planned, I'm done."

Jensen's eyes snapped back up to his face. "I told you to stop being a pussy."

When Trey didn't respond, he crossed his arms, revulsion coating his usual stoic expression. "The man I grew up with wouldn't have chosen to lay in a fucking bed when someone he loved needed him. When his *people* needed him."

"The man you grew up with is dead. What the fuck do you want from me?" he asked, leaning up until his neck ached and his bonds dug into his chest. "You want to help me? Then put me out of my gods damn misery, Jensen. That's what I choose."

"Even if that means leaving Vera blind when she returns, *for you,* and steps right into the viper's nest?"

He flinched, his heart squeezing and constricting in his chest. And it only made him angrier. "What do you all think I can do? Look at me!" he yelled, his lips finally wetting as they cracked open and bled.

Jensen darted a glance at the door at his outburst, and then turned back, leaning his face over Trey's. "I've seen you look worse. I seem to recall us both taking back-to-back beatings for each other from shithead kids around town when we were young."

"Funny, I don't seem to recall any of them torturing and starving me for days on end."

Jensen just smirked, making him see red. If he said one more gods damn thing, Trey swore he'd somehow find a way to knock his teeth in.

"Honestly, you should thank His Highness. You're far less ugly now," Jensen said, tapping a single finger over his eyepatch. "Bit more of a coward than I remember though—"

Rearing up as much as his bonds allowed, Trey twisted, punching him as hard as he could in the side of his face. The sudden movement hurt, the burning along his side telling him he'd ripped open a stitch or two. But hearing Jensen's barked curse and seeing him stumble to the side made it well worth it.

Fucking asshole.

Holding a giant hand over the side of his face, his friend straightened his spine, meeting Trey's furious gaze as a rare, real laugh burst out of him. "Took you long enough. Looks like there's some fight left in you after all, my friend."

CHAPTER 14

VERA

The featherlight brush of something along her back sent gooseflesh down her spine, and she shuddered, rolling her body deeper into the warmth encircling her. A responding rumble tickled her cheek, and she grumbled, snuggling in closer.

The sound deepened, vibrating along her jaw just before a spark of warmth flooded her chest, and a gravelly chuckle echoed out from above her.

"As much as I've loved waking to the feel of your ass beneath me, I think I might like this even more."

Forcing herself to raise her head, she arched her neck back and met a pair of heavy-lidded, emerald eyes. His lips, still busted and swollen, twitched as he stared down at her, affection and humor warring in his gaze. Brushing her wild curls out of her face, he dropped his hand to her hip, sliding it down along her thigh to hook behind her knee and yank it up over his own.

Neither of them had bothered to dress after their night together, and she flushed as he pulled her center hard against his leg, sending a dull ache pulsing through her lower half. If she hadn't already known she was going to be sore today, she did now.

After giving her more orgasms than she'd even known she could have, Jaren's entire demeanor had changed. His touches lost their bite, and he'd gotten up to wet a rag and had patiently cleaned her up, leaving gentle nips and kisses along her body as he did.

By the time he'd finished, she hadn't even remembered curling up and falling asleep, let alone him climbing in and pulling her into his arms.

She couldn't help the small smile that pulled at her mouth. She'd slept better than she ever had.

Something had irrevocably changed between them now that their bond had completely snapped into place, but she couldn't quite find the words to describe what, exactly, was different.

Her sense of him was stronger, more potent than before, but it was more than that. Her entire life, she'd felt like something was missing. She'd always thought it'd stemmed from her desire to leave the armory and see the world, but it hadn't been that at all.

It had always been him.

She wasn't sure how long they laid there, neither in a hurry to move as he ran a hand up and down her leg, massaging her muscles in ways that had her biting back a moan.

"Why have you never asked me about us?"

His question startled her out of her thoughts, and she frowned. "What do you mean?" They talked about their bond all the time, it was literally his favorite topic.

He shook his head, moving to her other leg and kneading her calf. "Not us now. I meant our childhood."

"I don't know. We were so young, I guess I just assumed you didn't remember much more than I did," she said, but it was only partly true. She also worried about *him*, about what those memories would do if he lingered on them.

"I remember every second."

Her breath stuttered at the way he looked at her. Like she was the last remaining star in a deserted night sky. "Let me guess, I was a complete pain in the ass, little kid," she joked, her skin heating under his stare.

"Oh, you absolutely were," he said, grinning. "You were like a second shadow, following me around everywhere, even when I was training and you were supposed to be practicing script."

"That explains why I can't read, I suppose." She laughed. "I bet you hated me back then."

He leaned up, cupping her face and caressing his thumb down her cheek. The gentle act sent butterflies off in her stomach, and she wished they could stay like that every day.

"You were the most annoying female on the entire island,

but no, not once have I ever hated you, little star. Not even when you left me in a piss-filled alley."

She narrowed her eyes, the butterflies falling dead. "You called me a thief and threatened to kill me several times."

In one smooth movement, he rolled on top of her, nestling his legs between hers and resting his hands on either side of her face. "Yet, even then, I wanted to fuck you into the gods damn floor."

A laugh burst out of her, loud and carefree. "You have such a way with words."

His eyes sparked; their color bright as they dipped to her mouth. He didn't seem to be breathing. "I will say anything you ask of me, if you just do that again."

Aware they were still very much naked, she fidgeted. The movement pulled at her skin, and she flinched, having forgotten about the multitude of bites her mate had bestowed upon her.

He grinned wickedly, rolling back off her to continue where he'd left off, kneading his fingers up her thigh. "Are you going to heal yourself?"

She blinked, trying to keep her eyes from rolling to the back of her head from the magic his fingers were currently working before she could comprehend his question. "What?"

He looked pointedly below her navel, indicating he wasn't referring to his bites, and repeated it, his tone suspiciously calm and even. Like he was putting up a wall to protect himself from the answer he already anticipated she'd give.

She flushed, embarrassment shooting through her at how

cowardly she'd been about the entire thing. He was a fucking ass, for sure, but it also wasn't his fault that they'd grown up so differently. She should've just been honest with him from the beginning.

His face hardened, and his arms tensed around her as he misunderstood the shame radiating from her. "No," she said, pushing up to a sitting position and wincing, the ache between her legs increasing with each movement. "No, I'm not going to heal, Jaren. I'm not ashamed of what we've done."

She smirked; glad she wasn't as red as a tomato for once. "I like the reminder."

His nostrils flared, and he slid his hand up over her ass, his eyes promising a multitude of morning scenarios as his fingers grazed just between her cheeks.

The heat that immediately blazed to life at his touch had her shooting up and knocking his hand away to grab one of the many blankets strewn about them. She ignored the dark chuckle from behind her as she shoved off the bed, wrapping the stolen blanket around herself.

Apparently, she was going to have to put some distance between them if they were to get anything accomplished today. Otherwise, she had a feeling they'd spend the day repeating last night rather than meeting anyone. The predatory look on his face as he watched her walk to their pile of belongings only confirmed her assumption.

"You didn't have to destroy my clothing, you know," she tossed over her shoulder, trying to lighten the mood as she searched for a clean pair of undergarments and leggings.

"Yes, I did."

She paused her rummaging to flick an amused look at him, raising one brow. He sounded stupidly proud of himself. "Well, now you get to fit shopping into your schedule again since you've dropped me down to only one pair."

"Considering I don't plan on you needing to wear them very often, I'd say one is all you need," he said, rolling his tongue over his bottom lip, eyes locked on her bare legs.

She squeezed her thighs together. How she could be so sore, yet so ready to do it again at just one look, was something she probably needed to contemplate later. But gods, the way he'd touched her—

A sharp rap on the door had her jumping out of her skin. Jaeros! Panicking and praying he didn't threaten to barge in like last time, she let the blanket fall to her feet and snatched up her clothing, yanking them on and ignoring the slight twist in them. She'd fix them later.

Grabbing one of Jaren's tunics, she'd barely pulled it down over her head before another knock echoed on the door. "Shit, hold on, I'm almost ready," she said in a rush, but the sound of the lock sliding back rather than Jaren's reply had her heart stopping.

Wide-eyed, with her hair an untamed nest all over her shoulders, she whipped toward the door, the too-large tunic slipping off one shoulder as she did. Her pulse took off so fast she feared she might pass out.

Jaren stood at the door to their room, casually leaning against the frame, and naked as the day he was born.

His scar-flecked skin, defined back, and well-toned ass was normally a sight she'd drool over, but it was quickly ruined when he flung the door wide open, revealing two males on the other side.

He grinned at them, the expression anything but kind. "And here I was thinking you were only lacking honesty and integrity, but apparently your patience is also missing," he said, standing to the side so they could step in.

Her mouth fell open. What the fuck was he playing at? He was fucking naked. If they wouldn't have already guessed by their combined scents still lingering in the air, they'd certainly know now.

Jaeros stepped through the doorway first, a frown marring his face as he noticed Jaren's busted lip before flicking his confused gaze over to her. His blue eyes widened, and he choked, stopping so suddenly she'd have thought *she* was the one standing proudly naked.

"Good gods."

Her face bloomed bright red, and she self-consciously patted down her curls, rolling her lips in, unsure what to do. What did you say to someone's father who just realized you had sex with his son? *Good morning, hope you had a great night. I sure did.*

Pulling her gaze away from his still wide, unblinking eyes, she watched the second male silently enter the room, passing by

178

Jaren with a single, clipped nod.

Jaren had warned her that Dedryn made Elric look downright friendly, but she had a feeling Dedryn's lack of a warm greeting had more to do with the venomous look his son was currently shooting at him.

Broad shouldered and standing even taller than his son, Dedryn was one of the most intimidating males she'd ever seen, second only to Jensen, a Matherin guard she'd nicknamed Boulder Shoulders.

Although not as large as Jensen, Dedryn's arms made her own look like sticks, and his trousers tightened and pulled around his tree trunk thighs with each step.

He stopped just behind his mate, towering over her even from several feet away. His hair was a muddied, auburn hue that looked like it'd curl if it wasn't cut so short. The color accentuated his light skin and almost golden eyes, and made the chiseled, inhuman features of his face sharper, more severe.

His protective posture and armed waist didn't help. Not to mention the hand he rested against Jaeros's lower back, as if prepared, even in their small room, to defend him if needed. At least she knew where Jaren got his personality from.

Where Jaeros had been an emotional mess at seeing her in Ocridal, Dedryn's expression remained stoic, revealing nothing as his eyes roved over her face, pausing on her ears before dropping. His jaw tightened, and he surprised her by using the common tongue. "Heal them."

She blinked, not expecting that to be the first thing he said.

Instinctively raising her arm to an ear, she brushed her fingertips over the scarred top. "Um…" He didn't actually expect her to be capable of that, right?

Jaren stood beside her, wrapping a possessive hand around her waist, and pulled her in close. Thankfully, he'd at least taken the few seconds she'd been watching his fathers to step into a pair of trousers.

"That's how you greet Bhasura's heir? The heir you were charged with protecting?" He scoffed. "I suppose I should've known better than to expect any form of apology from *you*."

While Jaeros flinched subtly at his unveiled hatred, Dedryn was an unmoving stone as he ignored his son and met her eyes. "We are running out of time. Your shoulder. Heal it."

Jaren's grip tightened, his voice containing a dangerous edge to it as he dipped his head and spoke in her ear. "Don't you dare."

She hadn't planned on it, but with how his fathers were staring at her, she found herself suddenly second-guessing her decision. Weren't mating bonds common? *They* were mated, themselves, so why did they seem so appalled?

Dedryn considered her for another moment before tilting his head down toward Jaeros. "Did you not tell them?"

Jaeros shook his head. "He was angry enough as it was," he said, giving his mate a knowing look. "I was far too tired to have it out with him again."

"Did you not think it more important than his self-centered anger?"

Jaren stiffened, and she covered his hands with hers, squeezing once. The last thing they needed was him to lose his shit. Especially with the long day they had ahead of them.

Jaeros rolled his eyes, gesturing in their direction. "They were exhausted and had not yet completed their bond, I wasn't expecting...well, you know."

"You were expecting your son to put common sense above the needs of his cock?"

Jaeros chuckled, gently elbowing him in the side. "Says the male who can't make it a single night without trying to mount my backside."

Vera's eyes darted back and forth, listening to them converse like she and Jaren weren't even there. Were they always like this? And did they often talk about sex so openly in front of others? She made a mental note to ask Jaren later if that was a *them* thing or a Magyki thing.

A rumble vibrated against the back of her head as he pulled her flush against him and growled. "Say whatever the fuck it is you came to say and get out."

Scratch that. She'd ask *way* later.

"We'd planned to take you two somewhere to talk, as I'd promised Veralie," Jaeros said, sobering. "However, it would appear the few servants who'd spotted her have already filled the halls with gossip. I wasn't exaggerating when I said she is the spitting image of her mother. King Vesstan demanded to see us at barely past dawn this morning and now requests your immediate presence."

Jaren cracked his neck. "Perfect. Let's go then."

Dedryn shook his head. "Not until she removes your mark."

Jaren just ran his hands over her shoulders, expelling a humorless laugh. "No."

Shifting closer, Dedryn's fists clenched and unclenched at his sides like he was fighting the urge to grip his son by the collar and shake him. "If you cannot control the urge to mark her, at least do it somewhere it cannot be seen."

A cruel smirk. "I did."

Dedryn snorted, his lip curling on one side despite himself. "You never did excel at listening," he said, crossing his arms. "Although, given what happened to her, I'd have thought you'd try a little harder this time around."

Jaren's grin dropped as his rage flared, and she instinctively reached a hand out, wrapping it around his bicep. "Jaren, maybe I should—"

He ripped her hand off, using it to pull her into him as he glared down at her, anger and hurt filling his eyes. "Why are you so gods damn forgiving of them? Is it some desperate desire for a father figure that has you rolling over? Or do you truly seek to keep hiding our bond?"

She shoved against his chest, knowing in her heart his anger wasn't directed at her, but his daggered words drew blood all the same. "Don't be an ass, Jaren, that's not what I meant."

"Then what is it? Are you afraid your father will disapprove of you because of me?" He snapped, teeth bared on the last word.

"He will disapprove of her simply because of her human

qualities. As will most others," Dedryn interjected.

She flinched, turning in Jaren's hold. Of course, he would. The happiness and hope she'd felt on the trip to Bhasura shriveled and died. She didn't fit in anywhere. She was too Magyki for Aleron, yet too human for Bhasura.

Noticing her reaction, something like regret flashed across his eyes, and Dedryn rotated his jaw like he had a bad taste in his mouth. "I only meant that King Vesstan will be conflicted about finding out where you've been all this time."

She nodded, trying to step out of Jaren's arms only for his hands to lock around her waist. "I know you said we're in a hurry, but what did you mean?" she asked, darting a look to Jaeros. "When you asked him if he'd told us?"

Jaeros shifted closer to Dedryn, eyeing Jaren nervously. "King Vesstan is not aware you are mated."

"Because he thought I was dead?"

"Because we never told anyone."

Jaren's nails dug into her sides, hard enough to break skin if she hadn't been wearing a tunic. They'd never told *anyone*?

"I don't understand." It didn't make any sense. They'd made him daggers, for fuck's sake! And King Vesstan had personally sent Jaren to Aleron. Right?

Her next words spewed from her like word vomit, coming out more like an accusation than a question. "Why would you not tell your King your son had mated to his daughter? You were obviously proud about it," she added, gesturing to where Jaren's daggers lay.

Nothing. Not a single flicker of emotion. "We do not have time to hash out everything for you right now. You've been requested, and it's only a matter of time before servants start wandering this way, more than happy to eavesdrop."

"Then I suggest you answer her question a little fucking faster," Jaren growled from behind her. His tone promised blood, but she could feel what lay under it, the truth he could no longer hide from her even if he tried. He hadn't known. Yet another secret to add to the ever-growing pile pressing down on him.

"To protect you and my *aitanta*," Dedryn snapped, irritation finally clawing through. "Use your head, Jaren. What do you think King Vesstan would've done if he'd have known you were with her? That *we* were with her? I serve my king, but I protect my family first." He glared at his son, daring him to contradict his claim.

Feeling Jaren's fury boiling beneath his skin, she caught him the second he lunged around her, aiming for Dedryn. Slapping both hands on either side of his face, she yanked him down to her level, forcing him to make eye contact.

"I am here," she said, brushing her thumbs down the sharp angles of his cheekbones. "I am with you. That is the only truth that matters right now." His nostrils flared, but she just pulled him closer, uncaring that he was practically bent in half.

"I cannot get through today alone, Jaren," she whispered. "I promise to piss you off later so you can rage at me, but right now I need you to be my constant." It was the most she'd admitted out loud about how she really felt, even to him.

Are you with me?

He said nothing for a moment as his chest heaved, but his eyes spoke volumes as he placed his hands over hers and nodded once.

Always.

Exhaling in defeat, he closed his eyes, bottling up his anger and shuttering it in whatever place he went to when he had to focus. He flicked his eyes up to Dedryn, his expression mirroring his father's. "Would revealing our bond to King Vesstan be unsafe for her?"

His fathers shared a loaded look before Dedryn answered. "I can't say. But Queen Vaneara did not want him to know. That was enough for us."

They stared off for several seconds before Jaren nodded minutely. "Fine," he said, reaching over and snatching her cloak off the chair she'd tossed it on the previous night. "But you will find the time to explain that later, or my mate will not keep me from extracting the information from your lips."

He slipped the cloak over her shoulders, running his fingertips along the curve of her neck as he fastened it.

"The things I do for you, little star."

CHAPTER 15

VERA

Jaren's fathers led them through the palace, each hallway just as massive as the next with the same eccentric torches and bright banners she'd seen the night before.

She didn't think she'd ever consider a palace comfortable or home-like, but at least this one felt livelier and warmer than Emperor Sulian's had.

Then again, she'd been convinced she was headed to her death when she'd walked through the Matherin palace, so there was a good chance her memory of it wasn't entirely accurate.

The farther they walked, the more servants and guards began to appear, and she swore she felt each one's eyes as they passed. She didn't dare speak, knowing every Magyki ear within the palace was probably on high alert, waiting to hear even the smallest tidbit of gossip to hint at who she was.

She stepped closer to Jaren, suddenly missing the armory with a passion. She'd never wanted to be the center of attention, and she still didn't. Knowing it would likely only get worse made her nauseated.

If the last hallway to the throne room hadn't already been obvious with the oversized archway and the long, maroon runner going down the center of the floor, she'd have known by the number of guards alone.

There were several stationed down along the walls and two standing at the very end, blocking the open archway. Each wore the same light leather armor she'd seen the guards outside wearing last night, including the long blades they sported on each hip.

Compared to the fully armored, masked guards in Matherin, these guards might as well have been naked. None wore masks or helmets, nor were their arms covered apart from their shoulders and wrists. Her brow crinkled at the sight. They may have been long-lived and fast, but they were still mortal.

Finally approaching the two males at the end of the hall, she arched her neck back, admiring the archway they stood before as Dedryn spoke quietly to them. It was impressive beyond anything she'd ever seen.

The pillars were thicker than two of her put together, extending high enough, she didn't think even Jaren could reach if he jumped. But the part that drew her in the most was the engravings that wrapped around the entire thing, reminding her of Jaren's daggers.

She made a mental note to drag him back there later and force him to read them out to her. She'd never been unable to read something before, Elric having been thorough in her basic education, and it was driving her crazy. If she was going to stay here, she definitely needed reading lessons.

Her attention dropped back down to the males before her when one nodded sharply and spun, walking through the archway and out of sight. She watched him disappear to inform King Vesstan of their arrival, and swore her stomach went in right along with him. With how fast it'd dropped, it was certainly no longer inside her body.

Any excitement she'd had about stepping foot in Naris was quickly overshadowed by her fear of what was about to happen now that she was here. She should be excited for this, for meeting her father, but all she wanted was to retreat to her room and avoid it completely.

The last time she'd entered a throne room, she'd been scared and insulted, only to then be squeezed into a gown and lied to about who she was. And that wasn't even mentioning the whole "let's marry and unite our people" conversation.

At least she could draw comfort from the fact that the last part wouldn't happen this time around. Staying positive was going to be the only way she'd make it through the day without vomiting on her boots.

She shifted, wondering what was taking the guard so long, aware of Jaren's heavy gaze on her face. He said nothing, but his silent, steady presence grounded and calmed her. He'd threatened her numerous times, blackmailed her, and marked her against her initial wishes, yet somehow, he was the only person left in the world whom she trusted with her life.

Taking a deep breath, she reached out and took his hand, grateful her arrogant asshole of a mate was with her. She focused on the steady beat of his heart, and was using it to help slow her own when the guard reappeared and nodded at them.

She wasn't sure why, but she found herself immediately looking at Jaeros. Maybe she was just hoping for an encouraging smile or something to hint at how this would go, but he didn't seem to be aware of her at all.

Her heart sped up, beating out of her ribcage all over again when she saw Jaren's fathers staring, unblinkingly, at one another, silently communicating in a way only mates could do.

She couldn't see Jaeros's eyes, but Dedryn's—which had been hard as stone all morning—had softened, the amber color warm and inviting as his lips tipped up in the barest hint of a sad smile.

But before she could ask if everything was all right, or even turn to see if Jaren had noticed the moment, Jaeros broke their gaze to speak to her.

"Before we go in, Veralie," he said, still using the common tongue for her, "I know you struggle to keep up with Thyabathi, and there is no shame in that. But even so, make sure you use it in there."

Not waiting for her to respond to his warning, he turned away and they both strove forward beneath the arch.

JAREN'S FATHERS WALKED IN SIDE BY SIDE IN FRONT OF HER, almost as if shielding her until the last possible second, and she wondered just how much of her nerves were painted on her forehead for them to feel the need to do that.

She took a deep breath, closing her eyes for a moment, and forced herself to release Jaren's hand. As much as she wanted the comfort of his skin against hers, she needed to stand on her own.

Because she wasn't just Vera anymore, nor was she just Jaren Barilias's *aitanta*. She was the *Nlem Snadzend*, the Daughter to the Throne. And she was strong enough to stand on her own.

Seeming to agree, or to at least understand, he didn't fight her for once. He just placed his right hand on the pommel of his dagger and grazed his other along her spine, ushering her forward.

Walking into the throne room, she'd fully expected to feel the same weight and oppression she had when she'd walked into Emperor Matheris's. The intimidating stone throne, the pristine floor-to-ceiling windows, the feeling of not being good enough to be there.

But it wasn't like that at all.

The room was surprisingly bare of almost everything, unlike the rest of the palace she'd passed through. There were no banners on the walls, no crests or greenery adorning the windows, no carpets leading to a dais. In fact, there was no dais at all.

The room was a decent size, but small in comparison to Emperor Matheris's. Rather than gray stone, it had a tan, tiled floor, and a single, empty throne sat at the end of the room. It was a deep, blood red, matching the runner that had led into the room.

The cushioned back was curved, and the armrests appeared to be made from the same yellowed gold she'd seen on the sconces. They swirled under, giving the throne a softer, more feminine appearance.

Given that the only three other occupants in the room stood off to the side of it, it was safe to assume it was the late Queen Vaneara's seat. Did King Vesstan ever use it, or was it set to be empty until...*she* took it?

She shuddered at the thought and came to stand next to Jaeros, glancing up at the room's occupants in time to see three mutually shocked faces.

There was a tense silence, a heaviness that saturated the air the longer no one spoke. She shifted awkwardly, feeling like a weapon that'd been laid out on a table to be inspected for balance and efficiency. If she'd thought her father would run to her with open arms, embracing her with tearful affection, she'd been painfully mistaken.

If it hadn't been for the gold-trimmed tunic and the power emanating from him, she wouldn't have even known which of the males was her father based on their twin reactions. The third individual, a female, stood slightly apart, suspicion already clouding her expression.

"Dedryn. Jaeros." His voice was smooth, caressing over the syllables of their language, yet somehow still holding an unyielding air of authority.

They bowed low at the waist, and she scrambled to follow their lead, realizing a second too late that she was supposed to curtsy. Amusement filled her chest, and she bit down on her tongue, tucking her hand behind her to pinch Jaren as hard as she could. He made a soft choking noise, struggling to hold in a laugh.

Awkward silence settled in, and she inwardly cringed at herself, raising up from her ridiculous bow only to be ensnared by a pair of gray eyes.

Sitting under well-manicured brows, King Vesstan's eyes were not quite silver like hers, but a slate gray, similar to what hers had looked like before she'd connected with the crystal. His brown hair, a shade lighter than hers, was slicked back, not a single hair out of place.

His warm beige skin was clean-shaven, and although looks were deceiving with Magyki, it still unnerved her to see he didn't visually appear much older than she was.

"So…this is the female who had my servants whispering in corners like senseless children last night."

"Yes, Your Majesty," Jaeros said, straightening his spine but keeping his head bowed. His peppered hair had draped forward over his shoulders, concealing his face from her. "She is here to claim the title of Veralie Arenaris, Daughter to the Throne."

"That is quite the claim," King Vesstan said, his voice pausing ever so slightly at the end, and she could've sworn the corner of his lips twitched. "But I must say, it is hard to refute even such a farfetched one as that with her face so clear before me." Another awkward pause. "They truly could be one and the same. Fascinating."

She turned her head, sneaking a glance back at Jaren who looked about as irritated as she felt. Her father was talking about her like she wasn't even there, with little to no emotion.

His initial surprise had faded, and he now neither seemed happy nor sad about it. As if her unexplained appearance was no different than a cook announcing they were having fish instead of chicken at dinner.

Her expression must have given her away more than she'd thought because he stepped forward, raising his palms out before his chest. "Apologies. This is quite odd for me. I can say with absolute certainty that I did not expect to ever see you walk into this room."

Odd for *him*? How did he think *she* felt? She lifted her chin. "I can't say I expected it either, Your Majesty." He motioned her forward and she obliged, ignoring Jaren's answering irritation.

Leaving his silent, unnamed companions, King Vesstan approached her, circling her like a prized mare. Coming back around to her front, he crossed one arm over his torso, resting his elbow on it, and cupping his chin as his eyes latched on to her ears.

"I cannot deny the resemblance, as even a blind human could see it, but I do not see how you could possibly prove it."

Anger flared hot in her veins at the clear implication she was lying. She was used to Jaren's demeanor, and even Dedryn's stone face hadn't bothered her, but she hadn't expected her *father* to be so emotionless.

She chewed the inside of her cheek, chastising herself. He'd lost his wife and child in the worst way possible, of course he was hesitant to believe her. After all, Jaren hadn't immediately known either, and they shared a soul.

If King Vesstan had known about their bond, that enough could have been proof, but her mother hadn't told him. Doubt crept into her heart. Was he just protecting himself, or was there something more to his lack of reaction?

"By your mutilated state, I deduce you were on Aleron." He waved a hand at her head, his lip curling up in a sneer before he could wipe it away.

He will disapprove of her simply because of her human qualities.

She steeled her spine. Regardless of her relation to him, she refused to feel shame for something she had no control over. "Yes, Your Majesty."

"She connected to the crystal while still on Aleron," Jaren said, speaking for the first time since they'd left their room. "Along with her resemblance, that should be proof enough." His tone was clipped, a protective edge to it he didn't bother to hide.

King Vesstan's tongue darted out across his lips, a flicker of something finally darting across his face, but it was there and gone before she could contemplate what it might mean. "That's not possible."

"I saw it with my own eyes. And she did it with ease." His hands fisted at his sides, and at a warning look from Dedryn, he tacked on, "Your Majesty."

King Vesstan stared at him long and hard, his eyes narrowing at whatever he sensed between them. "I suppose it could be possible if she truly shares Vaneara's blood."

He looked back to Vera, tilted his head to the side. "Vaneara's ancestors never stepped foot off their homeland," he said, pointedly raising a brow, "so we have no other instance to go on as to how far the connection could go. Interesting."

"Your power must be quite strong, indeed." The remark came from the female who had finally come to stand next to the king along with the other male. At first, Vera thought she was trying to compliment her in a way, but the look on her face said otherwise.

Although around the same height as Vera, she was her opposite in every way. Her blond hair was shaved bare on both sides of her head, accentuating her pointed ears and leaving the middle portion plaited down her back. Her hazel eyes were hard and unforgiving as she looked down her nose at Vera, and her cheekbones and jaw were nearly as sharp as Jaren's.

She wore the same light leather armor as the guards outside, every defined, thick muscle of her arms on full display. Vera would have swooned at her feet and begged her to spar with her had it not been for the death glare she was sending her way.

"Well?"

Vera shuffled uncomfortably under the pression of the five gazes currently on her. All except Jaren, whose eyes were trained with intense focus on Lady Death Glare. "She's not some weapon for you to try out," he snapped, stepping around Vera to stand at her side.

Casually placing a hand on the pommel of her weapon, she smirked. "You have much nerve to talk back to me, Jaren Barilias." Her eyes darted between him and Vera, noting the protective stance he held beside her. A blond brow arched high on her forehead.

"I wasn't aware you suddenly had authority to assign protection without my approval, Dedryn. Especially someone I have not personally vetted."

Vera started, eyes widening despite herself. Holy Aleron. This female was in a position of authority *over their guards?* She knew Bhasura respected its females in a way Aleron never had, but this was even more than she'd expected.

Tension thickened the air from her question, rolling off both Jaren's fathers. "I have not assigned anyone, Taeral. Though I know for a fact you are well aware his skill surpasses most of the individuals under your command." Dedryn aimed his attention at the king, ignoring the angry flare of Lady Death Glare's eyes.

"Your Majesty, I know we have spoken of Jaren to you before, but I do not believe you have seen him since he was not much more than a child." He stepped to the side, holding an arm out toward Jaren.

King Vesstan froze. "Your son, you say."

He tipped his head back, sucking on his teeth. "How fortunate our…children…seem to have formed such trust."

Jaren bristled, and by the twitch of King Vesstan's lips, he didn't fail to notice.

"Hm. There is apparently much more to you than meets the eye, *Veralie Arenaris*." He reached out a hand, and she hesitantly set hers into his, trying not to tense as he covered it with his other and smiled down at her.

"You must be hungry and eager to tour your new home. Jaeros knows the palace quite well given his occupation and would be more than happy to show you around, I'm sure."

He released her hand, nodding at Dedryn. "I will need to speak to my advisors about what to do with you. Stay within the palace, and I will send for you in a few days."

She swallowed, clasping her hands together to hide their shaking. Yet again, she was being restricted indoors and told not to be seen. Her chest tightened painfully. Nothing was different.

"Until then, I'll have you moved to more permanent quarters tonight with clothing appropriately fitted for your claimed station."

Setting a hand on Lady Death Glare's lower back, he steered her with him toward a back entrance Vera hadn't noticed until then. Dedryn turned toward her, bowing at the waist, before nodding at his husband and son and following the king's group out.

CHAPTER 16

EITHAN

He stared, unseeing, down the hall, slipping a hand in his trouser pocket and grasping the small object hidden there, the smooth spin of it along his fingertips immediately calming him. He'd been reaching for it more and more lately, the impulse to use it cutting into him deeper with each passing day.

The edge of the lid dug into the pad of his thumb as he tightened his grip. The thought of using it tonight was so deliciously tempting.

He cracked his neck, trying to ignore the weighted stare boring into the back of his head. Coleman said nothing, but his unease grew with each step they took down the hall, his good-intentioned anxiety practically bouncing off the walls around them.

His worry was oddly soothing, if not a tad annoying at times. Especially considering what Eithan's first-in-command might gain if Sulian's punishments ever went too far. His cheek twitched, and he rolled his neck, sparing a quick glance behind him. Thankfully for them both, tonight was just dinner.

The only pain Eithan was set to endure was a long, drawn-out evening of thinly veiled insults and alcohol-inspired lectures. There was nothing Sulian loved more—apart from watching Eithan's lessons—than informing him of just how disappointing he was.

Eithan's wounds had healed well over the last few days, with only a few that still itched and pulled whenever he twisted just right. He inhaled, testing his ribs. They'd received most of the abuse, but even they were on the mend, the coloring of his torso making them look worse than they were. Not that Coleman believed him.

Eithan, on the other hand, was glad he still ached. There was no greater motivation than the constant reminder of humiliation and pain. As they approached their destination, he spun the small vial once more in his fist, daring himself to use it.

"Your Highness?"

His fingers spasmed, but he forced himself to turn, releasing his grip and yanking his empty hand from his pocket. He wasn't sure how long he'd stood there staring at the door, but the worried look on Coleman's face told him enough.

He smoothed his palms down the front of his midnight blue tunic and considered the man. "How many more years would you say my father has left, Coleman?"

His guard visibly balked, his skin paling even more than his natural hue. "What do you—I'm not sure I understand your question, Your Highness."

"It's not a trick question. I'm not going to hang you for your answer, so stop gaping at me like a dying fish," he said, combing his hair back off his forehead. "I'm just curious how healthy he seems to you?"

If anything, Coleman paled even further, his body instinctually shifting back ever so slightly as he slowly blinked at him. A clear warning that Eithan was balancing dangerously close to the fine line he walked.

He mentally chastised himself. He knew better than to hint at such things. Maybe it was his unanswered letters that were driving him to the brink of madness, his desperation growing thicker with every day he received no reply.

Or maybe he'd simply become spoiled from the freedom of being able to vent his thoughts and desires to Gibson, with no consequence, that made him feel less confident in his mask than usual. Whatever it was, he needed to snuff it out.

He pressed his nails into his palms, digging in until his mind cleared. He'd be an idiot to trust Coleman in that way. To trust *anyone* he couldn't exact complete and precise control over.

"Never mind. I was just thinking about how precarious of a thing life is. You know how my mind wanders, don't mind me."

Coleman nodded, looking like he was about to reply, but Eithan reached for the door, cutting him off.

"No need to wait for me tonight," he said, smirking over his shoulder. "My father's not a fan of getting his own hands dirty, so he's unlikely to kill me over dinner."

THE TABLE WAS already set and loaded with steaming dishes when he walked in, Sulian apparently having grown too impatient to wait for him. The man in question sat at the head of the table, dressed in a loose, white tunic that was open at the collar, eyeing Eithan as he entered. His blond hair hung unbound, ending just above his shoulders to frame the same squared jaw they both shared.

Eithan silently took his seat, lifting a finger to the servant standing against the back wall holding a half-full decanter of wine. He'd never been a fan of any form of alcohol, usually abstaining when he went out with his men, but it was unfortunately a necessary taste he'd had to acquire, especially considering his sire's predilection for it. He eyed Sulian's drink, the already empty glass a silent confirmation.

"Father," he said, voice flat as he bowed his head, wishing more than anything he could wipe that gods damn title from his memory.

Sulian tipped his head forward an inch, the only sign he gave of acknowledgement as the servant moved on to refill his glass. Then he slouched back, silently appraising him. Eithan bristled, understanding the gesture as the underhanded insult it was.

The way Sulian's tunic bunched up around his stomach, the way he leaned his weight on his armrest as he sniffed his fresh wine. It was not a position the Emperor of Matherin would take in front of anyone he respected or cared to have respect *him*. He smirked over the glass, daring Eithan to say something.

But Eithan just picked up his knife, brandishing it with a little more flare than was necessary, and sliced into the perfectly seasoned pheasant wafting up from his plate.

Minutes passed in silence as they both ate, but he knew it wouldn't last long. Sure enough, Eithan had barely finished half his food before Sulian cleared his throat.

"Somewhere else you intend to be this evening?"

Eithan glanced up, lifting his fork to his mouth and chewing through his bite. *There are a hundred places I'd rather be. In what order would you like me to recite them?*

"Of course not, Father. Why do you ask?"

Sulian raised a brow, lifting a thick finger from his glass to gesture at him. "You and I both know you only dress in Matheris blue when you have someone to impress. Whatever whore you intend to rut into tonight, your name will impress her plenty. No need to ruin expensive thread."

He ignored the baseless jab. Sulian had spies everywhere among the court. There was zero chance he was unaware of the fact that Eithan hadn't taken a woman to his bed since he'd learned of Vera's identity.

He took another bite, focusing on the spice of the pepper as he forced down another piece. Sulian's obvious prodding was more insulting than his lazed posture.

"I am betrothed, Father. I have no one to impress until she is back safely. I didn't realize I needed a reason to dress akin to my station." The truth was his nicer tunics were less abrasive against his healing skin, not that he'd ever admit it to anyone, much less him.

Sulian's eyes narrowed, his crow's feet seeming deeper and more numerous these days. "Good," he finally said, setting his glass down and clasping his hands over his stomach, "that will make my news far easier to swallow."

"And what news is that, Father?"

"I'm sending you to the base near Midpath to welcome the next enlistment of men. You leave within the next few weeks."

Eithan's knuckles whitened around his fork, his chest constricting until he was sure it'd cave in under the pressure. "For what purpose?"

He smoothed his free hand down his beard. "The same reason I tried to send you before, why else?"

Eithan stared at him, lowering his hand to fist it beneath the table, wrestling to keep his face passive. "Is there any particular reason that you've decided it must be me, or is this another punishment for my failure?"

Failure. Saying it made him want to rip his own tongue out. He ground his teeth together, double-checking his mask to make sure not a single flinch made it through.

"I would love to hear your recommendation of who else to

send, as you've yet to find me a replacement for the Weapon's Master you arrested behind my back."

He inhaled, letting it out to the count of five. "I brought Lesta in for questioning, as I've previously informed you, and released him directly after. He's been back in the training yard ever since and is more than capable of working with a bunch of eastern farmers."

"Last I checked, Prince Eithan, I make the final decisions in my city. And until I decide his fate for doing the opposite of what I demanded he do with the Magyki heir, you will go in his stead."

There was a pregnant pause as they stared at one another, each testing the other's mask to see who, if either, would break first.

"Vera trusts me. It is vital I be here when she returns to make sure everything goes smoothly."

Sulian's expression hardened. "Don't patronize me by insinuating I require a mediator. I kept her in line for over a decade, boy."

Eithan bowed his head, sliding his hand in his pocket and gripping the vial. "I meant no disrespect. But she has her abilities now. She will not be so easily controlled."

"Says the boy who couldn't manipulate her for a single night even when she was without them. I stand by my order." Sulian sat back again, steepling his hands over his chest.

"Not that it will matter in the long run," he added, shrugging. "You'll be lucky if you live to see a handful more moons, let alone marry her."

Eithan forced his muscles to go lax, crossing one leg over the other and resting a hand over his knee. "Is that a threat, Father?"

Sulian scoffed, glancing out the window to the darkened landscape. "Don't be daft. It doesn't suit you." He cut his eyes back over. "Do you really think Vesstan Arenaris will accept our role in his daughter's disappearance? That he'll happily accept that his only child was kept here on Aleron and do nothing about it?"

He had to force his body to stay languid and not jut forward. Aleron couldn't afford a war with Bhasura. Not yet. Not without adequate leverage. "You expect him to launch an attack over it?"

"No, he wouldn't risk unintentionally divulging just how weakened Bhasura is now. He won't start a war he isn't guaranteed to win." His blue eyes darted back to Eithan, flaring in time with his smile. "He's more likely to send assassins to kill us in our sleep."

"Comforting."

"Indeed."

"And what do you believe he will do once his heir willingly returns?"

The sound of Sulian's calluses scraping over his beard was the only sound as he seemed to ponder Eithan's question. "If you are correct about Veralie Arenaris, her actions will not be done with his permission."

Eithan nodded, having already figured as much on his own.

If King Vesstan was anything like Sulian, there was no way he'd allow his only heir to run free. Not when it wouldn't benefit him.

"However," he continued, "Vesstan's pride and belief that we are below them will work in your favor. Marry his daughter, and he may still resist a treaty with us. Breed her and dilute their sacred bloodline with our own? He won't have much of a choice."

Sulian dabbed a napkin over his lips and stood, staring down at Eithan. "She carries the only direct line their people have left. He will not risk starting a war with her. So, *if* she returns, do what I told you to do the night we had her, and put a fucking child in her womb."

Eithan glared daggers into the bastard as he arrogantly gave him his back and disappeared through the doorway leading to the large hearth Eithan had once held Vera's hand in.

Fucking breed her. Like she was a pure-blooded horse Sulian sought to help fill his personal stables. He bit his tongue until he tasted blood, quashing his disgust at the man who'd sired him.

Sulian had always been weak, but his complete lack of ingenuity or aspiration to help better his own gods damn people infuriated him.

Children. That's all the Emperor of Matherin hoped to gain with Bhasura's sole heir? Fucking *children*? To intermix her abilities into their bloodline for a ruler years from now to use and enjoy? What good would that do for any of them in the here and now?

It was the most idiotic thing he'd ever heard. Obviously, he wanted to conceive a child with her someday. Who wouldn't? She was breathtaking and resilient, caring and strong. But there was so much more they could gain from her than that.

The Magyki had been using the relic of the gods to power and heal their people for centuries. But the truth was that it was never made for them, nor was it tied to them. Eithan didn't yet know what, exactly, it was or how they used it, but he was almost certain they could figure it out together.

Bhasura had hoarded it for long enough. It was time for the people on Aleron to be given the same chance. Living a long, healthy life shouldn't be a privilege only the Magyki could have.

He removed the small vial, holding it up to his face and admiring the liquid rippling inside. His people deserved the same gifts and privileges, and he'd do whatever it took to give it to them.

CHAPTER 17

VERA

Following Jaeros down the halls back toward the room she and Jaren had shared, Vera barely made it through the doorway before she lost it.

"What the fuck was that?" she demanded, pushing back tears as she crossed her arms and stared at Jaeros.

Her emotions were a complete and utter wreck, and she felt ready to break at any moment. What on Aleron had just happened? Had that seriously been her father? A male who had to believe she was who she claimed, who should *want* to believe she was, but who didn't appear to care in the least.

She'd waited all this time—all her life—for *that*? To be locked away again and told he'd send for her in a few days? Gods damn Elric had literally punched her on several occasions, and even he still showed her more affection than her only remaining blood relation had.

"I know you're upset—"

"No offense, but you don't know anything about me."

Jaeros settled down on the edge of the bed and ran a hand through his hair, combing it back and tying it at his nape. "No, I don't—"

"Which is your fault," Jaren chimed in, resting his hands on her hips as he stood protectively behind her.

"I need to know, Jaeros. And I'm not waiting for Dedryn. What was all that? And who the fuck was Lady Death Glare?"

He froze for a moment, likely at her nickname, before resting his elbows on his knees and massaging his temples. He suddenly looked a lot older. Like the entire morning had already been too much for him.

The feeling was mutual.

"Veralie, King Vesstan is…a very closed-off male. He not only lost his wife, but he had to end a bloody rebellion, learn how to lead an entire island alone, and deal with the consequences of Vaneara's death. He hasn't been the same since."

Jaren huffed a laugh, his breath coasting over the top of her head. "That's an understatement. He made Deds look downright chipper. He accused her of lying and didn't do a damn thing about Taeral running her foul mouth."

Taeral. That's right, Dedryn had called her that. Vera preferred Lady Death Glare, it was far more fitting.

She sighed, walking across the room to plop on the opposite

side of the bed. "I can understand that, I guess." And she could, but it still didn't change how the encounter made her feel.

"Jaeros," she started, looking up into his tired, blue eyes. "Why was I given to you? I know you hid me, and that the rebellion was because of me. But why? And why didn't you just take me home the night you found those males taking me?"

Why didn't you let me stay with you where I could have been loved and seen? Where I could have been raised unaltered and unafraid of living my life.

She had so many damn questions, and with each one, Eithan's words came to the forefront of her mind. His warning.

There's a reason your people went to war over you, Vera. It's not safe there.

Jaeros's lips tightened for only a moment, but she caught it. His uncertainty. Jaren either saw it, too, or sensed her own unease growing because he ground out, "Lie. I dare you."

His father snapped back, his patience with Jaren's constant verbal attacks finally thinning. "Stop acting like a damn child, I'm not going to lie to her."

Ignoring Jaren's answering growl, he faced her again, resting his hand on the bed between them. "We raised you because your mother asked us to."

Her heart beat so fast, she was surprised it was still within her rib cage. She'd been desperate for this information her entire life, having spent most of it believing she'd done something wrong to make her family abandon her.

"But why? Is that...normal? For females to be sent off to

live with their mates?" Maybe her living with them *hadn't* been to hide her. Maybe she'd lived there to be closer to Jaren, and the rebellion was just a coincidence.

Hope surged, and she ran her palms down her thighs, suddenly nervous.

"No, it's not usual for mates to live together before maturity. And even then, not all mates form a relationship."

She nodded. Jaren had once explained as much. Some mates rejected the bond completely. "Okay, so then..."

"Veralie," he spoke her name slowly, softly, and she knew she wasn't going to like whatever answer he was about to give. "Vaneara loved this island and her people with a fierceness I've never seen before, but she also had a secret. One she did not voice, even to Vesstan."

He paused, waiting for her to make eye contact. "She had no desire to ever get pregnant. Not with you, nor any other child."

Silence filled the room as his words sank in. The bed shifted as Jaren settled behind her, his warm hands wrapping around her waist and pulling her onto his lap. She burrowed back into his chest, blinking rapidly to fight back the sudden burning in her eyes.

She wasn't sure why, but some part of her had believed Eithan when he said her mother died to protect her. She believed it with every broken piece of her heart. And it couldn't have been further from the truth.

Jaeros shifted toward her before stopping and sitting back,

clasping his hands together. "Vaneara physically suffered, Veralie. Just like every queen before her. Every day, every year, she felt it."

He glanced back at Jaren once before finally scooting closer and setting his hand over hers. Jaren stiffened at his proximity but did not demand he remove it.

"She did not want that for you, nor any child she could ever have. She wanted her bloodline to end with her."

"Okay, so..." she swallowed, taking a deep breath. She asked for this. To know this. She needed to grow a spine and listen. She could be upset later when no one was around to see her break. "So, why didn't she..."

"End the pregnancy?"

She nodded. The procedure had major risks on Aleron, and very few healers would even entertain the idea, but here where females' choices were respected and they could heal themselves? It had to have been a viable option.

He squeezed her hand once before pulling it back. "I didn't know she was pregnant until after you were born, so I can't say for sure. All I know is when I voiced surprise, she was adamant that having you was the only option."

Jaeros rubbed a hand along his jaw, smoothing his beard. "She believed you were a sign from the gods. One that had to be protected at all costs. And before you ask, no, she would not tell me why."

Vera frowned. None of this was making sense. "So, that's why she gave me to you?" Maybe her mother had been slightly loose in the head, it was certainly possible if she'd suffered the way Jaeros had insinuated. Vera made a mental note to circle back and ask more about that later.

He shook his head. "No. She'd planned to travel to Cruiris and leave you at an orphanage until you were older. She had a bag packed and everything."

"Why didn't she?"

A fond smile graced his face as he glanced behind her at his son. "Because Jaren found you first. You'd barely breathed air into your lungs before he sensed you and tracked you down. I'd never seen anything like it."

Gooseflesh spread across her skin as Jaren's fingertips trailed up her arm, pausing to trace her shoulder before continuing up her neck and into her hair.

His nails scraped along her scalp, keeping her head taut against his chest as if to say, *I told you, aitanta. Our souls match. From the moment yours entered the world.*

Unaware of the simmering desire making its way through her body from Jaren's touch, Jaeros continued. "As much as she wanted to protect you, she was not willing to separate you from your mate. No queen had ever been mated before, including her. She saw it as further proof that you were different. Special.

"So, we agreed to take you and raise you as our own until she felt it was safe for you. It'd been several years since we'd adopted Jaren, so it wasn't a far stretch for anyone to believe we were ready for another."

She noticed that although Jaeros was obviously trying to

paint Vaneara in the best light possible, he'd never once confirmed that she'd loved her. Only that she'd thought she was important for whatever unknown reason.

But something else stuck out to her as well, something he'd said by saying absolutely nothing about it at all. "You keep saying *she*," Vera pointed out, forcing her fidgeting hands to lie still in her lap.

"You haven't once mentioned my—Vesstan." She stumbled over his name, unsure what to refer to him as. It didn't feel right to call him father when she still wasn't sure what his intentions with her were.

Jaeros placed both hands on his knees, shoving off the bed with a grunt. He really did look exhausted, and she wondered if he'd gotten any sleep at all the previous night, or if he'd stayed up filling Dedryn in on everything.

"King Vesstan wanted heirs. Neither he, nor the council, would've agreed to end the Arenaris bloodline. He didn't like what Vaneara went through, but he also believed it to be a necessary evil for the good of our people."

He sighed heavily, the lines around his eyes deepening as he added, "It's because of that, that your mother hid her pregnancy from everyone, including him."

"What? How is that even possible?" How on Aleron could someone hide an entire pregnancy from their spouse? She remembered Eithan saying the rebellion happened because her existence had been discovered, but she hadn't realized she'd also been hidden from her father.

Jaeros waved a hand. "A well-timed tour that I can explain some other time. My point is, King Vesstan didn't know until the rebellion. Tension increased each year the queen went with no heir, and when a rumor spread of your existence, only for the queen to deny it, panic and anger spread like wildfire."

So, all those deaths, all the fighting, really had been her fault. All because her mother believed her to be some type of gods damn blessing from gods who hadn't even been seen in centuries.

"You need to understand, Veralie. King Vesstan, like most of our people, has always believed that we are above those without power. I'm afraid he, like them, is not too keen on humans, or Aleron."

She raised her eyes, scrunching her face up in a 'yeah, you think?' expression. The king had ignored every single one of Emperor Sulian's efforts to start up trade and foster communication, so it was safe to say he wasn't keen on them at all.

Jaeros huffed a laugh at her face, dipping his head in acceptance. "Well, I will tell you now, given the overall decrease in the crystal's power over the years, his beliefs have only strengthened. He won't want to use you to cure the taint, but he will."

Jaren's arms turned to steel around her body, his chest vibrating against her back. "Will he hurt her?" he asked, his voice a terrifying, flat tone.

His tense posture screamed that he'd do whatever it took to

protect her, but she wasn't sure what that entailed anymore. He couldn't protect her from something that had already happened. Whether King Vesstan wished it or not, she was already connected.

"No," Jaeros answered, eyes firm as he stared at his son, knowing what was coursing through his mind. "He's not a monster, no matter how withdrawn he seems."

Speaking to her, he said, "Just don't let your hopes get too high, Veralie. He may be your father, but he will always be Father to the Throne first."

She had no idea what to say to that, so she didn't say anything at all, lowering her gaze to pick at her nails. Jaren said something to his father that she was too deep in her thoughts to catch, and then she heard the door open and close.

Her mother had never wanted her. Regardless of her good intentions behind the reason, the fact still remained. And it fucking stung. The only reason Vera lived at all was because of Vaneara's probably pain-induced, crazy belief that she had no choice.

Even Jaeros and Dedryn had given her up, sending her away for a reason they still hadn't explained.

She wasn't sure how much time had passed before Jaren loosened his hold around her waist and pulled back to run a hand down her spine. "Are you all right?"

"Yeah," she stopped, realizing she'd never be able to lie to him. Not when he could feel every emotion thrashing about in her head. "No."

216

Leaning down to whisper in her ear, he asked, "Would you like to sneak away to see the training yard?"

It wasn't really a question, so she didn't bother answering before she leapt off the bed, her legs carrying her straight to the door.

CHAPTER 18

VERA

The sharp clang and thuds of weapons clashing and bodies smacking into one another was like coming home. More so than anything else on the island had felt like.

An unexpected wave of homesickness crashed into her as Jaren led her down the last path leading to a large, empty field hidden within. She missed Elric. She missed the methodical motions of working with blades, the skill and concentration it took to perfect them, and the overwhelming smell of leather and steel.

She even missed the armory itself. Not being cooped up in it for hours, weeks, and years on end, but the comfort of waking up and knowing what the day would bring.

Even though she didn't yet have the freedom she'd hoped for, she didn't regret leaving. She'd spent her entire life wanting to see more of the world and go on an adventure of some kind, but she still missed the reassurance of knowing what was expected of her.

She had no idea what was expected of her here.

They pushed past the last line of trees, but she froze in her tracks when she set her gaze on the field of warriors training. Warriors of every shape, size, color, and sex stood and fought before her, mixed in together the way it should be.

Where some of the males were stronger, slicing their blades down with a power she could never naturally possess, the females were faster, darting out of the way before spinning back with their own strikes. It was the most beautiful thing she'd ever seen.

Her eyes burned, tears threatening as a joy she didn't know she could feel filled her heart, overshadowing every doubt that'd been coursing through her. She'd known she'd be treated differently here but being told and *seeing* it were two very different things.

Arms came around her, pulling her close and holding her flush against a firm chest. "You're like a warm ball of light in my chest."

"What?"

He grabbed her chin, arching her head back to look down at her. "You're happy," he said, smiling sadly. "And I didn't realize until now that I've never felt it from you before."

"I was already happy."

He shook his head. "No, not like this. I have felt many things from you, Veralie, but never this." He brushed his lips over her forehead and released her chin so she could look back at the field again. "I just wish I was the one who made you feel it."

She didn't know what to say to that, didn't know how to put words to how she felt. He might have been able to feel her, but as a Magyki male, he'd never truly understand what it had been like to have no power, no freedom, and no voice.

"Is anyone allowed to join?" she asked, changing the subject and stepping out of his embrace to gesture at the sight before them.

There was a beat of silence, but then he nodded. "They won't turn anyone down who is interested, but they do require you pass a test to join their rankings."

"What kind of test?" Guards on Aleron didn't have to pass anything in order to join. They just signed their names, swearing their allegiance to Emperor Sulian, and began training with the rest of them, no matter how much they struggled.

"A test of strength and skill."

"So, basically a sparring match?" she asked, giving him a side glance. That didn't sound so bad. Jaren was practically a rabid animal, and she'd beaten him. Once.

He cocked a brow, sensing where her thoughts had gone. "More or less, but Veralie—" he trailed off, cursing under his breath when she left the security of the trees, heading straight for the center of the field.

Snatching her arm, he pulled her in close, his breath coasting over her cheek. "No one here needs to know who you are. Not until King Vesstan has announced you officially."

"Yes, I'm well aware," she said, rolling her eyes. His own darkened in answer, and she immediately ducked under her arm, twisting out of his grasp. "And no one here needs to die if they beat me in a fair fight, green eyes," she added, giving him a pointed look.

"I make no promises."

Ignoring his comment and leaving him where he stood, she made her way up to the closest Magyki. Wearing the same light armor she'd come to realize was the basic uniform in Naris, he sat near the outer edge of the yard, his weapon resting across his thighs as he knocked back his head to guzzle from a waterskin.

His long, black hair was tied back, emphasizing the sharp jawline she was starting to realize almost all Magyki had. He had golden-brown skin and light brown eyes set above a slightly crooked nose that looked similar to her own.

Hearing her approach, he glanced sideways at her, uninterested, only to immediately freeze and do a double take.

She waved awkwardly, pretending not to notice Jaren's reaction to her approaching an almost half-naked male, alone. "Excuse me," she said, making sure both her hands were visible and he could see she was unarmed.

Focusing on her next words, she tried to make her Thyabathi come out as smooth and natural as possible. "Could you please take me to whoever is in charge here? Or point them out?"

His eyes trailed along her body before returning their

journey back up to her face, his full lips spreading into a slow grin. "And what if I told you I was the one in charge?"

"Are you?"

"For you, I will be," he said, standing to his full height and stepping a little closer than necessary. "Doren Panaeros, at your service."

An answering smile tugged at her lips, his comment reminding her so much of Trey, but it quickly fell when a lethal calm filled her chest, replacing the anger that had just been simmering there.

She internally grumbled, wishing she was close enough to kick Jaren in the shin. Part of her was tempted to flash a flirty grin just to piss him off, but the silent, killing calm radiating from him had her pressing her lips together and untying her cloak.

Letting it pool at her feet, she placed both hands on her hips, looking up in time to catch Doren staring at the collar of her tunic, where the outer edge of a mark could be seen.

His nostrils flared, and he immediately raised both hands, stepping back to put a more respectful distance between them.

See? She thought, shooting a glare over her shoulder. *No reason to go feral.*

"Well, Doren," she started, hoping he wouldn't notice she hadn't introduced herself, but his attention was no longer on her. It was past her, toward the tree line. He cleared his throat and took another healthy step back.

"*Well*, Doren," she repeated, "Can you help me or not?"

He didn't get a chance to answer before a harsh, clipped voice beat him to it. "You have no business being here."

Vera's stomach dropped as she watched Lady Death Glare step out from a group of female warriors just to the left of where she and Doren stood. Vera had been so excited; she hadn't even noticed her.

She should've expected it given what Jaeros said, but it still caught her off guard. Taeral looked the exact same as she had in the throne room, with the only difference being the fresh, bloody knuckles she now had. Vera glanced around, fully expecting to see someone laid out with a busted face.

"You shouldn't be here. We do not have time to satisfy your human curiosity, nor coddle you if you get injured."

She continued toward Vera as she spoke until she was only a few feet away. "This is no place for you. Your guard dog should have—" She froze, shock flashing across her face almost too fast for Vera to catch. And then her lips curled up in a cruel smile, giving her an almost feline appearance.

"Excuse me. I meant I'm sure your *mate* is more than capable of satisfying that for you."

Vera's exposed collar suddenly felt on fire even as her veins went ice cold. And every head twisted toward her, each trying to see her better and figure out who, exactly, she was.

"That's not why I'm here," she argued, adjusting her tunic to cover the mark, even though it was far too late to do so.

If Vesstan truly hadn't known she and Jaren were mated, he certainly would now.

Fuck, fuck, fuck.

The heat from the dozens of eyes on her was sweltering, more so than the sun beating down her back. "I'm just interested in training. I can fight. I'm not a beginner who needs one-on-one instruction on how to hold a blade," she added, since apparently Taeral had decided based on a single meeting that she was some pampered, naïve princess.

But the cackling laughter that exploded out of her armor-clad chest had Vera's hopes crumbling to dust. Taeral tipped her head to the side, eyes bright with unrestrained glee as she scrutinized Vera's body.

"Something tells me a fighter of Aleron is not the same as a fighter here. But by all means, human," she said, spreading her arms out. "Take your pick of a partner. It will not matter."

Human? Vera's hackles rose, anger sparking to life at the intended insult. The bitch knew she was no human. Even if they hadn't just met that morning, the lack of a point to her ears didn't overshadow all her other obvious Magyki features.

A low murmuring traveled around her as their surrounding audience circled around them, whispering among themselves. She'd known it was risky to come out here, but she'd hoped to be accepted and blend in. Now she'd be lucky to make it back to the palace before everyone was gossiping about the *daż* of the queen.

Smirking at the red hue Vera already knew was crawling up her neck, Taeral took her time sheathing her blade. Then, unarmed, she turned, giving Vera her back and walking away like she was no threat at all. The blatant insult had her seeing red.

More skilled or not, if Vera had ever pulled a disrespectful stunt like that to an opponent, Elric would've smacked the shit out of her.

Lady Bitch Face was beginning to seem like a far more appropriate name for her. She hadn't even given Vera a chance before deciding to hate her. But sadly for her, Vera just didn't give a shit.

She'd come all this way, crossed a horrid, rocky sea, and puked way more than any body should ever have to do, with the belief that she'd finally be allowed to train without fear of consequences. She certainly wasn't going to let some stuck-up female ruin it for her.

Holding her head high, Vera crossed her arms, letting a slow smile stretch across her face and flashing her canines. "What? *You* aren't up to the task?"

The entire yard went silent, the tension so thick she thought she'd choke on it. She swallowed, and pushed her anger down, hiding it along with what she could feel of Jaren. Him being near her wasn't helping.

Taeral stiffened, danger seeping from her pores as she slowly twisted back around. Her face contorted in pure hate, but before she could utter whatever reply was biting at her tongue, another voice spoke first.

"I'd love to play."

Vera whipped around to see that another female had

stepped forward behind her, a predatory glint in her dark brown eyes. From where she stood, she appeared to be a few inches taller than Vera, but with twice the muscles and curves. Wearing tight leggings and a sleeveless tunic, each ripple of muscle was on full display.

Unlike Taeral, whose hair was more shaved than not, the newcomer's hair was shaved on only one side, her black hair hanging in chin-length braids on the other. Her eyes were framed by long lashes, and she had dark brown skin, marked only by a single, long scar down her left cheek.

She was the epitome of gorgeous and intimidating and everything Vera could ever hope to be.

Nodding at a furious Taeral, she positioned herself in front of Vera and unsheathed the sword at her side. The very sharp, very *real*, sword.

Raising her chin, she didn't even bother turning around before calling to someone over her shoulder. "Suki, give her your weapon."

Immediately, a short-statured, blond female jogged toward her from out of the gathered crowd, sneering as she unsheathed her blade.

It was obvious Suki didn't appreciate the thought of Vera using it, but she did as instructed without uttering a word, shoving the handle into the palm of her hand with more force than necessary. The blade of the sword reflected in the sunlight, enhancing the fact that it was also, a very real weapon.

Vera's brows rose as she took in the female before her again.

226

Although Taeral had made it abundantly clear that she was in charge, this female held an air of command. Suki hadn't even batted an eye before complying, nor had she glanced to Taeral for confirmation.

"Reniya Virnorin," she said, introducing herself like they'd just met on the street rather than in the center of a circle full of sneering Magyki. Cracking her neck, she widened her stance, holding one arm in front of her, bent at the elbow, while the other held her blade in front of her chest.

"Let's see what you got, Arenaris."

Vera didn't get a second to react to her name being thrown out like a verbal whip before Reniya attacked, moving with a speed she hadn't anticipated.

She barely raised her borrowed blade in time, the unexpected hit almost sending her to the ground. The long sword was heavy in her hands, unlike the daggers she'd taken to practicing with on the ship. She grunted, using every muscle in her arms and chest to shove her back. The bitch had put her entire body weight behind that fucking hit.

Knowing her body strength wasn't nearly strong enough to withstand many of those kinds of hits, Vera lunged, going on the offense and aiming the flat of her sword for Reniya's shoulder.

She had no idea why anyone would train with real blades. The entire point of training was to be able to safely make mistakes, and regardless of their attitude toward her, Vera had no desire to physically harm any of them.

Her hesitation behind her thrust must have been obvious because Reniya flashed a terrifying smile, dodging her attack as easily as if she'd moved in slow motion.

"I am not afraid to bleed, Your Highness, nor am I afraid to draw yours. Fight me like a warrior or tuck tail and walk off this field."

Laughter echoed out around her, along with several shouts of agreement. Vera bristled, embarrassed. In her peripheral, she saw Jaren step through the crowd, arms crossed, and looking seconds away from ripping out throats. The Magyki around him shifted, giving him a wide berth.

"Well? What's it going to be? Are you—"

Growling, Vera attacked with a vengeance, refusing to be humiliated any further. Focusing on her anger, she put every ounce of it behind her strikes.

The bitch wanted a real fight? Fine. She'd give her a gods damn fight.

They met again and again in a clash of blades and limbs. But no matter how Vera came at her, Reniya met each of her movements with ease. She didn't even appear to be breaking a sweat while Vera was red in the face within minutes, her chest heaving as she darted in and out, ducking and lunging.

Her lack of sleep the night before wasn't doing her any favors, but she was giving it everything she had to avoid what would be a gruesome death if she missed. It didn't make any sense. Even the most hardened warrior should've been showing at least some form of fatigue at that point.

But then she sensed it, the pull she sometimes felt from Jaren when he drew on his abilities during her meditation. It was duller, barely noticeable, but there. Reniya was dipping into her power, healing her muscles and stamina as they sparred. So much for a fair fight.

She glared over her weapon, but Reniya just waggled her brows before coming at her again. The power behind her strikes reverberated down Vera's sword and up her arms, making her muscles strain and bulge, struggling not to buckle each time steel clashed against steel.

Jaren was incredibly strong, as was Elric, but neither had ever come at her with this kind of single-minded aggression and strength. The kind of unbridled strength that came from someone who was tapping into their fucking abilities to aid them.

She spun again, ducking just in time as Reniya's blade sliced through the air above her head, missing her by mere inches. Who the fuck aimed for the head during a spar with *real swords?*

The knowledge that Reniya wasn't even trying to hide what she was doing filled her with a blinding fury. Elric had held etiquette above all else during a spar, but apparently that didn't exist on this gods damn island, and Vera was having to concentrate far too hard to attempt tapping into her own power.

Growing angrier by the second, Vera twisted, throwing caution to the wind and aiming for Reniya's head right back, snarling a warning.

Reniya's eyes widened, surprise lighting them up as she

flung her blade up, ducking out of the way. But Vera was expecting it and already waiting for her. She pivoted, slamming her blade against hers again, just before ramming her foot into Reniya's stomach.

Reniya heaved, spit flinging from her parted lips as her body bent forward from the blow, and Vera wasted no time following through with a sharp elbow to her face, watching in satisfaction as Reniya's neck cracked back and blood dripped from her nose.

But rather than re-center herself to defend against another blow like she anticipated, Reniya's head snapped down, a wide smile on her face as she shot forward and swung her blade.

Vera cursed, her eyes barely tracking the movement in time to twist out of the way. But Reniya was relentless, increasing her speed and raining blow after blow down on her, each one as fatal as the last.

She whirled, heart hammering as she tried to keep up, but Reniya's blade came at her again, harder than any previous hit, and her arms buckled, warning her they wouldn't take another hit like that. Not without the ability to enhance her own strength in response.

Her only chance at winning was using the last bit of her stamina to dart in and catch her off-guard, but it was possible. Speed had always been what had given her the upper hand in the past.

Pivoting, she planned to strike low, hoping to knock her off balance enough to get her to the ground. All she needed was one second to get her blade up against her throat, and she'd win.

But instead of landing what should have been a guaranteed blow, Reniya anticipated it, twisting with inhuman speed and lunging.

Jaren's warning shout rang out over the excited yells of the other Magyki just before Reniya's blade made contact with Vera's chest. It sliced through her tunic and into the flesh above her breasts, ripping a scream from her throat.

Then she dropped, sweeping a leg out to kick Vera's right out from under her.

She flew back, the pommel of her sword falling from her hand as her shoulders slammed into the ground, pain shooting through her body like a battering ram.

She lay there, sprawled in the dirt in front of everyone, including her mate and motherfucking Taeral, blinking away the spots in her vision. She'd fucking lost.

Wincing, she lifted her head and glanced at her burning chest. Sure enough, both the new tunic and breast band Jaren had just purchased were completely ruined, her flayed skin visible underneath.

Curling her torso, she forced her throbbing arms to move, shoving up into a sitting position. Her entire body screamed at her, her torn tunic sticking to her chest, but she ignored it, biting her tongue hard enough to bleed.

She wouldn't utter a single groan of pain, refusing to give anyone the satisfaction of hearing it. Who the fuck tapped into their abilities when sparring with real weapons?

"Sorry about your clothes. I wasn't expecting you to miss an obvious hit, but at least I avoided your nipples."

Vera's nostrils flared at her jovial tone, and she seethed, more embarrassed than anything. She felt like a child training with Elric for the first time all over again.

"I would've blocked it just fine if it'd been a fair fight," she spat, finally glaring up at her.

Reniya's blade lowered, and she tilted her head to the side, looking genuinely confused. "Fair fight? You were armed just the same as I was. What'd you expect me to do? Cuddle you?"

Laughter barked out from the side, grating down her spine. "The *warrior human* didn't expect you to use your gods-gifted abilities in a spar," Taeral said, looking all too fucking pleased as she picked up Suki's discarded sword from the ground.

Vera's chest rumbled as an uncontrolled growl slipped past her lips.

Taeral's face snapped back to hers. "What? You don't like being called a human?"

She didn't bother responding. She just glared at her, hoping she could feel her hatred boring into her head.

Taeral held the blade out, letting Suki come reclaim her weapon before replying to Vera's silent loathing.

"You sound like them, you move like them, you fight like them. So, until you prove otherwise, you haven't earned any other title." She lifted her chin, the unvoiced dig loud between them. Magyki wasn't the title she was insinuating, and they both knew it.

Vera's face and neck flamed, the stares of the surrounding

Magyki burning off the last protective layer of her pride. She lowered her head, fighting back tears. This had been the only thing she'd wanted, and it'd just been thrown in her face.

She stared at the ground, refusing to meet anyone's gaze, least of all Jaren's. Her own shame was too strong to sense his, but she didn't doubt it was probably there. Maybe if she sat there long enough, everyone would magically disperse so she could crawl away to mope in private.

Something shot out in front of her face, and she instinctively threw her arm up to block the strike. But the attacking hand stopped a few inches from her face, its owner releasing a loud snort.

"Embarrassment doesn't suit you, Daughter to the Throne."

She looked up from the outstretched hand to find Reniya standing before her, wearing a wide-ass smile on her face.

CHAPTER 19

VERA

After the taunts and shit she'd just pulled during their fight, Vera didn't at all trust Reniya not to humiliate her further, but she couldn't exactly ignore her either. Not without simultaneously looking like a bitch and a sore loser.

And the last thing she needed was for the whispers that were still spreading through the Magyki around them to state she was unskilled *and* a fucking asshole.

Taking a deep breath, and hoping for the best, she reached her arm out, accepting the offer of help.

Reniya wrapped her hand around hers in a firm grip and yanked her up so fast, she lost balance, falling into her like a lover seeking an embrace. Mortified, she shoved back, hissing from the throbbing pain in her chest at the impact.

The cut wasn't deep enough to warrant immediate

attention, but fuck, it hurt.

Her ears were raging infernos on the sides of her head as she righted herself. It was going to take time before she was used to everyone around her being so gods damn strong.

Reniya just laughed, reaching out to brush off bits of gravel that still covered Vera's tunic. "I like you, Daughter to the Throne. You need a lot of work," she said, running her eyes down Vera's form and back up, "but I respect your fire."

"Thanks," she muttered, putting more space between them and wondering how she'd known who she was.

The Magyki around them still stared, refusing to move until Taeral began shouting angry commands, threatening to disembowel anyone who didn't get back to work.

Vera watched them slowly disperse, avoiding meeting any of their gazes. This wasn't the first time she'd lost a spar, both Elric and Jaren had beaten her more times than she could count, but it was the first time she'd ever lost to an audience.

She turned, forcing her feet to walk at a normal pace when she wanted nothing more than to run as fast as she could to the cover of the tree line. She teetered, feeling slightly lightheaded. Gods, she needed a bath and a damn nap.

"Tell me, Your Highness," Reniya called out, jogging to catch up and make pace with her, "is he your *zisdemyoz*?"

Vera's brow creased, not recognizing the last word. Was she talking about Jaren? "My what?"

"Your *zisdemyoz*," she repeated, as if saying it again magically explained what it meant.

"I know what you said," Vera muttered, "I just don't know what it means." She could feel Reniya's gaze as she stared at the side of her head. "I'm not perfect at our language yet," she reluctantly admitted, trying to walk faster.

Reniya kept up, either not taking the hint, or—more likely—just didn't give a shit.

"Would you be more comfortable if I spoke like this?" she asked, her mouth and tongue twisting in an almost endearing way as she enunciated her words in the common tongue.

"No," Vera snapped, her embarrassment somehow growing even hotter. Would she just leave her alone?

"I am fluent in both," Reniya continued, despite Vera's obvious irritation.

Stopping in her tracks, she pressed the pads of her fingers to her eyelids and audibly exhaled. Of course, she was. The female was apparently good at *everything*.

"What do you want, Reniya?" she asked, pointedly using Thyabathi. "You and Taeral made your point quite clearly. I get it. I'm leaving."

Reniya slapped her hand against the sword sheathed at her side, pointing at Vera and then herself. "*Zisdemyoz*. A guardian. I am to be yours."

Vera frowned, still not understanding what she was rambling on about. "Like a personal guard or something?"

Reniya nodded. "King Vesstan assigned me to you not an hour ago. I begin this evening after I set up my replacement here."

Vera balked, her thoughts immediately going to Eithan. She hadn't even considered the fact that she might be expected to walk around with a guard following her. Just the thought made her cringe.

She'd assumed Jaren would be enough. But considering how Taeral had reacted to him, and that King Vesstan would soon learn what he was to her—though she still didn't understand why that was bad—she shouldn't be all that surprised they weren't allowing it to be him.

She shook her head. "King Vesstan did not discuss protection with me. He didn't seem to—We didn't speak for very long," she finally said, not trusting Reniya enough to say more about how their interaction had gone.

Reniya grinned, switching back to Thyabathi. "Well, now you know. I think we will have fun, you and I. I have a feeling things with you are about to get very interesting."

Vera blinked, unsure how to take that.

"Get lost, Virnorin. She doesn't need you."

They both turned at the clipped words. Jaren had made his way through the crowd and was standing just behind them, glaring daggers at her companion. His arms were crossed over his chest, and the hostility vibrating from his entire body was visceral.

Reniya didn't bat an eye, completely unaffected by the violent death he was all but promising her. She raised a brow, the curl of a smirk on her full lips.

"Good to see you again, Barilias. Thought maybe you'd

237

decided to stay on Aleron this time around. It's been a while."

Jaren didn't answer, but a hint of frustration trickled down their bond. She glanced between them. They knew each other? And apparently well enough for Reniya to have noticed his absence.

She frowned, a weird sensation coiling in her stomach. Jaren looked like he wanted to murder her, but given the fact that he hadn't, even after she'd sliced Vera's chest open, he clearly trusted her. More than his attitude was letting on.

She considered the beautiful female again. Technically, Reniya hadn't done anything wrong besides best her in a fight. And since both King Vesstan and Jaren apparently trusted her not to murder her in her sleep, there was no reason Vera shouldn't as well.

So, why did she suddenly feel like sinking her fingernails into Jaren's skin and snarling in Reniya's gods damn face?

Jaren cleared his throat, glancing sidelong at her. Amusement flickered in his eyes, dampening the fury that'd been swirling there just a moment before.

Stupid fucking bond.

Reniya huffed a laugh and waved a hand dismissively. "Last I checked, Barilias, you didn't rank so high. Since when do you speak for the long-lost Daughter to the Throne?"

"Since now."

Reniya's nostrils flared as her eyes darted between them, pausing on Vera's shoulder and then her chest, where yet another of Jaren's fresh marks was visible below her cut.

"Ah. I see," she said, a knowing grin creeping across her face. "But with you as her guardian, who will stand watch at her door while you're mindlessly burying your tongue inside her, I wonder?"

Vera rolled her lips in; certain her face was going to be permanently stained red at that point. At least that answered her question about open discussions of sex. Apparently, it *wasn't* just a Jaeros and Dedryn thing.

Jaren's face didn't change, but she felt his uncertainty flare at her words. Reniya had found the one weakness he had and twisted it, making him question whether he, alone, was enough to protect his mate.

Because he hadn't been the last time.

Vera's heart lurched, wishing she could wrap her arms around him and soothe the hatred creeping back into his heart, but knowing he wouldn't want her to in front of everyone.

Reniya lifted her chin, somehow looking down her nose at him even as he stood above her. "You and I both know I'm the best one to protect and train her, Barilias. Don't let your pride get in the way."

His eyes darkened. "Says the one who announced her identity to everyone here."

A savage smile appeared on Reniya's face as she unsheathed a small knife at her side and began picking at her nails. "I saved her ass and her reputation. You're welcome."

Vera balked, wincing as her chest screamed at her with the movement. Saved her reputation? Was she serious? "We have very different ideas of that, I think."

Reniya didn't bat an eye. "King Vesstan may have spoken to me, but until he claims you publicly, every Magyki here has only Taeral's word to go on. Not only did they think you a liar, but they thought you *weak*. They'd have found you later and beat the shit out of you."

"How did our fight possibly help? I lost."

"Yes, as does everyone who fights me," she said, looking at Jaren and winking. She pointed the tip of her blade in Vera's direction. "But seeing how long you lasted? They now question what they know of you. They still won't respect you because of your human qualities, but they will second-guess touching a hair on your head."

Perfect. Day one and she'd already disgusted or disappointed literally everyone she'd met. She was off to a great start.

"Thanks for that, I guess," she said, pressing a hand to her chest and grimacing. She needed somewhere to sit and focus on healing where others weren't going to witness her struggle.

"Don't look so put out, Your Highness. They hate what they think they know of you. I will teach you to fight like a Magyki, and you will earn their respect, yes?"

The offer was tempting. Reniya was skilled, not only in the physical sense, but also with her abilities. A skill Vera very much needed help with. There was no hurt in trying, she couldn't be a worse teacher than Jaren.

Vera met her eyes. There was one thing she needed to know

first. "Why do you care, Reniya? Are you offering because you believe your pretty words, or are you offering because you were ordered to?"

"I was only ordered to protect you."

"Then why train me?"

"Her mother was Queen Vaneara's guardian," Jaren interjected before she could respond.

Wait, what? "Did she—"

"Die trying to protect her?" Reniya said. "Yes. She failed that night and they both paid the ultimate price."

Vera pressed her lips together, shuffling her feet awkwardly, unsure what to say to that. But Reniya's expression didn't waver or look upset. Only pride shone through her brown eyes.

"And before your mate runs his mouth again, yes, that is part of the reason. But, no, that is not the only one. I told you, I respect your fire." She smirked. "And I also enjoy pissing off my aunt."

"Your aunt?"

She hiked a thumb over her shoulder to where Taeral had disappeared, something dark flickering through her eyes. "She hated both my mother and yours and is as insufferable off the field as she is on it, trust me."

She was Taeral's *niece*? Wait. "Taeral's sister was my mother's personal guard?" she asked, eyes wide remembering the way King Vesstan's hand had settled onto her lower back as they'd walked out of the throne room that morning.

Reniya nodded. "Half-sister, but yes. I may be second-in-command, and share her blood, but there is no love lost between us. It'd bring me great pleasure to prove her wrong about you."

That would certainly explain why Suki had listened to Reniya's order without a second thought. Well, that and the fact that she could probably kick everyone's ass.

But as much as Vera would kill to see her and Taeral go head-to-head in a full spar, she'd much prefer being capable of knocking the bitch down, herself.

"All right then, Reniya, I accept. Let's piss off your aunt."

Reniya flashed a wicked grin as she stepped forward, reaching out as if to pat her on the shoulder. But Jaren's arm shot out before she could make contact, smacking it away.

She sent him a warning look but lowered her arm. "We will return here tomorrow when the sun has barely entered the horizon, and we will work on...this," she said, gesturing to Vera's body.

Vera's eyes narrowed, but Reniya just winked, stepping past her and strutting back toward the others. "See you later, Barilias."

JAREN

SHE'D BEEN BREATHTAKING.

It was no wonder she'd bested him that night in the alley before he'd known who she was. No matter what baseless taunts Taeral tried to spit, Veralie didn't fight like a human. Nor did she fight like a Magyki. She was something in-between, moving in a way he'd never seen before.

She'd taken down several guards the day they'd left Aleron, and he'd sparred her every morning during their trip across the Dividing Sea, but until she'd faced Virnorin and raised her blade before her face, he'd never been able to just sit back and *watch* her.

Gods. Even though he'd felt his mate's exhaustion, felt her muscles cramping up and screaming, she'd never once wavered or so much as lowered her blade an inch. Every Magyki in Naris could run their mouth about her appearance and choppy Thyabathi all they wanted, but there was no denying her strength.

She'd moved with a grace some trained Magyki still didn't have, and as much as he hated to admit it, Virnorin was right. Very few lasted that long against her.

Virnorin had been younger than Jaren when her aunt had thrown her into training, and he'd yet to meet another even remotely as skilled as she was. But even so, he was positive that if Vera had had control of her senses, that arrogant ass female wouldn't have stood a chance.

"You should have expected her to use her abilities," he said, dipping a clean cloth into the wash basin and wringing it out before carefully wiping around the long cut across her chest.

She winced, squeezing her eyes shut. "Oh? I wasn't aware mind reading was one of my gifts. I'll have to practice it more."

Giving her a mock glare, he reached down with his free

hand and pinched her side, drawing a satisfying yelp from her enticing lips.

They'd walked back to the palace, Veralie all but running to get there, only to be immediately tracked down by a set of palace guards who insisted on taking "King Vesstan's guest" to *her* new quarters.

As if her father thought there was even a chance she'd be staying there alone. Jaren had just flashed them a terrifying grin and walked in the room right along with her.

King Vesstan could assign her a single-body, medical cot, and he'd still find a way to fall asleep with her in his arms.

But luckily for them both, her official room—clear across the palace from where they'd originally been—was the size of a small, city home, and had a bed large enough for four grown Magyki to fit in. Which he had every intention of taking advantage of very soon.

By the time Veralie had toured the room, mooned over the large windows and equally large bathing chamber, and gasped in horror over the gown-filled closet, she had dark circles under her eyes, and her tunic had all but crusted to her skin.

She'd wanted to sink into a hot bath, but he worried she was too tired, the image of her face down in the inn tub flashing through his mind like a whip. So instead, he'd taken her by the arm and led her to the bed, wanting nothing more than to take care of his mate before curling up behind her.

Hair a fan of dark, frizzy curls about her head and gloriously topless, she lay sprawled in the center of the bed as he checked for debris and cleaned the dried blood away from her cut.

She winced again when he pressed around a deeper part of the cut, scraping off flecks of blood where the dagger had first pierced her skin. "I'm almost done."

Cracking open an eye, she sighed. "If you'd have just let me heal myself, I'd already be done and asleep by now."

He grunted, believing it. Her exhaustion was so heavy it was even weighing *him* down. Between feeling hers and his own, he was barely keeping his eyes open, and it was only after mid-day.

"I told you, if you heal wounds before they're clean, they will still scar. Your power speeds up and enhances your body's natural ability to heal; it doesn't pick out dirt and pebbles first."

"Is that why Doren's nose looked like it'd been broken? He'd just healed before setting it or something? And why Reniya has that scar down her cheek?"

Jaren's lip curled at the mention of them, especially that gods damn male who'd eyed her like a ripe fucking fruit, but he nodded. "It's possible. Although Reniya has had that scar for as long as I can remember. Since before she was old enough to be able to heal it."

He looked back down at her chest, careful not to snag the edges of the flayed skin as he worked. "You, however, will not have that problem."

She scrunched her lips, shrugging. "What's one more scar? I'm sure I'll have even more if I take her up on her offer to train."

He flicked his gaze up to the thin, white line above her collar, grinding his molars together when his eyes threatened to move higher. To her ears.

"You have enough scars," he growled, tone dark.

"So do you."

"They're not the same."

She reached up, running the tips of her fingers over his cheekbone before moving lower, the light scrape of her calluses sending gooseflesh down his arms. She trailed them along the edge of his jaw, over his chin, and then up to his opposite brow.

Tracing his scars.

"Will you tell me about them? Were they bad fights?"

He huffed, gently removing her hand, even though he didn't want to, so he could lean back over her chest and finish taking care of her. "No, most of these were during normal training. I was younger than most when I started and had a bit of a temper. I messed up often."

"That sounds about right," she said, giving him a sleepy smile. His heart beat hard against his ribs at the sight, soaking it up and tucking it away with every other one she'd given him.

"Were you also too young to know how to heal them, or did you do the unthinkable and not clean them first?" she teased.

His fingers froze for only a blink of a second, but she noticed, her eyes growing clearer as she focused in on him.

"Neither."

Her smile fell, and he immediately wanted to kick himself in the jaw. "Jaren?"

He sighed, refusing to make eye contact. If he did, she'd see straight through him, right to the center where he shoved every single broken piece of himself from the world. The pieces he hated.

"The first years without you were the worst years of my life, Veralie. I'd failed you as my mate and as my best friend, but I'd also failed our people.

"So, I threw myself into my training, caring about nothing else, and vowing to never again be as weak as I was the night you d—the night I lost you."

He dipped the cloth back into the water, wringing it out one last time before continuing. "But every injury I got, every fight I lost, only reminded me of that failure. I left each one to heal on its own as a reminder."

"So...even as a child, you were dramatic, then?"

His head whipped up, stomach roiling at the thought of her making fun of his naked truth, but she wore a sad smile, her silver eyes fierce and swirling as they finally met his.

Wrapping her small hand around his, she pried the damp cloth from his fingers and dropped it into the basin on the side table. Then she pulled on his arm, gaze firm as if to say, *get over here.*

He obeyed her silent demand, unable to resist even if he'd tried, and let her guide him down until his head rested on her stomach, and his chest pressed flush to her thighs.

"There's so much more to you than just fighting and protecting, Jaren," she said, running her fingers across his forehead and down his nose, soothing the tension in his face. "And I'm sorry that you couldn't see that growing up. I'm sorry their choices took that away from you."

He swallowed, and then swallowed again, feeling a burning in his throat as she gave voice to the pain that he'd held onto all these years. Gave voice to it and accepted him anyway. "It doesn't matter anymore."

His eyes fluttered shut, and he groaned when her other hand worked its way into his hair, massaging his scalp. "Yes, it does."

Humming in pleasure, he turned his face down into her bare torso, letting the steady rise and fall of her lungs drive away everything else. "I like it when you say my name," he mumbled, wrapping his hand around her side.

She chuckled, and pressure built in his chest as his heart swelled in a way he'd never felt before, not even in the last few weeks with her. The feeling reminded him of the tug of their bond, but different. Stronger.

As if, even without it, even without their history, their connection, or any of it, he'd still be completely and irrevocably hers.

Her muscles tensed beneath his cheek, her skin growing hot just before a flash of light sparked behind his eyelids. He mumbled again, aware he needed to do something, but his mind grew hazy, and his eyes refused to open.

A moment later, her sigh of relief hit his ears, and her body went soft beneath him while her hand continued its lazy circles over his scalp.

And for the first time in his life, he felt like he was home.

CHAPTER 20

VERA

Consciousness came too soon. She groaned, not yet ready for another early morning of pain with Reniya. It'd been six days since Vera had met King Vesstan and gone to the training field, and Reniya had made a habit of kicking her ass every single morning since.

She was starting to wonder why she'd ever agreed to it. Her body ached more than it ever had in her entire life. Elric hadn't been lax by any means, but no matter his skill, he'd certainly never hit with the power of a confident Magyki.

She wanted nothing more than to curl into Jaren and steal a few more minutes of sleep. Maybe wake him slowly with soft kisses and convince him to rub her calves. And feet. And also her shoulders. Fuck, she was sore.

Feeling the steady beat of his heart, but not feeling his body heat from his usual position behind her, she rolled to her side only to grunt in pain when something stabbed her just under her ribs. "What in all of Aleron is that?"

She winced, flopping back off it. If Jaren fell asleep with one of his daggers in the bed again, convinced someone was going to murder her in her sleep, she was going to whip him in the face with it.

A breeze hit her bare skin, and she shuddered, leaning her head up and cracking open an eye only to freeze in place.

No.

No. No. No.

Her stiff muscles pulled and screamed at her sudden movement as she shot up to a full sitting position, scrambling to cover herself with a blanket, only to grasp handfuls of pebbles instead. "Oh gods, not again. Please, no."

She looked beside her, where Jaren should have been, but her only companion was the sharp, glowing rock embedded in the ground that she'd rolled on. Jaren, their bed, the room, all of it was gone. Her heart sped up as she frantically darted her gaze around, still groggy from sleep.

Or maybe she was still asleep, and this was just a dream this time. She placed her hand on top of the stone and pressed down, slicing her palm open and grimacing. Did people feel pain in dreams? She'd certainly felt the pain of water filling her lungs during the last vivid one she'd had.

Feeling nauseated, she shoved the memory of drowning to the back of her mind. It wasn't going to help. Just the thought of it had her lungs burning.

"Jaren?"

Nothing. A hint of his scent hit her nose, but it was faint, likely from the residual release that'd dripped out of her during the night and dried on her thighs. She'd been so depleted; she'd made him do all the work and then promptly passed out naked after he'd cleaned her up.

And although she couldn't see him now, she could definitely *feel* him. She'd been too panicked in the lake last time to notice him until he'd raced to find her, but she was significantly calmer this time with both feet on land.

She closed her eyes and rubbed at the center of her chest, focusing on Jaren's heart. It beat in a steady rhythm, indicating he was still asleep next to her. So, if anything happened, he'd sense it immediately and wake her. She could do this.

"Stop being a child, Vera. Come on. Figure it out."

Biting back a groan, she placed both hands on the ground and pushed to her feet, her knees popping as she did. It was unfair to still have the bruising pain of sore muscles when she was fairly confident her actual body wasn't even moving.

She turned in a slow circle, taking in her surroundings. The first thing she noticed was the endless lake to her left, its unmoving black water taunting her. "Yeah, I recognize you, you piece of shit."

She subconsciously stepped away from it, already feeling a cold sweat break across her skin over the shadowed memory of it rising over her chin.

She still needed to find time to add swim lessons onto her list of things to do, along with reading Thyabathi, training, and learning how to use her abilities at will. No biggie.

The rest of the cavern appeared the same as it had during the brief explosion of light she'd created when she'd dove into her power. It wasn't as bright as that had been, but it wasn't dark as night this time either. The glass shards she'd seen all over the ceiling and walls were now emitting a soft glow, like a wild collection of natural lanterns.

She shivered, crossing her arms over her naked chest, and arched her neck back, her mouth popping open at what she saw. "Holy gods."

It was like standing in the middle of the night sky, stars surrounding her for as far as she could see. Appearing in an array of colors and vibrancy, they also varied in size, some smaller than her palm while others were several arm spans wide.

Careful not to impale her feet on any shards growing from the ground, she worked her way toward one of the walls, keeping her senses on high alert for any movement or sound.

It was unnaturally silent, the echoing movements of her body making her feel like a damn bear stomping through a forest.

Following along a wall, hoping it would eventually lead her to another room, or an exit or something, she looked closer at the pieces embedded within it.

Every single chunk was unique, jutting out in uneven, random directions. She stepped closer to a large, pink-tinted shard, reaching out a hand to touch it. The soft glow it emitted flared brighter, blinding her until she had to squint to see.

Deciding she shouldn't touch an unknown, glowing rock, she yanked her hand back, watching as it dampened back to its original state. Stepping up to another one, this one smaller and darker in color, she reached out again, and just like the first, it reacted.

She glanced behind her where she'd woken up and noticed what she hadn't before. The rock she rolled on was no longer glowing either.

"What the fuck is this place?" she murmured, pulling her hand back to stare at it. Was it her, or did they react to any kind of body heat? Chewing her lip, she took several steps away, avoiding touching any pieces on the ground.

Unsure how to force herself awake, she darted a look over her shoulder, desperately hoping to catch sight of an exit, and nearly screamed when a dark figure stood only a few yards away. She lurched back, whacking her head on the wall and felt her heart leap into her throat.

It was a person. Or, at least, she was pretty sure it was. Whoever it was, was completely obscured.

They wore a dark cloak, their face hidden beneath a deep hood. If it wasn't for the bare feet she could see poking out from the bottom, she'd have thought them to be some omen with the way they'd appeared out of nowhere.

"*Kültha?*" she called out hesitantly, squeezing one thigh over the other and tightening her arms around her chest. Why did she have to be *naked?*

Whoever it was didn't so much as flinch at the sound of her voice. Seeming unaware of her presence, they turned away from her to face the nearest wall, placing a single hand on it.

Her heart picked up, fear beginning to rise at who this figure might be, or whether or not this was their land, and she was trespassing.

She had nothing but the skin on her back to defend herself with if they attacked, while they could easily be hiding a weapon or two beneath their cloak.

Fuck, she couldn't even tell if they were human or Magyki, and if Reniya had taught her anything over the past week, it was that her physical skills meant nothing compared to a Magyki in control of their abilities.

Fuck, fuck, fuck.

All right, kill them with kindness, right? It wasn't *her* fault she was there, and maybe they were in the same predicament and just as confused as she was. And if they weren't, then that meant they'd had to have entered from somewhere. Which meant she could exit. That's what she needed to focus on.

"*Kültha!*" she called out again, raising a hand and jogging forward. She only made it a few feet before she stumbled, slicing her foot on an exceptionally sharp shard she hadn't seen.

She hissed, jumping back and balancing on her good foot. Her blood coated the glowing rock, and she watched as it faded back to an almost invisible gray.

She cursed, darting a nervous glance to the stranger, but

they still weren't looking at her. It was like she wasn't there at all. They just continued staring at the wall, tilting their head as they analyzed the softly glowing shards.

"Hey!" she yelled, automatically switching to the common tongue as pain radiated up her leg and panic began to build. Why couldn't they hear her? "Can you help me, please? Or tell me where I am? Hello?"

She frowned when her chest suddenly warmed, but it was quickly followed by a flicker of confusion that didn't belong to her.

Jaren.

Her heart squeezed. Even asleep, he'd sensed her pain and immediately woken to check on her. She took a deep breath, the knowledge calming her racing heart. Knowing she wasn't alone, even when she felt like it, gave her the confidence she needed.

Jaren wouldn't let anything happen to her and would wake her any second now.

Steeling her spine, she walked faster, clenching her teeth through the pain radiating up the arch of her foot. She needed to use what time she had and figure out why her mind kept transporting her to this gods damn place.

When she was only a couple feet away, the stranger's back still to her, she ran forward, reaching out to grab their shoulder, hoping beyond hope, she didn't get stabbed.

By the blood still leaking from her burning foot, it was safe to assume a dream dagger to the heart would hurt just as bad as a real one.

"Please, can you just—shit—" she cut off with a curse, watching in horror as her hand passed straight through their shoulder. Not because *they* weren't solid, but because *she* wasn't.

Unable to stop her momentum, she teetered to the side, attempting to regain her balance. But the second she threw her weight onto her injured foot, it gave out, slamming the side of her face into the wall.

Pain exploded from her temple, blurring her vision, and she instinctively shoved backward, stumbling and landing hard on her ass. She threw her hands out to catch herself, a cry bursting from her lips when more shards stabbed into her thighs.

Tears burned in her eyes, and she clutched her chest, feeling ice-cold fear fill it as Jaren's heart took off. Rolling off the now-bloody stones, she raised a hand to her forehead, her fingers coming back sticky and warm.

Movement caught her attention, and she dropped her hand, staring up with wide eyes as the stranger finally lowered their hood, revealing a mane of dark curls, a smattering of freckles over warm ivory skin, and pointed ears.

"Mbi thothori trush zhu," she whispered, noting the crushing weight contained in the female's pale gray eyes, and the deep creases along her forehead and cheeks. She had to be old indeed if her healing was no longer making a difference.

Vera watched in silence as she hovered her hands over a shard in the wall. It was about the size of both of her hands, but for whatever reason, it didn't glow brighter from her proximity as the others had done to Vera.

The female swallowed, her hands shaking and eyes lining with silver. Whatever she was doing, she didn't want to be doing it.

"Gods, please forgive me." Taking a deep, shuddering breath, she placed both hands on either side of the shard and twisted, screaming at the top of her lungs as she did.

The sound of it tearing from the wall cracked through the cavern like thunder, and the ground shook, nearly tossing her on her ass next to Vera.

"What the fuck did you just do?" The words flew from her like word vomit, followed by a squeak when the female whipped around to face her.

Vera could do nothing, limbs frozen in shock, as they locked eyes for the first time, the female's mouth opening just before a sudden, sharp pain lanced through Vera's shoulder.

Instinct had her ramming an elbow back into whoever it was attacking her from behind, but there was no one there. She craned her neck, attempting to see what had cut her this time, only for the panic in her chest to skyrocket just before something ripped into her shoulder.

She screamed, slapping a hand over the bleeding wound, and lurched back, eyes darting around in fear. But she could make out nothing as all the shards began to dim, causing the cavern around her to fade like parchment in water.

The last thing she saw was the female pulling back her cloak to tuck the broken shard in a concealed bag. A flash of metal on her empty sheath glimmering against it before everything went black.

Vera lurched up off the bed, her head barely avoiding smacking into Jaren's as he darted out of the way.

"Oh, thank the gods. Breathe, Veralie, you're all right. I got you." Warm hands cupped her cheeks, pulling her face up to his. His pupils were blown wide, stark in the soft morning light, and his hands shook as he seemed to stare into her very soul, checking it for injury.

"You're all right," he repeated, soft and broken, like he was reassuring himself more than her.

She shifted her weight and winced when a throbbing pain worked through her shoulder and up her neck. Something tickled her collar, and she carefully craned her neck down to see blood dripping from a vicious bite mark.

It was deep and the edges messy, like he'd clamped his jaw around her only to rip away in a wild panic.

"I'm sorry," he said, running his hands down her arms like he couldn't convince himself to release her. "I didn't know what to do. You were in pain, and I couldn't wake you."

She looked up to see blood smeared over his chin and a flash of terror still lingering in his eyes. She hated it. Hated the fear he couldn't seem to overcome about losing her. She wanted her gruff, asshole mate back.

"So, to wake me, you decided to cause me *more* pain?" she asked, arching an eyebrow.

His lips twitched, accepting her distraction. "I figured if anything could wake you up, pissing you off would do it."

Laughter bubbled up, and she cringed when the act pulled at her shoulder. She shifted, trying to get a better look at it, and phantom pains shot through her foot and thighs.

Clenching her teeth through the pain, she shoved Jaren back, sitting up to look down at her foot, expecting a nasty gash. But nothing but bare skin greeted her.

She twisted it back and forth, perplexed. It definitely hurt, as did her hand and thighs, but not like they had in the cavern. "It wasn't real," she whispered.

"Was it the same dream? In the water?" he asked, picking up her foot and digging his thumb in, massaging it in a way that had her eyes nearly rolling to the back of her head.

"Yes and no," she said, groaning. "It was the same cavern I saw before with the same monstrous lake, but I wasn't in it this time."

Closing her eyes, she replayed the dream in her mind, trying to describe it for him as best she could. "It was like the cavern could sense me, like it *knew* I was there, even though I wasn't." Not really. She remembered how her hand had passed straight through the female's body and shuddered.

"But you're fine," he said again, holding her foot tighter. "I don't know why I couldn't wake you this time, and I don't like it at all, but it was just a dream, Veralie. The only thing that actually hurt you was me."

His eyes darted back to the nasty wound on her shoulder. She'd need to heal it soon, not just because it fucking hurt, but because it'd also hurt *him* to do it.

"Jaren," she said, chewing on her lip. She remembered the glint of the buckle on the stranger's sheath, the family name she'd seen engraved along the edge. "I don't think they're just dreams."

He sat back, brows drawing low as he focused on her. "What do you mean?"

"I mean, I think they're visions of things that are real. Or, *were* real a long time ago," she said, aware that what she was about to say was completely crazy. But she couldn't fight off the feeling that she was right.

"I think I just saw Queen Alean steal the crystal."

CHAPTER 21

VERA

Finished healing, she shot up, energized, and rolled to the edge of the bed, slapping her hand on the side table in search of a pair of clothes. The past few nights, she'd been leaving a set there to throw on before getting up since Jaren had a habit of ripping them off if she even dared climb in wearing anything.

Her hand hit nothing but solid wood, and she groaned, forgetting they'd all been taken away to be laundered. The only tunic and leggings left in the room were the ones she'd worn the day before, and she'd rather strut naked through the palace then put those back on.

Gods damn Reniya had her sweating like a pig each day.

"Do you have any clean tunics?" she asked, looking over the shoulder that was still covered in residual blood to the frozen male staring at her like she'd lost her mind.

"Not besides the one I'd be putting on my own body, no. Why?"

She threw her head back and groaned again, louder this time and significantly whinier. She was in too much of a hurry to try to convince Jaren to go buy her more—since she wasn't allowed to wander Naris yet—so she'd just have to settle for something else for now.

Rolling her head down, she glared at the closet on the other side of the room. The one King Vesstan had made sure was filled wall-to-wall with dresses of every color and numerous formal gowns.

She tried not to let it bother her, since he was just trying to be thoughtful, but the idea of him having someone estimate her size and choose what she was, and wasn't, allowed to wear, rubbed her wrong. It reminded her far too much of Emperor Sulian demanding she dress up for their dinner.

She hadn't hated that dress; she'd actually felt more beautiful in the shimmery lilac gown than she'd ever felt, especially with how Eithan hadn't been able to keep his eyes off her. She just hadn't appreciated being *forced* to wear it just because Emperor Sulian wanted something nice to look at.

Part of her wondered if the servants would even bring her tunics back, or if they'd all somehow magically disappear while being washed.

Anxious from her dream and irritated over her current predicament, she stomped across the room, naked as the day she was born, and disappeared into the closet to find the least restrictive dress possible.

Reniya was going to kill her for not showing up for training today, but she couldn't. She needed to figure out what the truth was behind these gods damn dreams before she got stuck in another one she couldn't get out of.

She'd figure out a reasonable excuse to give her between now and when Reniya showed up later. Because if the last few days were anything to go by, Vera would find her stationed outside her room, standing guard. Even Jaren hadn't been able to convince her to stop.

The female was adamant about being her personal guard until King Vesstan said otherwise, and after the second day, Vera had given up. What was one more demanding Magyki to follow her around?

"Where are you going?" Jaren asked, his voice moving as he wandered the room to find his own clothing.

Finding the stack of underclothes neatly placed in a short dresser, she yanked them on and snagged the first lightweight, plain dress she could find. The fabric was deep green and flowy, with a wide, belted-looking leather corset. It'd have to do.

She worked herself into the garment, shouting behind her, "To the library. I'm assuming they exist here, do they not?"

A pause. "And what exactly do you plan on doing there?"

"Oh, you know," she said, frowning down at the corset-like contraption in her hand, "Find a good chair to curl up in and peruse all the books I can't read. It'll be fun."

Hands wrapped around her waist, pulling her back against a taut body as lips brushed across her neck. She shuddered, automatically arching to give him better access.

He nipped her earlobe. "If you're intent on avoiding training with Virnorin, I can think of several other activities I'd rather spend the day doing than staring at dusty books."

Heat flared to life in her middle when she felt his hard length press flush against her back, but she pushed it down, determined not to let his touch and smell distract her.

"I want to read up on the history of the crystal and Queen Alean. I'm hoping maybe a scribe will translate some for me." She shrugged. "Or, I suppose, my doting mate who has nothing else better to do could translate for me."

He released her, shifting back with a sigh, and she looked behind her in time to catch sight of the bulge fighting against his trousers. He ran a palm down it, readjusting himself.

"Naris's main library is located clear across the city, and you, Veralie Arenaris, are not supposed to leave the palace."

She sucked on her front teeth and tilted her head, placing her free hand on her hip. "I also don't listen, so are you coming with me, or shall I bring Reniya? Something tells me she'd be up for sneaking out."

He glared. "If you even consider sneaking out of this palace without me, I will hunt you down and smack your ass until it's raw."

She glared right back. "You have any better ideas, green eyes?"

For a second, she worried he might actually throw her over his shoulder right there and then and follow through with his threat, but he eventually sighed, running a hand through his hair.

"Though not as large, there is also one here. Jae used it for my studying materials growing up because the other was too far away for him to visit after his dinner shifts in the kitchen."

"Perfect," she said, smiling widely and gesturing to the contraption in her hand. "Now hurry up and help me lace this up because I have no idea what I'm doing."

A QUICK, DRY breakfast that Jaren had all but forced her to swallow down, two shy servants who looked ready to bolt at the sight of her, and three wrong turns later, they finally reached the palace library.

She wasn't sure what she was expecting, but a two-level, dark, musty room wasn't it. Although there were a multitude of sconces along the walls and lanterns on each table, they did very little to shed light throughout the maze of shelves.

"Was it everything you'd hope it'd be?" Jaren asked, bumping her arm.

She scrunched her nose, somehow convincing herself *not* to elbow him in the gut. "I'll admit I'm a little underwhelmed. I thought libraries were fancier."

"It's two levels of texts and scrolls that are older than our grandfathers' grandfathers, written by ancient, stuffy Magyki who loved to hear themselves speak. There's nothing fancy about that."

She craned her neck back to look at the higher level, which looked even darker than the first. "How does anyone even read what they pick out? It feels like a crypt in here."

Granted, she'd never been in one of those either, so maybe all her assumptions were set to be wrong.

"The scribes know where everything is at, and they just read them at the tables."

"Oh." Duh.

He chuckled, taking her by the hand and leading her between the sets of tables until they reached a large, wooden desk in the center of the room.

Seated behind it was, in fact, an ancient, white-haired, stuffy looking Magyki. By the skin spots and creases across his skin, he had to have been pushing one-hundred-fifty years old at the youngest.

"We're looking for any information you have on the history of the gods' blessing," Jaren said, sharp and to the point.

The male's face crinkled, almost folding in on itself as he directed Jaren where to go. He lifted a shaky arm to point up the lone, spiral staircase behind him, only to smack it to his chest and rear back with a gasp when his gaze landed on her.

Moving faster than anyone his age should be capable of, he shoved away from the desk and fell to his knees, disappearing behind the desk as he did. His joints echoed out through the silent room, and she could do nothing but stare at the spot he'd vacated.

She snapped her mouth shut, glancing at Jaren to silently ask *What do I do?* But he was too busy biting his lip to keep from laughing to answer.

Giving him a vulgar gesture, she muttered a quick thank you over the desk and practically ran for the stairs, suddenly grateful for the dark aisles she was headed toward.

How did Eithan deal with people floundering and bowing around him all the time? How had her mother dealt with it? Vera had only known who she was for a matter of weeks, and already she was panicking.

There were two sides of her warring against the other, one wanting nothing more than to crawl back into the armory and never leave it again, and the other wanting to see what her future could hold. She honestly wasn't sure what she felt anymore.

"I THINK I found something."

Stepping back from the most recent shelf she'd been looking through, she walked his way, hoping he'd finally found something worth their time and effort. Or, *his* time and effort, at least. She wasn't much help besides looking for the few words she could recognize.

It'd taken longer than they'd thought to find anything on Queen Alean, and she was starting to grow frustrated.

There were numerous texts and scrolls about her family line as a whole, but it was almost like each account actively avoided talking about Queen Alean besides a casual mention on a family tree.

"Is this who you saw?" he asked, leaning the book down so she could see the portrait he'd found.

The depiction was old and faded, the colors having long since lost their luster, but she froze all the same. The head of dark curls, the pale, gray eyes. It was her. The same female she'd seen in her mind. Yet at the same time, she looked different. Her face was softer, the edges less sharp, and she looked younger. Happier.

"That's who I saw."

"You're certain?"

She nodded. "Arenaris was engraved on her sheath, and I didn't notice at first, but when she spoke...it was the same voice I'd heard the first time."

My name is Alean Arenaris, and I seek entrance.

She frowned, staring down at the young, carefree face held within the book's pages.

"She looked haggard and worn down, like her soul was already two-hundred years old, and she had dark circles under her eyes and deep, worry lines. But at the same time, she still looked young in a way. I'd guess around one-hundred years old, maybe?"

He was already shaking his head before she finished. "No. If who you saw was truly Queen Alean taking the crystal, she wouldn't have possessed abilities yet. She would've still been human."

She blinked, dumbfounded. She hadn't even thought of that. She looked at it again. What on Aleron had Alean gone through to make her go from the soft, hopeful queen in the portrait to the distraught one she'd seen in the cavern? They were missing something, something their history was being very careful not to recount.

"What does it say?"

"Not much I wasn't already taught," he said, flipping to the next page. "It's mostly just about her reign, with the same known story about the gods bestowing her with the gift of health and fortitude to share with the Bhasurians. All in thanks for their unwavering belief and protection of their resting place."

He turned the next page, his fingers freezing over the next painting. She leaned in closer, moving his hand out of the way. It was a smaller depiction of Queen Alean. She was kneeling, grateful tears streaming down her face while a hand held a crystal above her upturned hands.

The visual was quite different than the agonized scream that had erupted from Alean's mouth when she'd violently ripped it from the wall and stashed it in her cloak like a thief in the night.

Jaren twisted his face toward her, and his breath tickled her ear. "If my education hasn't failed me, I believe it was only a decade or so later that the name Magyki was adopted. Only history texts use the term 'Bhasurian' anymore."

She nodded, remembering that being mentioned even in the Aleronian history texts she'd read. Though those had discussed it in a negative sense, citing the Magyki as prideful. Considering the name 'Magyki' literally translated to "gifted people," they weren't wrong.

"Anything else?"

He closed the text, shaking his head. "Nothing more about the crystal, no. Just pieces of her reign and who she married. She had three children but only one daughter. Queen Alyana was the first queen on record to notice something was wrong. She eventually died in her sleep, as did almost every queen after her."

"Comforting."

"Indeed." He set the book back on the shelf—not at all in the correct place—and pulled her in close, pressing a kiss to her forehead.

She sighed, leaning into his touch. "All this did was confirm what we already knew. Queen Alean was never blessed. But even Emperor Sulian had assumed as much, so it doesn't change anything." She shoved a few loose curls from her face, frustrated.

Something wasn't adding up. Everyone seemed to know the truth, but purposefully ignored it, determined to believe the lie with every fiber of their being. Because there was no way their people believed Queen Alean was cursed right after being blessed.

The queens just started up and dying in their sleep too young, and no one batted an eye. It didn't make sense. She couldn't stop thinking about what Jaeros had said. That her mother had suffered so much, she hadn't wanted a child.

That was Vera's future. And Jaren's future if he chose. Because as much as it had hurt to hear, she couldn't blame her mother's choice. She wasn't sure when she'd start to notice, or even if, she'd start to notice the affects, but she couldn't imagine wanting to pass it on to an innocent child.

"Come on," Jaren said, pressing one last kiss to her temple, "let's find you something more substantial to eat before we deal with Virnorin."

She chuckled at the way he practically spit her name. "You can't hold a grudge against her forever just because she always kicks your ass in a fight."

"Yes, I can."

Still laughing as they turned the corner to head back toward the staircase, she yelped, barely avoiding crashing into the body standing just on the other side.

Before she could recover or even blink, Jaren had snatched her back, flinging her behind him, hand gripping the pommel of a dagger.

"May the God of Death take me!" A voice squeaked out.

She rose on her tiptoes, looking up over Jaren's shoulder to see a short, blond-haired male staring at them with owl-like eyes. They drifted from Jaren's death glare to the top half of Vera's face, widening even farther until she was sure they'd pop clean out.

"My apologies," he said, beginning to fall into a bow before stumbling and rearing back up. He rolled his lips in, looking unsure if he was supposed to bow or not. Shuffling a stack of scrolls in his arms, he stepped back, putting several feet between him and Jaren.

"Wait," she said, trying to move around her statue of a guard. He tightened his hold on her arm, flashing her a warning look. She rolled her eyes, using both hands to shove past him. *We're in a library, what in gods name could happen?*

Green eyes darkened behind lowered brows as his chest rumbled. *A great many things, little star.*

Ignoring the sudden heat scorching a path all the way down her spine, she swallowed, looking back at the speechless male before them. "You were there the other day, with King Vesstan."

His head bobbed. "Yes. I'm Onas Dornelin, Miss Veralie."

"Do you believe yourself above using her title, Onas Dornelin?" Jaren asked, his tone dangerously soft.

"N-no. She has not yet been c-crowned. I don't—"

"It's okay, Onas," she said, raising a hand out to stop his panicked rambling. Seeing Jaren tense beside her, she raised her other hand to him, feeling ridiculous. "He's right, Jaren. It's fine. It's nice to meet you, Onas. You can call me, Vera."

"No, he can't."

She wasn't going to kill him. She wasn't going to kill him.

Onas's eyes bulged all over again, and she wondered how much time he actually spent around other people besides the king.

"I was actually looking for you, Miss Veralie. I stopped by y-your room and your guardian said...w-well, she indicated I might find you here," he finished, ducking his head.

Gods, did she even want to know how Reniya had figured out where she was? By the way Onas was turning red from his ears to his neck, she probably didn't want to know what her new trainer had said about her.

"Why were you looking for her?" Jaren asked, hand still firmly attached to his dagger.

"King Vesstan has requested your presence at dinner tonight. A-alone."

Jaren's answering chuckle had her skin breaking out in gooseflesh. She made to frown at him, just in time to see him blessing Onas with a terrifying, wide-toothed smile.

Slapping her palm over his mouth, she tried to smooth over his psychotic expression with a soft smile of her own. "Ignore him, Onas. Thank you for letting me know. Where am I to meet him?"

He fidgeted, shifting farther toward the stairs and away from Jaren, who had gone preternaturally still beneath her hand. "Your guardian knows where and agreed to escort you."

Vera nodded, mentally preparing herself for the fight she and Jaren were certainly about to have over that tidbit.

"It really is strange," Onas said, tucking his bundle closer to his body.

"What is?" she asked, lowering her hand before her mate decided to bite a finger off.

"How much you look like her."

Her heart flipped, pleased, only to notice the way his eyes

twitched, his lips pursed like he'd tasted something bitter, and it sank. "Why do I feel like you don't mean that as a compliment? Was she considered really ugly or something?"

Jaren snorted.

"No! No, of course not. I didn't—I mean, it's just so odd to see you, given—it's just…a lot to take in," he stuttered out, looking more uncomfortable by the second.

He took a deep breath, trying to compose himself. "You just look like her, especially wearing her clothing. For a second, I thought you *were* her. That's all I meant."

Vera's breath caught in her throat, and she instinctively placed a hand on Jaren's arm. "The dresses that were put in my closet were my *mother's?*"

She looked down at the flowy green dress, unsure how to feel about that piece of information. Still unsure how she felt about her mother, period.

"The entire room was hers," Onas said distractedly, looking behind him toward the stairs as if considering whether or not he could make it to them before they caught up with him.

She shared a look with Jaren. They'd passed the royal wing during their search for the library. King Vesstan's room definitely wasn't in the same hall as hers.

"They didn't share a room?"

Onas's head snapped back to them, his eyes flaring before he quickly squeezed them shut, shaking his head. "I just meant that she used that room. If there's nothing else, I really must be going."

She watched him beeline for the stairs, tripping in his haste before disappearing from view. She honestly felt a little guilty about how frazzled seeing her had made him. What did he even do for the king?

"Don't even think about it."

She groaned, turning to look up into a pair of furious green eyes. "It's just dinner, Jaren. And I'll have Reniya with me," she said, raising her hands like she was calming a wild stallion. But it was the wrong thing to say.

He growled. "Is it a game to you to see how far you can push me? Do you enjoy it? I'm already angry enough without you gallivanting off with fucking Virnorin to dine with someone who treated you like a last thought," he spit, jaw popping with how hard he was clenching it.

"Already angry? What could you possibly already be angry at me about? Onas?"

His arm whipped out, snatching hers and dragging her behind him while he maneuvered around the closest aisle, hiding them from view. Snarling, he twisted, stepping into her and forcing her to retreat until her back bumped a shelf.

"From the moment you were born, my sole purpose has been to protect you. Nothing else. *You.* And you dangle it in my face every time you brush off my attempts to do my job."

She blinked, trying to separate his racing emotions from her own. It was like he couldn't decide whether he wanted to fuck her or throttle her, or both.

"If we were in any other circumstance I'd understand, but

come on, Jaren, did you see him? The poor male was shaking harder than a leaf in a winter storm. What was he going to do in the middle of the library? Throw a scroll at me?"

Arms bracketed her head a second later, his scent swirling around her as he leaned down in her face. "That's the second time you've hinted that you're safe just because you're within the palace walls, *Daughter to the Throne*."

The wood behind her creaked beneath his hands as he stepped flush against her. "May I remind you it was in this exact palace that I lost you the first time."

Was it hot in there? She swallowed, lungs pressing into her ribcage as her breathing became more labored. "We were alone then. We're not alone in here. There are scribes wandering everywhere," she said, hoping he didn't point out that they'd only seen one on their way up there.

"Really? Because I could do whatever I wanted to you right now, little star, and there's not a fucking thing those walking parchments could do to stop me."

"Good thing I'm perfectly capable of it then."

He rolled his hips into hers, growling in her ear. "Is that a challenge?"

CHAPTER 22

VERA

Fire met steel in her veins as she lifted her chin, her core accepting the challenge even as her eyes and voice told him differently.

"When will you learn that threats and demands don't work on me?"

He hummed, continuing to grind his hard length against her center, sending sparks of pleasure shooting down her spine. "When will you learn that I like you better when you're angry?"

Placing both hands on his chest, she shoved, nostrils flaring when he didn't so much as budge. Well, then. "You must not be feeling too confident about winning if you're already tapping into your strength."

Only flashing her a wicked grin, he dropped to the ground, sliding both hands up under her dress. She stiffened, darting her head side to side to make sure no one was around. "What are you doing—*fuck*."

A sharp sting engulfed her hips and thighs, and then the sound of ripping filled the room. He'd fucking torn her underclothes clean in half, yanking them completely off her body.

He stood tall, six feet of pure male arrogance as he tossed the ruined garment like a shooting star to the other side of the upper floor. "What were you saying?"

She could only blink at him, shock making itself a home in her chest. He was crazy.

Taking advantage of her reaction—or lack thereof—he ran a hand down her thigh and gripped the underside, wrapping her leg around his hip and hoisting her up so her other foot grazed the floor.

"Go ahead, Veralie. Stop me," he murmured, his voice rough and gravelly as lust speared through him. His scent assaulted her, drowning out every other thought in her head.

"You're going to get us kicked out," she breathed, even as she gripped his shoulders and hiked her leg higher, giving him better access.

He released a dark chuckle, scraping his canines against the shell of her ear. "The chance of that happening is entirely up to you."

He pressed against her, shoving her back against the shelf again. Scrolls rolled off, littering the floor around them, their ends clanking loudly in the silence, but she couldn't have cared less anymore.

A second later, he dug his fingers into her other thigh and yanked, wrapping her leg around his other side and lifting her completely. Aligning himself at her bare center, he rolled his hips sharply, hitting that perfect spot and drawing a moan up her throat.

He hummed approvingly into her neck, licking and nipping his way down while his fingers caressed and squeezed her thighs beneath her dress.

As he molded his lips over her shoulder and sucked, she could only crane her neck for him, submitting to his touch. "Please, Jaren."

He raised his head, clicking his tongue against the roof of his mouth. "Unless you want an audience, I suggest you find a way to stay very quiet, little star."

"Asshole." Her breathing hitched, and she tightened her hold on his shoulders with each steady roll of his hips against her center.

"Don't tempt me," he said, lips curled in a smirk. "I'll take that with no remorse and have you screaming out to the gods until your throat is raw."

Desire pooled in her core as a shudder coursed through her body. She dug her nails in and opened her mouth to answer, but a hand wrapped around her throat, squeezing just hard enough to stop her from speaking.

His breath danced across her lips as he leaned in and whispered, "Undo my trousers."

More than happy to follow that order if it got him inside her, she did, practically tearing them in the process. He shoved her harder into the shelf, holding her up with only his hand around her throat and her legs clamped around his waist.

Slipping his other hand between them, he removed himself, sliding his fist up and down his stiff length. She licked her lips, watching as beads of white dripped onto his fingers.

"Not one sound, Veralie."

He released her throat, dropping his hand to yank her dress the rest of the way up to pool around her waist, baring her naked skin to the cool air. Squeezing her ass hard enough to bruise, he shifted back just enough for his tip to finally brush through her wetness.

"Feel free to bite down on something if you must."

Her breathing hitched, but she covered it with a scoff. "Don't tease yourself with something that will never happen. I'm not biting you." She angled her hips in, relishing the feel of him prodding at her entrance, silently urging him to go farther. "I won't need to anyway. I can be quiet."

"Would you like to bet on that?"

"Maybe. Won't matter," she said, leveling out her voice even as her heart raced. "You'll lose."

"Yeah?" He purred, pushing in an inch only to pull back. "Let's see just how hard I can fuck you before you break."

Gripping her ass with both hands, he slammed in, sinking all the way to the hilt in one go, her body accepting every glorious inch with pure fucking glee.

JAREN

THE SECOND HE SANK INTO HER WELCOMING HEAT, A roaring filled his veins. He'd been the one to initiate this, knowing there were Magyki in the lower level of the library capable of hearing them if they wished. For all he knew, they'd all already seen her undergarment fly over their heads as he'd launched it across the library.

He'd been the one to tell her she had to be silent. But fuck, the second she'd agreed, all he could think about was how much he wanted her to fail.

Her muscles squeezed and pulsed around him with each thrust he gave her, begging and urging him to fill her. Her neck arched beautifully, hands gripping, and jaw clenched as she desperately tried to stay quiet while he ground into her.

It wasn't enough. Seeing her struggle and feeling through their bond just how good it felt for her to have him pounding in at this angle, had sweat beading across his brow and his balls tightening. But it still wasn't enough.

An animalistic urge rose inside him, taking over. He'd fuck her as long as it took until she broke her silence. Lurching forward, he slammed the rest of her back against the shelf, knocking more shit off as he placed both hands at the crease of her thighs, lowering his thumbs to spread her open.

"I want you to watch me fuck you, Veralie. See how gods damn good you look taking me."

She grunted, barely biting back the sound as he dug her spine harder into the shelf, scraping the skin of her lower back on the edge as he rocked her body against it over and over.

Her skin was flushed and clammy, her dark spirals sticking to her neck and jaw as her head lulled forward. It caused more strands to drag across her shoulders, falling to rest over the tops of her breasts.

He growled, wishing he could rip the entire gods forsaken dress off as well. He wanted to see her tips harden in the air and feel her curls brush his face as he took her perfect nipples in his mouth, sucking and biting until she broke.

Fuck. He *wanted* someone to hear them. Wanted someone to see just how gods damn exquisite his mate was, see how her body clutched and begged for him and wish they could have that. Only to know, with every violent thrust they watched him force on her, that they'd never find anything like it.

Inching a thumb farther over, he began to work her clit, still driving unrelentingly into her. Her heavy-lidded eyes stayed focused on their connection, blood beading along her bottom lip as she bit down, watching him drive into her.

Circling his thumb faster and listening to her body for the exact pressure she needed, he lifted his other hand to grip her face, ripping her lip out from between her canines and sinking his own into it. She groaned loudly, bucking against him as she chased her climax.

Their bond thrummed to life, heating his chest, as she approached the edge, and he slammed up harder, using enough force for the shelf to creak in protest. He bared his teeth, fighting his own orgasm. "Give it to me, Veralie."

He plunged as deep as he could, grinding up to hit that spot in a way he knew would have her seeing stars. She made a choking noise, squeezing her eyes closed as she bit back a cry.

But sadly for his *aitanta*, her valiant efforts were in vain. There was no way in this world, or any after it, that every Magyki there couldn't hear the groaning wood and the delicious fucking sound of him claiming her.

The wet slap and slide of their bodies echoed out into the enormous room, making him teeter dangerously close to his own finish.

"*Now*, little star." He moved harder, faster, reveling in the mixture of pleasure and pain radiating from her as her spine screamed and her body exploded.

She gasped, carving bloody trails into his arms as her orgasm finally crashed into her. Her thighs tightened around him, squeezing his torso, and he immediately followed, clamping his jaw around her neck as he poured himself into her with a burst of wild, unhinged thrusts.

Spots danced across his vision, and he felt almost drunk as the combination of both their climaxes coursed through him at once, knowing she could feel the same. He groaned into her skin, refusing to slow his hips until the last wave of pleasure left their bodies.

He lifted his head, panting as he smiled at her, watching her droop back against the almost empty bookshelf. He was honestly impressed it was still standing.

"I want to praise you for how well you took me, and in the same breath, damn you for not screaming my name out to the gods."

She grinned, her heart beating a chaotic rhythm as her chest rose and fell rapidly. "I told you I could keep quiet."

Even their hushed voices seemed too loud in the now-silent room, and he twitched inside of her, feeling his release start to drip out. And just like that, he already wanted to carry her to the closest chair and bend her over to do it again.

But he sighed, knowing they needed to leave if she had any chance of being ready on time, yet still wishing he could keep her all to himself all the same. Pulling out, he slowly lowered her down his body, maintaining her weight until both feet touched the floor.

Her nose crinkled as she situated her dress back down—sans underclothes to his immense satisfaction—and he couldn't fight his smirk, knowing his release would be seeping out of her with each step she took back to their room.

He tucked himself into his trousers, not bothering to tuck in his tunic. She wouldn't have time for a bath before dinner with the king, which meant she would absolutely reek of him throughout the entire meal. His chest rumbled at the thought, knowing he would be right there beside her relishing in it.

Because father or not, *King* or not, if she really thought he'd let her meet with Vesstan alone, she'd lost her gods damn mind.

He didn't give a shit why Queen Vaneara hadn't wanted her

husband to know about their bond, in the end, it didn't matter. King Vesstan would've been told by now, and whether her father liked it or not, Veralie Arenaris was *his*.

AFTER WALKING PAST more than one glaring scribe, who'd all conveniently come out of hiding to stand near the main desk, they'd finally left the library and were making their way back toward their room. His star walked silently beside him, but she was anything but calm.

The post-orgasm bliss that had filled her before was gone, and he could feel her nerves clashing with the unsteady beat of her heart.

"I can feel how hard you're thinking even from way down there, Veralie. Talk to me."

Her lips tipped up, but there was no humor behind the tired expression. "What do you think he wants to discuss tonight? King Vesstan, I mean. He said so little the first time, I guess I'm not sure what to expect now. I'm assuming Taeral would've told him about us by now."

He tipped his head down, watching as she worried her lip, pulling at the torn skin from the damage their canines had caused earlier.

Each time she sparred Virnorin or when she pushed back at him, refusing to yield, she seemed so fierce and strong. And then there were times like now, when he remembered just how sheltered she'd been. How new she was to simply *living*.

He inhaled slowly, letting the sadness and fury flow out of him. He'd never be over it, but right now she needed him to be her constant. His heightened emotions would only worsen her own.

"Do you think he'll still act as walled off as before, or maybe…" she fisted her hands at her sides, trailing off, and he immediately wanted to strangle his king. She'd never admit it, but she craved her father's acceptance and approval, and he hadn't even tried to give it to her.

And what worried Jaren the most was that he didn't think she'd ever get it from him. Not in the way she wanted. "I don't know, Veralie. I don't think he knows what to believe or do with you."

Sadness filled her chest, flowing into his until he couldn't resist reaching out and taking her hand, threading his fingers through hers.

"Do you think he blames me? For my mother's death? I know what Onas said, but that doesn't mean he didn't care about her."

Jaren didn't answer right away, gently running his thumb along her skin as he considered it. He wanted to immediately deny it, demanding she throw the thought out and never give it space in her mind again, but he couldn't.

Because it *was* possible, and as much as he hated not being able to comfort her the way he wanted, he also refused to lie to her. They were surrounded by enough of those as it was.

"Maybe." Her face fell, but he continued, lowering his voice. "However, I think it's more likely that he's scared of you."

"What?" She stopped in her tracks and looked up at him, cute creases appearing between her eyes. "Why would he be scared of me? I can't even control my abilities. That alone will practically make me a human in his eyes."

Jaren glanced around them, making sure they were completely alone before he replied, lowering his voice even further until it was barely above a whisper.

"Because of what you mean for *him*. I know you don't like to think about it, but you are, in fact, the Daughter to the Throne, Veralie. You have the ability to take the crown from him. Power here lies within *your* bloodline, not his.

"Whether your parents were in love or not, their marriage was, first and foremost, a political pairing to provide her with the strongest offspring possible. Vesstan had no real power until she died. Despite what Taeral insinuated, many will expect him to step down for you. And very few give up power so willingly."

She rolled her lips in, face contemplative. "But Jaeros said he'd always wanted an heir. That he believed the connection to be a necessary evil."

He shook his head. Jaeros had said that, but Veralie didn't know him well enough to notice the small spasm of his fingers as he'd said it.

King Vesstan may have wanted an heir, but Jaeros didn't trust him. What Jaren didn't know was whether it was because of Vaneara's decision to keep secrets from him, or another reason.

"I don't know, Veralie. I could be wrong, but I just don't see him stepping down for someone who knows next to nothing about our people."

She flinched, and he immediately regretted the harsh words. Gods damn, he wasn't good at this. Saying shit like that wasn't going to help her nerves.

But she was already squeezing his hand and starting back down the hall before he could smooth it over.

"It's all right," she said. "You're not wrong. I couldn't even read a book about our history without help."

Her lips twisted as she stared at the passing sconces, watching the flames flicker. "I don't desire the crown, not in the way I would have if I'd have grown up here. But I made a promise to Eithan, and I want to keep it. I want to help both our lands, and I doubt I can do that without accepting my role."

Jaren stiffened at hearing the *chinbi srol's* name on her lips, but he somehow convinced himself to keep his mouth shut. He might've wanted the bastard dead, but that didn't mean she was wrong. They stood a better chance at garnering peace with him than Sulian.

"I'd like you to be there tonight."

His heart flipped in his chest at her sudden, soft admission, and the way she'd subconsciously tugged at their bond while she'd said it. He'd have gone tonight either way, but her words pleased him enough, he opted not to point that out.

"Always, little star."

CHAPTER 23

TREY

"What the fuck are you doing back?"

He glared at the giant of a man peeking past the doorway, his scruffy face whipping back and forth as he checked to make sure the coast was clear. "Don't fucking ignore me, Jensen."

"Shut up." He glanced into the hallway one last time and then shoved inside, leaving the door cracked open an inch behind him.

"All right, listen up. You're about to have company. If ever there was a time to act like the pissed-off man I last saw, and not the mewling infant you started off as, it's now."

"Fuck off," he seethed. What *company* could he even be talking about? Lesta?

"Perfect," Jensen said, shooting him a shit-eating grin that boiled his blood. If Trey ever got out of these damn restraints for more than a few minutes to use a chamber pot, he'd track the asshole down and break his fucking nose.

Jensen just continued to smile, his best friend of decades knowing what he was thinking without him even having to word it.

Raising both arms, Trey gave him a double vulgar gesture, happy he had the energy to do so this time.

He'd actually felt better in the last few days than he had since before everything had happened. Healer Perry was annoyingly good at his job, and he'd even replaced his full-body restraints with smaller ones around his ankles, giving Trey the freedom to push up into a sitting position.

All of that combined with the regularly appearing meals, he'd even started to put weight back on. Nothing like the muscle he'd once had, but it was something.

But no amount of healing or food would ever fix what was truly broken. Even as his wounds turned to scars and his bed sores faded, there was no erasing the memories. He willingly took the elixir Perry handed him each night to fall asleep, but even that didn't always keep the nightmares at bay.

Jensen ambled his way, his long-ass strides bringing him to his cot so fast, Trey barely caught sight of something in his hand before Jensen was shoving it into his face.

He reared back, trying not to fall over as he blinked at the small object. "You risked your life to come here and bring me *alcohol*?"

Jensen scoffed, pressing the mouth of the flask onto his lips. "It's water. Next time, I'll find you a fancy, leather waterskin with your initials engraved on it."

He glared daggers at him, but Jensen just whacked his cheek with it. "Drink the damn water, Gibson."

Cursing, he snatched it from his grasp and lifted it back up to his mouth, his lips cracking as they opened to fit around it. He'd just planned to take a sip to get Jensen to shut up, but the second the cold water poured over his dry tongue, he almost groaned.

He guzzled it, trails of water leaking out of the sides of his mouth and disappearing into his unkempt beard as he choked, his body unable to keep up with his desperate pulls.

Jensen yanked it back, grunting. "I'm surprised to see you up. You look better."

Trey wiped at his face, a wave of loneliness shooting through him when he saw the almost tender look on Jensen's face. One he hadn't seen since they were kids. But then he cleared his throat, tucking the flask into his pocket and stepped back.

For the first time since Eithan had taken him, Trey realized he missed his life. And he wasn't sure what to do about that. But it was that exact reason that he needed to protect his friend from his own stupidity.

"Brex, I don't know what game you and Lesta think you're playing at, but you'll lose. That bastard is always one step ahead, and Lesta is living on borrowed time already. Don't put your life on the line, as well. Whatever it is you're doing isn't worth it."

Jensen crossed his arms and glanced back at the cracked door; head tilted like he was listening for something. "Getting you out of this shithole is worth it, tenfold."

Trey shook his head. "That's not all there is to this, and you know it."

Jensen's smile dropped a hair, his gruff demeanor wavering. "You know I'd put my life on the line for you, regardless of the reason or risk. But you're right, there's more to it. I don't have the reach to sneak you out of this place alone, but Lesta does."

"How'd you convince him to bother? He's in enough shit all on his own without adding me into the mix."

Jensen cocked an eyebrow, like he couldn't comprehend Trey's train of thought at all. "I didn't have to convince him, Gibson. Our Weapon's Master is loyal to *all* his men. That includes you. It's just a bonus that your family's connections could help with his end goal, as well."

"What connections—" He cut off, bile immediately replacing his words as the door behind Jensen swung open and another man passed the threshold.

His heart fell, fear like he thought he'd never known filling his body at who stood before them, taking in the entire scene with wide, unbelieving eyes.

They were so completely fucked.

"Gibson? No, that's not…that's not possible." His voice hit a higher pitch, his words stuttering out in utter shock as he stood frozen in the doorway, staring at him.

Walking around the statue-like man with a hand on his blade, like he was prepared to defend Trey if needed, Jensen came to stand between him and Eithan's first-in-command, Wes fucking Coleman.

"What on Aleron is going on?"

"What do you mean?" Jensen asked, feigning innocence. "You're the one who showed up unannounced."

Trey's mouth fell open. Coleman was the company he'd been talking about? He'd lured, not just any of Eithan's guards, but his *first-in-command* there? What game was Jensen fucking playing at? Coleman would run right back to Eithan, and then Jensen would be right where he'd been, screaming for mercy.

"He's dead. You're dead," Coleman continued, his eyes lingering on Trey's eyepatch as he took a single step forward.

Trey raised his chin, desperately trying to hide his racing heart and the nausea pushing at his throat. "Whoever told you that, I wonder?"

At his words, Coleman's face drained of color. "You were sentenced to death for treason. His Highness—"

"His Highness is a lying psychopath."

In a blink, Coleman's hand was on the pommel of his sword, knuckles white and face guarded. "Take care how you speak."

"Or what?" Trey laughed, the sound coming out as psychotic as he'd just accused Eithan of being as his anger overrode his fear.

Regardless of when Eithan chose it, he was going to die no

matter what. And Jensen, the gods damn idiot, had dug his own grave now. There was no point in rolling over for any of these assholes anymore.

He seethed. "Take care how I speak? About a man who prances about during the day, lying to his entire fucking continent, only to rip out eyes for fun at night? Because I sure as hell didn't tie *myself* down and sink a blade under my—"

"Gods, *stop*."

"What? You don't like the truth about your prince?"

Coleman released his sword only to fist both hands at his sides. "You have no idea, absolutely none, about what His Highness has been through," he said, voice low, but his eyes gave him away. His uncertainty.

Trey's jaw clenched. "I promise you, I know a whole lot more than you *think* you do. And that man is a demon."

Whipping his head to Jensen, who had been slowly inching toward Coleman, ready to halt him from sprinting out if necessary, he spit, "Why the fuck would you bring him here? If you truly thought he'd believe less of his perfect prince just because my ass is cursed to keep living, you're fucking suicidal *and* stupid."

"Why." The word came from Coleman. It was more a statement than a question, but Trey knew what he wasn't asking. He relaxed his hands, realizing he'd been gripping the cot in a death hold ever since Coleman stepped into the room.

"His Highness," he said with as much vitriol as possible, "believed I was hiding something from him about Vera."

"Were you?"

"Yes."

"Why." Again, not a question.

"Eithan lost my loyalty when he sent men to track down a woman and force her to marry him. A woman who'd been kidnapped and locked away her entire life." He paused, remembering she wasn't technically a *woman*, but the point remained all the same.

"And instead of putting me out of my misery after your perfect prince got what he wanted from me, he brought me here."

Coleman's brows creased, and a muscle feathered in his jaw. "Let me get this straight. You hate him because of what he did, but you also hate him for healing you. Makes sense."

Jensen chuckled, shaking his head. "I tried to warn Lesta. You really are a blind fuck."

Coleman whipped around, stepping dangerously close to a man who could easily crush him with barely a thought. "Then open my eyes."

But it was Trey who spoke. "Whether you open your eyes or not, Wes, that's on you. But Eithan Matheris is a lunatic who has his sights set on Vera. Or, more accurately, Veralie Arenaris. He won't stop until he has her. If his current plan doesn't pan out, he'll just come up with another."

Coleman threw his hands up, looking seconds away from a panic attack. "So, what is this? A coup? You idiots do realize killing Eithan won't remove his father from power, right? What are you hoping to gain?"

Jensen darted a glance out the door, then stabbed a thick finger at Coleman's chest. "Sulian is in power for now, yes. But he won't be forever, and with Eithan gone, the crown would be up for grabs."

Trey's eye widened despite himself. He thought Lesta was just trying to free him to help Vera, he didn't realize he was trying to completely change who retained power on Aleron. There had never not been a Matheris on the throne.

Coleman glared up at him. "What would you have me do? Kill my own Prince in the hopes that someone nicer comes along to take his place?"

Jensen stepped even closer until they were chest to chest. "You know what."

The look Coleman sent him would've had a lesser man fearing for his life. He looked seconds from pulling his blade out right then and there and stabbing Jensen through. "You don't know what the fuck you're talking about."

"Don't I? Lesta seemed pretty gods damn sure," Jensen threw back, before glancing back down the hall again, like he was expecting someone to come walking by at any moment. "We're running out of time."

Stomping across the room, he grabbed Trey's hand, removing a small dagger from his belt and smacking the handle in his open palm.

"If you want to die, it's your call. I'll leave this damn dagger. But if not, you'll have one chance to get out of here. One,

Gibson. So, you better fucking figure it out soon."

He straightened back up, pulling his hand away like he already knew what answer Trey would give. And for a moment, he considered it. It could all be over right now. The pain, the unknowns, the nightmares. He could be at peace.

But there was another part of him, a darker part that was growing larger by the day, that didn't want peace. That wouldn't have it until that bastard was bleeding on the floor, begging for his own life.

So instead of tucking the blade away and listening to the quiet voice that wanted to roll over, he opted to listen to the angry one. The one that snatched Jensen's hand back and slapped the dagger back into it.

His friend's eyes widened almost imperceptibly as they met his, and he knew there was no sign of the man he'd once been in his face as he spoke. "I want in. Whatever political game you're playing, I want in. And if we succeed, if we survive all of this, Eithan Matheris is *mine*."

Relief filled Jensen's eyes, there and gone in a blink, and then he gave a stiff nod, clearing his throat. "Stay strong, then. Eat your veggies and shit until I come back."

He didn't give Trey time to give him another vulgar gesture before he was grabbing Coleman's arm and whispering furiously into his ear before dragging him toward the door.

Coleman darted one last glance at him, his face paling at whatever Jensen said, before they both disappeared, the door shutting behind them.

And then he was alone again. And with the silence came the doubt, then the panic, then the anger.

He flopped back down to the cot. What the absolute fuck was all that? And what had Jensen been talking about when he said Coleman could do something? What was he whispering to him to make him pale like that?

The entire thing pissed him off, even more so *because* it pissed him off.

He shouldn't care. He shouldn't care whether or not Coleman was going to rat Jensen out. He shouldn't care where they were going now or wish he could go too. He shouldn't hate that he gave the dagger back in the spur of the moment, shouldn't want to open his eye anymore.

But gods damn him, he fucking did. And part of him hated Jensen for it.

Lost in his thoughts, it took him a minute to realize he could hear the sound of boots clipping down the hall. He shoved up to an elbow, brow raised, wondering what else his suddenly talkative-as-fuck friend needed to say.

But when the door swung open again, it wasn't Jensen or Coleman who stood at the entrance.

Although the multicolored bruises had faded from his face, the man who stood before him looked more disheveled than Trey had ever seen him. His blond hair hung in greasy strings around his face rather than tied neatly at his nape, and he had dark circles under his eyes, like he hadn't slept in days.

His expression was haggard, his lips pressed thin, and his

tunic was half untucked, like he'd yanked it out on his way there. But it was Eithan's eyes that had ice engulfing Trey's spine. His eyes were the same dead, emotionless blue they'd been in the dungeon. When he'd said little but done so much.

"What has you looking so perky and awake, Gibson? You pleased to see me?" he asked, voice eerily flat.

Trey swallowed, mentally urging himself not to shake or stammer a single syllable. Nothing that would give away what had just transpired. Because if they were lucky enough that Eithan hadn't passed them in the hall, Trey sure as shit didn't want to be the weak link that signed their death warrants. Not even Coleman's.

"It does tend to get quite lonely in here. The walls aren't the best at playing cards," he pushed out, lowering back down.

Eithan chuckled, but it didn't reach his eyes. Walking silently across the room, he stopped at one of the tables against the wall, running his fingers along the edge as he admired Healer Perry's tools and supplies.

Picking up a scalpel, he turned and rested his hip against the table, looking over to Trey as he spun it in his fingers. "I just had dinner with my father."

Trey's heart felt like solid iron in his chest. Eithan never referred to Sulian as his father, not so casually, and definitely not without a sneer or sarcastic raise of his brow.

He watched the sharp blade as it continued to spin in the bastard's hand. "By your tone, I'm guessing he overcooked the pheasant."

Eithan's fingers froze, his eyes narrowing as he pushed off the table and ambled closer. "Since when did you start joking with me again, dear Gibson?"

Fuck. This is why Jensen needed to stay the fuck away from him. He'd shook him up, confusing him, and it'd only end horribly for them both.

"I told you," he said, pushing all of his misery into his words, "it gets lonely down here. Even Healer Perry has stopped coming by as often."

"Yes, I informed him his services weren't needed anymore."

A tingling filled his body, warning bells going off in every direction. "So, am I being moved to the guest suite now?"

"You could call it that. It's certainly perfect accommodations for temporary guests, and much more entertaining since you're so bored here. Lots to listen to there, at least."

Trey's eye widened. He couldn't have blinked if he tried. His tongue felt three times its size as he got out, "And where is that?"

Eithan didn't answer right away, looking again at the scalpel in his hand and edging closer until he stood only a foot away, the sharp blade uncomfortably close to Trey's arm.

He could still feel the phantom pain of the last one Eithan had used on him, and nausea climbed up his throat as he subconsciously shifted toward the far side of the cot.

"Sulian informed me over our lovely meal that he's made the decision to send me to Midpath. Spewing some ill-conceived lie about me overseeing the guard in place of Lesta, of all things."

He huffed a laugh, hatred coating the sound, the first emotion he'd given since entering the room.

"But the truth is, Sulian believes, just as I do, that Vera will return. And he wants to sink his claws into her, himself," he growled, squeezing the tip of the tool until blood bloomed beneath it.

Vomit filled Trey's mouth, and he swallowed it back down, desperately trying not to show how completely unnerved he was by Eithan's unpolished demeanor.

"He's not planning on her marrying you?" he dared to ask, praying that he was right. Maybe Emperor Sulian had realized how fucking stupid it was to risk a fight with an island of gods damn Magyki all for the hope they'd give him whatever it was he wanted.

Eithan spit. "I wouldn't be surprised if he locked her away and stuck a child in her himself, just to remove me from next-in-line."

Trey blanched, his nose wrinkling at even the thought. "Your father may have political power, but even he cannot physically force Vera to do that."

Eithan nodded, rubbing the blond scruff along his jaw with his non-bloodied hand. Then he cracked his neck and sighed, leaning down closer to Trey's face.

"Anyway, I don't know when I'll be back, and I certainly can't leave you here to cause trouble, so I'm afraid it's back home for you."

Trey's two-story, childhood house in Southterres immediately came to mind. The blue paint, his mother's beautiful garden out front, the fence's gate that creaked no matter how many times he'd worked on it. But he shoved the images out, tucking them away. That wasn't the home Eithan was referring to, and they both knew it.

"When?" he croaked.

"Soon." He squatted down, grabbing the longer straps that had hung loose for days, and began securing them back over his body, tightening them until it felt like they were cutting into his blood flow. Then he removed a white cloth and wadded it, holding it up to Trey's mouth. "Open up."

He shook his head, lips pressed together, thrashing against the restraints. He took it all back, every word he'd said to Jensen. He'd do anything to have that dagger in his hand again. Anything.

Anything. Anything. Anything. Anything.

"I suggest you listen and open up," Eithan warned, pressing the cloth against his closed lips, "because I'm really fucking angry."

And it was those words that had his mind finally snapping, his fear dissipating on the wind as a soul-crushing fury overwhelmed him. *He* was angry? That spoiled-ass bastard didn't know what fucking angry was.

Twisting toward him, Trey lurched up as far as he could and slammed his head directly into his nose, reveling in the sound of Eithan's surprised yell and the tool clattering to the floor.

Eithan's head whipped back, and his hand flew to his face to hover over his gushing nose. He blinked rapidly, trying to clear the spots Trey was sure were swimming in his vision, but he didn't move closer.

Unease flashed across his watering eyes. "You broke my nose."

"Yes," Trey spat. "And if you touch me again, I swear to the gods, I'll fucking kill you."

CHAPTER 24

VERA

S he stared at her reflection in the mirror, her eyes wide as they lowered down her form, taking in the steel gray dress Reniya had helped her into.

"Don't you think this shows a little more cleavage than necessary?" She scowled, placing her fingers over the deep plunge of the gown, ending just a few inches above her navel.

Reniya's face peeked out over her shoulder from where she was currently pinning Vera's plait around her head like a makeshift crown. "You can never show too much cleavage. Now, be still," she said, disappearing behind her head again and yanking sharply on her hair.

Remembering the way Reniya had scared the shit out of her, sprawled out in a chair in front of her hearth, spinning her dagger as she and Jaren walked in, Vera opted not to make a comment.

Reniya hadn't even let her remove her boots before she'd lit into her, reminding her so much of Elric as she reprimanded her for wasting their limited training hours.

"You want to hump Barilias all night, be my guest, but don't you dare blow me off for it again."

Vera's face had heated, painfully aware that Reniya could smell the release still plastered to the inside of her thighs. "I was reading up on our history."

Her guardian's eyes had immediately narrowed, and she flared her nostrils, overexaggerating her deep inhale. "I certainly hope your reading included the proper use of *truik elixir*."

Vera fidgeted before the mirror, her ears warming all over again just thinking about the grin Jaren had shot Reniya in answer.

She cleared her throat, wiping the memory from her mind, and focused back on the reflected version of her staring back. If she was honest, besides the amount of cleavage it showed, the gown was absolutely stunning.

It fit her like a glove, showcasing what curves she had while also not suffocating her like the gown on Aleron had. The corsets here were much different, more for pushing up her breasts and accentuating her natural shape than making her appear as thin as possible.

She'd been baffled when she'd discovered this particular dress even had one built into it.

The bodice had intricate detailing and beads sewn

throughout, making it appear like an array of stars, while the skirt was made of a soft velvety texture, swaying as she moved.

A sheer cape flowed from the straps over her shoulders, making her collar and neck stand out and doing absolutely nothing to hide her multitude of marks. Including the scar on her throat.

Whether her guardian had intentionally done it or not, she'd made her look like a fucking queen.

"Reniya?"

"Hm?" She grunted, pressing her chest into Vera's back as she lowered her arms over her head, securing a glittering, silver necklace around her neck. It had a single, thin chain that dropped between her breasts and down the front of her dress.

Vera wasn't sure when she'd come to enjoy the gruff, female's presence—she still kind of terrified her—but she found herself hoping she'd say yes to what she was about to ask.

Reniya was feisty and blunt as shit, but she was also funny and loyal. She didn't owe Vera a single thing, yet she'd shown up every morning to help her even when it wasn't part of her duties as her guardian.

And she was *still* willing to do so even after Vera had selfishly blown her off that morning.

Their training sessions certainly weren't enjoyable, leaving her with more bruises and winces than she'd had in all her twenty years combined, but she enjoyed Reniya's company and considered her a friend. Her first one since Trey.

The thought circled around her heart and squeezed.

"Will you be attending the dinner with us?"

Reniya's hands froze in her hair, and she angled her head to meet Vera's eyes through the mirror. "Do you want me to?"

She shrugged, trying to brush off her nerves. Jaren would be with her, so it wasn't like she technically needed a second guard just to attend dinner. "I was just wondering."

"That's not what I asked, Your Highness. I asked if you want me there."

A muffled bang sounded from the other room, interrupting her reply, and she frowned, glancing at the door. Jaren had already washed up and shaved while she'd been picking out her dress with Reniya. What on Aleron could he possibly be doing?

Low murmured voices hit her ears before she realized it'd been a knock she heard, not Jaren banging around.

Finished anyway, she twisted toward the door, trying not to trip over the tall, spiked shoes Reniya had crammed onto her feet. But Reniya darted in front of her, exiting first.

Gods, maybe she didn't want her going after all. Between her and Jaren, there was a good chance they'd cause her to lose her mind by the end of the night.

Entering the main room to see who had come by, she made toward the door only to stop in her tracks when her gaze landed on Jaren. His back was to her, his fitted, black tunic showing off his broad shoulders and trim waist.

She let her eyes consume the sight, lingering on the way his dark trousers pulled at his ass before disappearing into his boots.

She wasn't sure where, or when, he'd purchased the

clothing, but it was the cleanest she'd ever seen him. And if it wasn't for the second male standing in front of him, she might've kicked Reniya out just to rip the clothes right back off him. She sighed, tucking the idea away for later.

Dedryn stood just inside their room, dressed in a sleeveless, maroon tunic with gold trim and tan trousers tucked into sleek, black boots. His face was clean-shaven and sharp, his golden eyes hard as they moved from his son to focus on her.

Noticing his change in attention, Jaren whipped around, his eyes flaring and his mouth falling open as pure, unfiltered adoration filled her chest. And before she could even process the heightened emotion he was pumping into her, he closed the space between them, his hands tenderly grasping her face.

His eyes were bright and glassy as he tipped her head back and whispered, "You are mine."

The words weren't a claiming or a demand like every other time he'd said them, but a breath over her lips, like they'd been pulled straight from his heart, and he didn't quite believe them.

Heat filled her cheeks under his penetrating stare, and she fidgeted, aware of their audience. "I didn't realize you cleaned up so nice, green eyes."

He blinked rapidly, almost like he was coming out of a trance, and then a slow, sinful smile spread across his face.

Dropping his mouth just above her ear, he whispered, "You're fucking ethereal, *aitanta*. A star incarnate. But I am going to have so much fun tearing this gown to shreds as I remove it from your body."

"Don't you dare," she said, shoving him back. He chuckled, turning to stand beside her as she rolled her eyes and looked to Dedryn.

A muscle feathered in his jaw. "Are you quite done?"

Jaren's arm pulled back only to smack her on the ass, pulling an embarrassing yelp from her throat. "Now, I am."

Oh, my fucking gods.

She wasn't sure, but she could've sworn Dedryn's lips twitched as he shook his head and turned to Reniya. "King Vesstan has dismissed you for the night. Jaren and I will escort her back."

Reniya nodded that she'd heard, but instead of bowing and taking her leave, she made direct eye contact with her, refusing to move. Vera frowned at first, until she realized Reniya was waiting for her to answer her question from the bathing room.

Eyes stinging, she smiled and nodded. "I'll be all right. Go enjoy your evening, Reni."

Her entire body went rigid at the nickname, and a comical look crossed her features before she shook it away, bowing quickly and marching out of the room.

The second she disappeared through the door, Jaren's neutral expression dropped. "What are you doing here?"

"Onas Dornelin arrived to our meeting earlier quite frazzled. He informed King Vesstan that it was highly unlikely Vera would come alone this evening. I seconded his assumption," he said, lips thinning in reprimand or to hide a smile, she wasn't sure.

Jaren's hands fisted. "Let me guess, King Vesstan sent you to try to prevent me from going."

Dedryn shook his head, surprising them both. "No, he said it would be educational for you to attend." He gave his son a warning look. "I am simply here to make sure you behave and to prepare you. Note, Taeral will also be present as his guardian."

Vera barely held back a groan. Great.

Jaren reached down, lacing his fingers with hers and made to step around him, but Dedryn threw out an arm, halting his attempt. Holding a finger to his lips, he lowered his voice until she could barely make him out with her normal hearing.

"Listen to me carefully. You two met on Aleron by the happenstance of fate. You brought her back for the sole purpose that she was your mate, no other. Jaeros noticed her similarity to Queen Vaneara and informed me of who he suspected her to be."

Jaren opened his mouth, fire all but spewing from his eyes, but one look from Dedryn had him snapping it shut again. A silent communication passed between them.

"You never found Vaneara in the woods the night Veralie was born. She never lived with us. Do you understand me?"

Veralie squeezed Jaren's hand, fear creeping up her spine with the power emanating from Dedryn. His hand slipped around the pommel of his blade as he stepped nose to nose with Jaren before continuing.

"I will protect you and your *aitanta* with my life. Always. But if you endanger Jae because you can't rein in your gods forsaken pride, you will answer to me."

Vera chewed on her lip, unable to watch the emotion the two males exchanged as Jaren nodded in understanding. And for the first time, a thread of hatred for her mother worked its way into her heart.

Her mother had done this. Forced Jaren's fathers to carry a secret that was never theirs to carry. Made them terrified of it being discovered to the point of hurting those they loved in the hope of keeping their promise. Forced them to fear for their safety and the safety of their son.

Jaeros had said her mother loved her people with a fierceness he'd never seen, but the more Vera learned of the female who'd given her life, the more she wasn't so sure she believed it.

THE ROOM DEDRYN led them into was surprisingly small, especially given what she'd been expecting. Only big enough to comfortably fit a table set for ten, it had a servant's entrance to the right, and three large windows against the back wall, overlooking what appeared to be a private garden of some kind.

King Vesstan sat in the center of the far side of the table, rather than the head of it as Emperor Sulian had. Taeral, indeed, sat on one side and looked so different in her pale pink gown, Vera might not have recognized her if it wasn't for the familiar sharp cheekbones and the hazel death glare plastered to her face.

And standing on King Vesstan's other side, just behind him, was Onas. Unlike the others, he wasn't dressed up, and instead wore the same plain tunic and trousers she'd seen him in before. His head was down, and he was clasping and unclasping his hands, refusing to make eye contact.

And then there was King Vesstan. Wearing a deep green tunic, with gold thread embroidered on each hem, he was a striking contrast to Taeral's soft pink. Not a single hair stood out of place, his jaw clean and his brown hair slicked back from his face as he frowned at the table, appearing to be reading something.

The three of them crossed the few feet into the room, stopping just a foot away from the empty chairs of the table. Remembering to curtsy this time, she lowered to the ground, wondering if it would ever not be weird for her father to appear so young.

"It's a pleasure to see you again, Your Majesty, I..."

She raised up to see him holding a hand out in front of him, palm out toward her to wait. She rolled her lips in, not knowing what to do as he kept his head bowed, ignoring her completely as he continued reading whatever parchment lay before him.

When he finally finished, he made a disgusted sound in his throat, dropping his hand to roll it back up. She caught a glimpse of a familiar navy-blue emblem before he handed it to Onas, whispering something in his ear.

She squinted, studying the parchment now clasped in Onas's shaking hand, trying to catch another look. She hadn't seen enough to be certain, but she could've sworn she'd seen the letter 'M' in the center of it. But too quickly, Onas tucked it into his cloak and out of sight, bowing and scurrying out.

Vesstan cleared his throat and stood, running his hands down his sides. "My apologies. There seems to always be something in need of my attention. Even uninterrupted dinners are hard to come by these days."

Not even bothering to stand, Taeral smirked, the expression oddly arrogant given the circumstance. What could she possibly feel vindicated about already?

Vesstan looked her up and down and nodded, clearly pleased with what he saw, and gestured to the empty chairs across from him. "Please, take a seat."

Dedryn bowed again, murmuring a greeting, and took the seat on the far right. Vera stepped forward to take the seat next to him, not wishing to be directly in front of the king, but Jaren's hand landed on her lower back, directing her to the next chair over so he could slide in between his father and her.

Overprotective ass.

King Vesstan watched them with an amused look on his face before he popped his lips awkwardly. "Forgive me for not introducing my companions last time. I was quite distracted, as I'm sure you can understand. Though, from what I hear, you've conveniently run into both since our last meeting."

Yeah, Veralie thought. *That's what happens when you tell your newly discovered daughter to fuck off for a week.* But on the outside, she nodded, confirming his statement.

He twisted his head, his eyes hungrily running down the frame of the female next to him. "This is Taeral Virnorin," he said, stretching his arm out beneath the table to rest somewhere on her lap.

"She is my *zisdemyoz* and first-in-command of my warriors. There is not a single Magyki on this island who exceeds her skill." He shot Taeral a secretive smile before breaking his gaze away, adding, "Though her niece is an acceptable second."

Vera cleared her throat, not sure if he meant that as a dig toward Reniya or not, and she was more than a little uncomfortable. Guess his fondling at least answered her question of whether Taeral was in some form of relationship with her father.

According to the history she knew and understood, only her bloodline, the Arenaris bloodline, could assume the throne. So, she wasn't really sure what to make of it. He'd introduced Taeral as his guardian, not his wife, so maybe they were just...casual companions? She shuddered, shoving that thought very, very far away.

King Vesstan continued, oblivious to the storm of questions brewing in her mind. "And, of course, the male who just exited is Onas Dornelin. He's one of Naris's best historians, and a new private advisor of mine."

She nodded absently. The historian part made sense, given the huge armful of scrolls and texts he'd been carrying in the library, but an advisor? The male was a walking nervous breakdown.

King Vesstan leaned forward, resting his elbows on the table and laced his fingers under his chin, considering her.

"He told me you go by Vera, but that is not your name. Is that something the humans called you?"

"Yes, Your Majesty," she said, trying not to physically react to the way he'd said *the humans*.

"Hm. And you allowed them to shorten your formal title in such a way?"

Allowed? Did he not realize she'd been a child? But then she realized, he might not. Her father had no idea what she'd been doing all these years, so for all he knew, she'd been much older when she set foot on Aleron.

"I suppose, Your Majesty. I was very young. It was my mentor who called me that." She smiled at the memory. Elric loved telling that story. "He said my full name was too—"

"You can call me Vesstan when we are in private company, Veralie," he said, waving a hand and enunciating her full name.

She started, taken aback by his blatant interruption. "Oh. All right," she muttered, feeling Jaren's hand wrap around her thigh and squeeze.

Vesstan's eyes latched on to the movement, his expression unreadable as he sat back, grabbing his glass of wine and taking a drink. "So, what can you tell me about Emperor Sulian? Did you meet his heir?"

She froze, midway through brushing a rogue curl back from her face. What? Why would he ask about Eithan?

He seemed intrigued by her silence, as if it answered for her, but Taeral straightened, her lip pressed thin in a look of hatred that Vera was beginning to think was permanently etched there. "I'm curious why you appear so surprised that your king would ask that."

Inhaling and mentally reminding herself she couldn't throw her wine in Taeral's face, Vera dropped her hands in her lap, answering coolly. "I guess I just wasn't expecting it to be my father's first question since he expressed such uncertainty about my identity."

The male in question raised a brow, talking slowly like she was a mere child unaware of adult conversations. "I assumed inviting you here was proof enough that I accepted your claim."

She clenched her jaw, fighting the sudden urge to cry. It was just more mind games. This dinner was just a ruse, no different than the one Emperor Sulian had put her through. They were all the fucking same.

Jaren's hold loosened, and his thumb moved soothingly back and forth across her thigh. She relaxed, letting his touch ease the tension out of her shoulders.

Don't let him know how you feel. Don't give him that power.

Steeling her spine, she asked, "Are you not at all curious what I've been doing for the past fifteen years?"

Vesstan didn't immediately reply, gesturing to a servant across the room to begin bringing in their meals. "I may have planted the seed inside your mother, Veralie, but I did not parent you in any other way. Your mother made sure of that.

"So, I apologize if my order of importance is not what you

hoped for. We can discuss your life on Aleron if it would bring you comfort, but given I can clearly see you are healthy and back home, I feel it would be a waste of both our time. Wouldn't you agree?"

Her nose burned with the effort of preventing tears from filling her eyes. She flared her nostrils, staring down at Jaren's calloused fingers resting against the gray of her dress, and took a deep breath.

She would *not* shed a tear in front of these two. Swallowing back the lump in her throat, she sat up and took a sip of water, letting it soothe her throat. "You're right. The past isn't important."

Although she refused to look at him, for fear of breaking apart, she could practically hear how hard Jaren was grinding his teeth, fighting to keep his mouth shut. Beside him, Dedryn sat stiff as a board, like he was just waiting for complete and utter chaos to ensue.

"As for Emperor Sulian, I'm afraid I don't know much at all," she said. "I was within the capital, but I lived in the armory and rarely left it. I only spent one evening in his presence."

"He kept you in the armory?" The question came from Taeral, a sneer ruining her mouth.

Vera bristled. It may have been true, but the way she'd worded the question made it sound more like an insult. "Yes. I lived under the guidance of the Weapon's Master. He..." She darted a look back at Vesstan. "He raised me."

Taeral scoffed. "You must've been quite a pathetic sight for

Sulian to believe you were no threat around weaponry."

Jaren growled, his grip like iron around her leg while his other fisted over the table. "I suggest you take care of how you speak to the Daughter to the Throne. You have seen with your own eyes that her skill exceeds many here, even *without* her abilities or the teachings of a Magyki."

Taeral pushed off the table, half standing, but Vesstan wrapped a large hand around her bicep and yanked her back down. A warning look from him had her snapping her mouth shut.

"I understand your urge to defend your charge, young Barilias," Vesstan said, "but you would do well to remember that any conversation tonight does not stand in place of her official crowning ceremony."

His *charge*? Gods, at this rate, they'd never make it to the end of the night before Jaren launched himself across the table at one of them.

She snatched up a glass and took a healthy sip of wine. Fuck, she missed ale.

CHAPTER 25

VERA

The stilted conversation throughout their meal was no better, and she'd officially downed enough wine that her head was beginning to feel fuzzy around the edges.

Vesstan had asked every manner of question about Aleron, the makeup of the Matherin capital, what form of training the guards received, and Emperor Sulian, himself.

With each unhelpful answer she gave, he grew more agitated, his brows drawn and his tone clipped. Finally, after he asked yet another question about Prince Eithan, she set her glass down, harder than she'd intended.

"I don't know, Your Majesty. I told you, I wasn't allowed to leave the training grounds. I only walked through the palace once, and the only time I ever spoke to Emperor Sulian was when he was lying to my face about who I am."

His lips thinned. "You only met his heir once, as well?"

Only years of training under Elric kept her from rolling her eyes. What was his obsession with her relationship with Eithan? "No," she said, tossing her napkin over her plate. As amazing as the food had been, she was too irritated to take another bite.

"I met him on a few occasions, but I didn't know him if that's what you keep implying. Emperor Sulian wished to marry me off to him, but I ran away that same night."

"Interesting."

His favorite word, apparently.

"And what of your abilities? Young Barilias claimed you connected to the crystal, which I'm inclined to believe despite the fantastical nature of the idea, due to your appearance."

She looked to Jaren, wishing she could climb in his lap and curl up against his chest. He'd had the same questions once upon a time, but he'd never once made her feel like she was being interrogated. She'd still felt like a person. Important.

Jaren's eyes flared, speaking the words he couldn't say. Her chest warmed, and she straightened her spine, preparing herself for her father's incoming look of disgust.

"I have them, yes. But I can't really control them."

"How so?"

She sighed, subconsciously pressing a hand over her heart, where the pool of power resided. "I struggle focusing it, especially with things such as my hearing or sight."

Taeral chuckled, clanking her fork onto her plate. "You expect us to believe you're powerful enough to connect to our power source all the way from Aleron, but you can't enhance your sight? Vesstan, this is ridiculous. The only power she possesses is the ability to lie through her teeth just like her mother."

Jaren snarled, causing every head to whip his way. Dedryn muttered his name and leaned toward him, ready to intervene if necessary, but Jaren waved him off.

"Veralie contains more power than you could ever dream of. I have not only seen it with my own eyes, but I've *felt* it. It is not her fault if you're incapable of acknowledging her superiority to you."

A single breath. That's all it took for the night to take a drastic turn. Jaren hadn't even finished the last word of his rant before Taeral erupted.

A feral sound ripped from her throat as she launched up and hurled her dinner knife across the table at him like an arrow releasing from its bow.

The world seemed to stop, everything around Vera moving in slow motion as she watched it fly. She felt her chest explode, fire shooting down her limbs as she watched the blade aim straight for her mate's heart.

One second a scream was threatening to spill from her lips, and the next she was whipping out her arm, wrapping her fingers around the knife and snatching it midair.

The entire room seemed to hold their breath, the pressure around her building until she thought it'd smash her into the floor. She sensed each one of them dip into their own power, as she lowered her bleeding hand and tossed the knife to the floor, seething.

But it wasn't until she met Taeral's wide eyes that she realized her body was pulsing with light, her skin itchy as it began to stitch itself shut without her even trying.

Beside her, Jaren reclined back in his chair, all but oozing satisfaction and grinning from ear to ear, even as his father stood beside him, staring at her in horror with his hand over his sheath.

Jaren hadn't even flinched at Taeral's attempt to stab him in the heart. He'd known. He'd trusted that she would react, had bet on it and antagonized Taeral to prove his point.

Vera growled, hoping he could sense just how much she was going to kick his fucking ass. The flare of anticipation confirmed he very much could.

"Did that make you feel better?" he asked, flinging the question over the table.

Taeral's lip curled, her hand hovering over her own weapon, but her eyes stayed pinned on Vera. "If you think—"

"That's enough," Vesstan snapped, slamming his hands on the table and causing several empty glasses to tip over, clattering onto other dishes. "Taeral, you're dismissed."

The female's entire body rioted against his command, but she clenched her jaw, pivoting and making her way around the table toward the door, her chin held high and her eyes promising retaliation.

Vesstan waited until the door had closed before he leaned forward, rubbing his thumb and forefinger between his eyes. It was the first time he'd looked his age.

When he finally raised his head, he eyed Jaren disapprovingly. "That was unnecessary. I already stated I believed it, and my opinion is the only one that matters."

Vera bristled. Taeral's entire presence had been unnecessary, not Jaren's defense of her. She'd have thought, as king, he'd understand a mating bond a little bit better.

"I'm assuming, based on your calm demeanor, this is not the first time her instincts have reacted in such a way," he said, cleaning up some of the mess in front of him.

Jaren's lips twitched, pride shooting down their bond. "She killed a man with a rock."

Oh my fucking gods.

But Vesstan nodded like he'd simply remarked on the pleasant weather. "Even so, the truth stands that you cannot control it. And that, combined with your overall lack of...knowledge, is indeed, a problem."

She put a hand to her temple, feeling suddenly dizzy. Gods, how much had she drank? "So, what do you suggest I do? I can't help what I wasn't given the opportunity to know."

"Agreed, but that doesn't change anything. You are not fit to lead a people you cannot even write a summons to, let alone understand the geography of the island, or the differences between the cities and their citizens."

She wanted to argue, to steel her spine and tell him she *could*. But he was right. Gods damn him, he was right.

"I'm sure you understand."

She darted a look at Jaren, who stared at her wordlessly, his eyes hard. *I told you, little star.*

"Okay," she said, exhaling and running her palms down her thighs. "So, what do you suggest?"

"I've spent the last week pondering what to do with you," he said, sitting back and resting an arm over Taeral's empty chair. "Don't look so nervous, I'm not going to lock you in an armory."

She forced a smile to her face, knowing it's what he wanted. But the last thread of hope she'd held about him fell away at his words. What kind of father made jokes about his child's trauma?

"You will obviously start with learning how to read and write, and then move on to basic geography and history. Then, of course, you will need to know both Vaneara's and my family lines by heart, and successfully pass a round of etiquette classes."

Next to her, Jaren choked on his drink.

Great. "And at what point will I be deemed ready?" Three months from now? Six? It couldn't be *that* hard to learn to read and do whatever the fuck etiquette classes entailed. Just as long as it didn't take away from her training with Reniya.

"I would think a handful of years should be sufficient."

She fought the urge to look at Jaren again. "Years?"

Vesstan waved his free hand, brushing her off like an annoying insect. "You'll be so caught up with getting to know your people and the excitement of choosing a life partner and starting a family that you won't even notice the years that go by. I have faith you'll do splendidly."

She blinked at him, certain she had to have misheard him. "Um..." she felt Jaren's gaze searing into the side of her face, and she fidgeted, beyond uncomfortable.

"We're not there yet," she said, neck and face hot under Vesstan's scrutiny. "And until someone here finally explains my connection to the crystal, I don't even *want* to have children." She and Jaren hadn't talked about it, but she knew he'd agree.

Vesstan shook his head, looking every bit the regretful father. "It's not about what you want, Veralie. Very few Magyki, or even humans, get to choose their path in life. It's just not the way the world works."

Her fingernails carved crescent moons into her palms. She was well aware that not many got to choose their path. Did he think she'd *chosen* to live her life the way she had?

He rested his elbows on the table, clasping his hands and leaning his chin on them. "When you meet your chosen partner, you will come to realize, just as your mother did, that some paths are chosen for you for the good of everyone."

Her stomach roiled, and she sensed, more than saw, Jaren's entire body go preternaturally still. But Vesstan carried on, unaware of the silent violence beginning to swirl inside the male beside her.

"I'm not sure I understand completely," she said.

King Vesstan nodded. Taking a rather large sip of wine, he picked up his napkin and dabbed at his lips before he bothered to answer.

"You should've been wed when you turned eighteen. You

are behind, not only in your intelligence and abilities, but also in that regard."

He paused, setting his napkin on the table and smoothing it out. "There is much you need to catch up on, so the faster you get started, the better. I plan to announce your crowning and coupling within the next three moon cycles."

Her head throbbed. He couldn't be serious. "I am mated, Your Majesty."

His eyes flicked to Dedryn, lingering for a heavy moment before moving on to Jaren. "I was made aware. However, you are set to take the throne. You need to be matched to best continue your line. It is not to be cruel. Every previous queen would've made the same choice, if mated."

He said it like she was an outlier, like the gods had cursed her rather than given her a gift like her mother believed. But then he opened his mouth again, and it got so much worse.

"We do not know the history of your mate's bloodline. Dedryn confirmed today that they adopted him at infancy and were never aware of his parentage. Mixing your connected bloodline with an unknown is…unwise."

Jaren lurched toward her, arm out and mouth parted to speak—what would likely be a very dangerous comment—but Dedryn snatched his extended arm, pulling him in and whispering something in his ear.

The king was still watching him, shaking his head slightly. "I understand where your anger comes from, Jaren Barilias, but this is bigger than you. Mates are a beautiful, wonderful thing, but they are not always in the best interest of our people. Sometimes we must make sacrifices for what is most important to the whole."

Anger simmered under her skin. Vesstan sang how gifted and special the Magyki were, but he was no better than Emperor Sulian. He could claim it was for their people all he wanted, but all he cared about was marrying her off to whoever would be most beneficial for *him*.

And she refused to be used. "Then I will be unwise, I guess."

Something dark flashed across his eyes, and he slowly laid his hands flat on the table. "Being of royal blood, you are inherently privileged to have anything you could ever want. Clothing, books, parties, food and drink. Any of it. I do not believe a lack of *one* choice constitutes such a response."

As if she was being selfish by refusing to reject her bond.

She raised her chin, unwilling to back down. Because if she didn't change his mind, she estimated the king had two minutes left to live, unless Dedryn, who had not uttered a single word, stepped in to block her mate.

"I disagree, and I'm willing to bet our people would too," she said, hoping and betting she was right. Something told her that her mother wouldn't be the only Magyki to believe her mated status was a sign from the gods. Especially after the last decade.

By Vesstan's flared nostrils and clenched jaw, she'd wagered right. He stood, brushing his hands down his sides.

"I can sense you are both too emotional to continue this

conversation at this time. But I ask you to take some time to think it over, Veralie. You are no longer living responsibility-free, and you need to think about the consequences of your actions."

She stood as well, immediately followed by Jaren and Dedryn. Thank the gods it was over. She wasn't sure how much longer she would've lasted.

"You may take your leave for the night. Your guardian will escort you to your first lesson tomorrow after you break your fast. Don't be late."

Following Dedryn's lead, she curtsied, officially counting the minutes until she could be back in the safety of her room. Vesstan tipped his head and walked out the side door without another word.

The second it clicked shut, she leaned forward, resting a hand over her stomach and exhaling heavily. The next time she was forced to attend a family dinner, she'd avoid the damn wine.

She jumped, nearly tripping over her shoes when the door behind them opened. She spun around, bumping into Jaren's shoulder, to find both Jaeros and Reniya standing in the doorway.

Reniya grinned. "Well, that could've gone better."

CHAPTER 26

VERA

Reniya and Jaeros parted, letting their group exit the room into the otherwise abandoned hall. The look on Jaeros's face as he examined his mate was answer enough of why he was there.

Whatever emotions Dedryn had been pushing through their bond had concerned him enough to head their way, just in case. But Vera had no idea what the other individual was doing there.

"I thought you went home for the night, Reniya?"

"Did you really think I'd miss all the fun just because Deddie over here told me to?"

Jaeros snorted, slipping his arms around *Deddie* in a hug. Or to restrain him. Either was possible.

"Rein your eye daggers in, I'm kidding. I was doing rounds

and saw Jae heading this way, so I decided to keep him company. Can't say I regret it one bit."

Vera cringed, squeezing an eye shut, and then grimaced when the action made her head hurt even more. "How much of that did you hear?"

"Enough to wish I could've attended. However, I feel like I will have just as much fun, if not more, escorting you to your *etiquette classes*," she said, wiggling her eyebrows.

Vera laughed despite herself. Leave it to Reniya to find a way to make her feel better about the shitshow that just occurred. She shifted her weight, wincing. She was more than ready to toss these death traps off her feet.

Jaren cocked his head, his eyes roving over her before he stepped closer and dropped to the ground, grabbing the hem of her dress.

She squeaked, vividly remembering what he'd done the last time he'd dropped to his knees before her in a public setting. But he only lifted one foot and then the other, slipping off her shoes.

She groaned, feeling the blood rush back to her squeezed, abused toes. "Oh my gods, thank you."

He nodded, dangling them off one hand and leaning down to press a kiss to her temple. She looked past his shoulder and smiled when she saw Dedryn and Jaeros in almost the exact same position.

Dedryn whispered something in his mate's ear before brushing his lips over his forehead and turning away from him. His face was its usual stoic mask, but she could have sworn pride swam in his eyes as they met hers.

"If you don't mind, Veralie, we would like to have a word with our son. I had planned to escort you back, but since Miss Virnorin has taken it upon herself to be present," he added, throwing a disapproving look her way, "She can do the honors."

Vera nodded. She didn't care who walked her back, just as long as her shoes were off, and she was heading somewhere with a bed. But like an aggressive animal, Jaren's chest rumbled, and he immediately opened his mouth to spew the gods only knew what.

Still feeling lightheaded and not possessing the energy to defend him in any more altercations, she twisted into his body, wrapping her arms around his waist.

"Nothing is going to happen between here and our room, Jaren," she said, relaxing into his chest and breathing him in. His earthy scent swirled around her, instantly calming her mind and settling the dull throb in her head. She smiled into his tunic when he scoffed.

"Veralie," he said, somehow making it sound more like a warning than her name.

"Hm?"

"Do you actually expect me to let you out of my sight after everything he just said in there? After he just tried to take—"

"Yes," she said, pulling back to gaze up into his dark, angry eyes. "I promise it'll be fine. I'm not going to marry some attractive, Magyki noble on the way to my room."

He growled, imprinting his fingers into her hips.

"Just let them talk to you. The faster you listen, the faster you can catch up with me." She pushed up onto her toes to press a soft kiss to his unmoving lips. "And if you're nice, I'll let you do whatever you want to my dress."

He hummed against her lips and kissed her back before tipping his forehead down to hers, sighing. "The things I do for you, little star."

Desperately trying to ignore the fact that she'd just hinted about having sex with him in front of his fathers, she huffed a laugh and stepped back, taking her shoes from his hand.

Then, before he could talk himself out of it and attach himself to her hip, she turned, following a cackling Reniya down the hall.

SHE STARED AT Reniya's back as they made their way through the palace, waiting until they were far enough away to avoid Jaren eavesdropping.

"I know you didn't run into Jaeros, Reni." It didn't make sense. Dedryn had sent her home for the night. There would've been no reason for her to have been doing rounds as she'd claimed.

"Technically, I never said *where* I ran into him."

True. "Did you come because of me, or because you found out Taeral would be there?" Because if there was anyone Reniya didn't trust, it was her aunt.

"The better question, oh Daughter," she said, clearly deflecting, "is, are you excited for dance lessons and script in the morning?"

Vera groaned. "Don't remind me, my head hurts just thinking about it."

Reniya threw her arms out, cackling, "The proper way to eat a meal in front of fancy people."

She groaned again, rubbing at her temples. Is that really what Vesstan planned on having her do? For *years*? He wasn't even trying to hide the fact that he was buying himself time.

"Whining is unbecoming of you, Your Highness."

She glared at her friend's back. "Apparently everything about me is unbecoming. If Vesstan could trade me out for someone else and still retain the connection he needs, he'd do it in a heartbeat."

Reniya glanced back at her, a brow raised. "He's preparing you to take your mother's place. Are you saying you believe you're ready to do so *now*?"

Dropping her gaze to her feet, she grumbled. Just the thought alone was making her feel sick. "No, but I mean, years of etiquette classes? Really? How does that have anything to do with leading people? Wouldn't our citizens appreciate seeing someone more like them?"

"Well, you're not really like them either though, are you?"

Vera's vision spotted, and she tucked her shoes under her arm so she could press her palms into her eyes. "I guess not. I think it's mostly the marriage idea I can't comprehend."

Reniya didn't refute that one. Who could? Her father wanted her to give up a mating bond just to push out, what he believed, would be the perfect heir to continue their precious connection.

"Just give it time, Your Highness. Maybe he'll change his mind once he gets to know you better."

More spots entered her vision, and she stumbled, blinking rapidly. "Reniya?"

Her friend continued walking. "If you're about to ask me to help you play hooky, think again. If you don't show up tomorrow your father will come for *my* head, and I am quite attached—"

"Reni." The name had barely rolled off her tongue before Vera stumbled again, dropping her shoes, and slamming into the wall. Her shoulder screamed as it bounced off the stone, all but throwing her to the floor.

She gulped in air, hearing steps run toward her but unable to see anything. Her head was fucking pounding.

"Your Highness?"

Hands grasped her arms, holding her steady as her upper body swayed. Her chest heaved in and out and her muscles felt seconds from giving out as even the weight of her head felt too heavy.

Inhaling slowly, she tried to calm the swirling in her head, but the second she tried to push up off the floor, a stabbing pain shot through her skull. She cried out, twisting her face away from Reniya in time to vomit all over the floor.

"Oh gods." She couldn't think past the pain, and her eyes—

gods—her *eyes*.

"Your Highness? Veralie! Tell me what's wrong."

Vera heaved again, feeling tears run down her face as she continued to blink blindly. "I can't...I can't see."

"What is it? Can't see what?" Reniya asked, alarm creeping into her voice.

"*Anything.*"

Panic overtook her, threatening her consciousness completely as another ear-splitting pain shot through her skull. "Jaren." She needed Jaren.

"I can't leave you."

Vera fell forward, placing both hands on the floor and focused on the cool chill of the stones to center her. It was fine, it was just a headache.

More tears streamed down her face as she squeezed her eyes shut and tucked her knees up under her, curling in on herself and trying to swallow down another wave of bile.

Mentally talking herself through the pain, she rocked forward only to hiss when a sharp sting sliced into her knees.

Her eyes instinctively shot open to see what had cut her, and her suddenly clear sight had her rearing back and falling onto her ass.

A glowing cavern surrounded her, and she had to squint, letting her eyes grow accustomed to the glow as thousands of shards pulsed around her in hot, angry bursts.

Crashing echoed out, startling her, and she twisted, hissing when more shards pressed into her thighs. The lake roiled a few feet away from her, the roar of the waves unimaginably loud as they slammed furiously over the shore, each one reaching farther than the last.

Still unable to stand, she scooted back on her ass, desperate to put more space between her and the water. Her head was still pounding, and terror filled her chest. She'd never come here awake before, and Jaren wasn't around this time to help pull her out.

Gods, Reniya would have no idea what was happening. Was her body sitting in a trance of some kind, or had she completely passed out in the middle of the damn hall?

Her breathing came out ragged, her lungs working double time as she searched for her friend, knowing in her heart she wasn't there, but unable to keep herself from looking anyway.

She cursed, slapping a hand to her chest and feeling her heart slam against her rib cage, when a male stood a few yards behind her, his body facing the wall. A dark-haired, very muscular, very *naked*, male.

Alarm bells rang in her head, some animal-like instinct warning her that whoever he was, he was dangerous. She slowly eased a hand to the side, trying not to make a sound as she blindly felt around for a rock of some kind, keeping her eyes on the stranger.

Like Alean, he didn't seem aware of her. At least, not yet. He stood in the same spot she had, his head tilted and hands fisted at his sides as he stared at a large, dull crystal embedded in the wall.

A large, *broken* crystal. His tan body radiated fury, and a new wave of nausea rolled through her at the absolute power pouring off him as he slowly raised a hand to the crystal's jagged edges.

She held her breath, watching him press his palm into it, not a single twitch as he impaled his hand on the shard. With trails of blood dripping down his forearm, he only tipped his head back, murmuring something she couldn't quite make out.

The entire cavern swelled at his words, each crystal glowing brighter than a star, and then her neck snapped back, mouth open on a scream, as agony like she'd never known speared through her body.

And then she knew nothing at all.

JAREN

HE GRUNTED, PRESSING A HAND TO HIS HEAD. LEAVE IT TO his fathers to give him a gods damn headache before they'd even started talking. A hot soak with his mate sounded pretty fucking good right about now. Better than this, at least.

He still wasn't sure how he'd let her convince him to leave her side to go somewhere private with his fathers to talk.

Cracking his neck, he made to follow them into one of the palace's advisory rooms only to stop in his tracks when another dull pain throbbed behind his eyes.

"You all right?"

He glanced up to see Dedryn paused in the doorway, brows drawn in concern.

"Fine," he snapped, straightening his spine. "It's just a…" he broke off, whipping around to stare back down the hall as Veralie's nerves took off, panic sweeping through her until he felt his own heart race in time with hers.

What the fuck was Virnorin saying to have her completely freaking out? He stilled, remembering the look Taeral had shot Veralie on her way out. It hadn't even crossed his mind that she might have gone to their room to wait for her.

He closed his eyes, trying not to panic himself. That's not what it was. He'd sense anger or disgust pouring from his mate if she'd found Taeral waiting for her. And he'd definitely be able to sense if she'd been attacked.

No, it had to be gods damn Reniya. He glowered, hating that he wasn't there to kick her out for upsetting his mate after she'd done so well holding it together tonight.

"Then come on, we have things we need to discuss," Dedryn said behind him, impatience lacing his tone.

"No, *you* have something to discuss. I don't even know why I bothered—" The throbbing in his head increased as fear shot through the bond. He gasped, staggering forward like a rope had wrapped around his middle and *yanked*.

"Jaren?" Both his fathers were suddenly before him, hands grasping at his shoulders as Dedryn's face leaned down into his. Understanding hit his eyes a second later and he shot up, looking down the hall as well. "Is she hurt?"

Jaren closed his eyes, inhaling slowly to steady himself, and focused on her. He didn't feel anything besides the pain in his head and her fear, but he was beginning to think the headache wasn't *his*.

"I don't know," he said, shrugging off Jae's hands. "But I need to get to her. Something's wrong."

He dipped into his power, letting it fill his body, and prepared himself to sprint all the way to their room when a sharp, excruciating pain shot through his chest, taking the heart nestled next to his and lighting it on fire.

He crashed to the ground, unable to hold back the choked cry that ripped from his throat. In his peripheral, he saw Dedryn kneel down, saw both of them reach for him, and heard their voices, but he couldn't focus on any of it. Nothing except the swirling agony coursing through his mate.

He'd left her. He'd fucking left her.

And then her scream split the air, coming from every direction and surrounding him, taking his soul and shredding it into a million pieces.

CHAPTER 27

EITHAN

His breath came out in short, erratic puffs as he wrapped his hand around his shaft, arching his neck back until his head rested over the edge of the tub.

Squeezing, he could only imagine what her lips would feel like gliding up and down his length, her sharp canines scraping along his sensitive skin with just the right amount of pain. He closed his eyes, allowing himself to fall deeper into the image of her before him.

Her dark curls would be loose, wild and thick about her shoulders, and he'd sink his hands into it, knotting his fingers in the spirals and holding tight so there would be no chance of her pulling away.

Then, just as those inhuman, silver eyes met his, he'd slam forward, watching himself disappear down her throat until her nose pressed against his abdomen.

Throat constricting as she gagged around his shaft, tears streaming down her cheeks, and nails scratching at him as she silently begged for air, she'd look fucking beautiful.

Ever since his first time, he'd never gone this long without sinking inside a woman, and it'd surprised him how much he didn't miss it. He didn't need or desire it the way most men he met seemed to. He'd only ever done it to help slake the pull of his demon and smooth out his perfected, rakish image.

But the last few days had been different. Harder. He still didn't need *sex* per se. He just needed *her*. And with each day that passed without her, it grew worse. His body fucking craved and begged for her, driving him near madness.

It was like a physical ache he couldn't shake no matter what he occupied himself with. Training, drinks, cards, nothing. Absolutely nothing had worked to satisfy the raging hunger he had for her.

Maybe if he hadn't come so gods damn close to having her, he'd feel more in control. But he had. He'd grazed his fingers along her body, pressed his lips to her warm skin, and felt the addiction crawl through him like a street drug.

"Fuck," he spit, ramming up into his fist harder, listening to the water slosh and spill around him, wishing it was her moaning and begging instead.

Releasing himself suddenly, he gasped, gripping the edge of the tub until his knuckles turned white. He refused to keep fucking himself each night like some uncontrollable adolescent.

It wasn't helping. If anything, it was only making it worse.

He took a breath, holding it in and counting, before letting it trickle out. Maybe if he satisfied his fantasy, fed the craving in the only way he could, then maybe, just maybe, he'd make it until she returned.

He wasn't unfaithful if he imagined and wished for his bride the entire time, right?

Relaxing one of his hands, he leaned over, pulling the string attached to the bell on the wall. His servant, an older, white-haired man, rushed in seconds later, arms saddled with clean clothes to assist him with drying and dressing.

Eithan shook his head, the motion sending a pang through his still-healing nose. Gods damn, Gibson. "I will not be needing those just yet, Cal. I find myself desiring a warm body to keep me company, and I'm not feeling very patient."

Cal nodded, a knowing smile curling on his face. Eithan actually liked the old man, more than he liked most of the individuals around the palace, at least. He'd been working for him for years, ever since the last had bled out and died on Eithan's floor. The man was quite used to his requests.

He turned to go, but Eithan snapped his fingers, stopping him in his tracks.

"Lean frame and curly brown hair, Cal. I don't care about anything else. But her hair must be a long mess of dark curls."

His servant nodded again before turning and slipping out of the room. As soon as the door latched shut, Eithan stood and stepped over the lip of the tub, silently watching rivulets of water run down his naked form and pool at his feet.

No matter who showed up at his door, she wouldn't be good enough. She wouldn't have the innocent, wide eyes, or the perfect dusting of freckles he dreamed about every night.

He clenched his jaw. He'd have to resign himself to taking her from behind, because if he even saw a flash of a face that wasn't Vera's, he'd lose it.

Caressing a hand down his still painfully erect length, he sighed. Guess it wouldn't be a mouth he fucked tonight.

Grabbing the pair of trousers Cal had set down, he threw them on over his wet skin, leaving them undone and ignoring the way the fabric immediately stuck to his thighs. It's not like he'd be wearing them long anyway.

He dried his hands and made his way over to his bookshelf, counting the spines from the left, and picking up the fourth book. Letting it naturally fall open in his palms, he removed the key he'd hidden inside, and placed the book back on the shelf.

He moved to his desk, opening the bottom drawer, and removed the paper and quills inside of it. Then he reached in, pulling up the faux bottom to reveal the locked, hidden compartment beneath.

The one he kept all his private texts and journals in, as well as his favorite mementos.

Shifting a stained, ceramic shard to the side, he grabbed the most recent Bhasurian scroll he'd borrowed from the scribes and closed it all back up, returning the key to its original spot.

He'd write another letter while he waited, and then, after

he rid himself of this raging fucking need and cleared his mind, he'd spend the remainder of the night studying. Just like he had every night for weeks. Thyabathi was a lot harder than it looked.

And with Sulian sending him to gods damn Midpath to oversee the guard, he'd need every night of studying he could get. Especially now that he had nothing else to do. He certainly wouldn't visit Gibson anytime soon, nor did he have any great desire to visit any of his other usuals down there.

Eithan had taken Gibson back to his cell as promised, but he hadn't touched him. Something had changed in the man's expression that warned him off. His eyes had held a fire that shouldn't have been there.

And as much as he wanted to, Eithan didn't have the time to figure out how or why. Not right now. But he'd find out eventually. As long as Hayes kept Gibson alive until he returned, that is.

He looked back down at the text, wishing he could take it with him to Midpath. But it wasn't worth the risk of Sulian finding out.

The bastard would have him beaten within an inch of his life if he ever discovered Eithan was learning a language that he, himself, didn't know. Which only further proved how pathetic of a leader he truly was.

ABOUT TWENTY MINUTES later, he heard the door scrape

against the floor as it opened behind him, but he didn't bother turning or even pausing his writing.

"My—"

"Don't speak," he interrupted, barely letting the woman get so much as a word out. He didn't want to hear her voice. It would ruin everything. She was his bride-to-be. The woman—female—who was set to be his.

"If you speak, or if, at any point, I see your face, this evening is over."

He finished the letter, signing his name at the bottom and dropping his quill back into its pot. "If that is something you can do, tap twice on the door. Otherwise, you may take your leave."

There was a slight pause, and then two raps echoed out. He closed his eyes, dragging his palm down his quickly hardening length, and imagined it was Vera standing at his door.

Vera who waited for him. Vera who was completely inexperienced and too shy to speak.

He squeezed his eyelids tighter, working his shaft harder. She stood naked beneath a white, sheer robe, her breasts heavy and nipples hard, the tips pushing against the fabric as she pressed her thighs together.

It was *Vera* who would be bent over, shoving her ass into him again and again in silent demand, needing him to cure her insanity. The same insanity he felt for her.

He placed both hands on his desk, leaning over it as lust shot through his body and his heart beat faster. "I want you to walk over to the hearth and get down on all fours, Vera.

Forehead to the rug with your ass up and thighs spread."

Hearing her footsteps lead over to where he'd instructed, he wasted no time removing his trousers and letting his length spring free. He'd been lusting for her for weeks. He needed to be inside her.

Two raps hit the floor, signaling she was ready without instruction. Good girl.

Finally daring to turn, he made his way toward the hearth, a shudder coursing down his spine at the sight of Vera before him. Naked skin, up and bared for him, while brown curls fanned across her back.

She was fucking perfect.

EPILOGUE

ELRIC

He glared at the letter in his hand, grinding his teeth until his jaw popped. It was meticulously written, each word chosen specifically to mean something to Vera, while not raising alarm bells to anyone else.

And as much as Elric hated to admit it, he had to give it to the boy. The snake knew what he was doing.

It was the second letter Elric's men had been able to intercept, catching the messenger before he'd even left the city and bribing him to disappear.

But he knew there were more that had slipped past their notice. According to his contacts within the palace, Prince Eithan had sent at least half a dozen since Vera left.

Sighing, he rolled the parchment back up, staring at the 'M' in the center of the navy-blue emblem. Eithan Matheris was going to be a bigger problem than he'd originally anticipated.

"What does it say this time?" A gruff voice asked from behind him. "Has the bastard claimed you're dead yet?"

Elric tucked the letter into his belt and turned, resting his hands on the table behind him. The same table Vera had once sat on as a child, watching him with big, gray eyes while he worked, taking in every movement.

The same table she'd later worked at, herself, sharpening blades and smirking as she goaded him and said something infuriating.

His heart squeezed at the memories, and a wave of sadness washed over him before he shoved it down. He didn't have time to feel sorry for himself, or her.

"The same as last time," he finally answered, clearing his throat. "Are you prepared for tonight?"

Brex Jensen nodded. "I'm ready. He's set to meet with me just after sunset, along with Gibson if all goes to plan."

Elric ran a hand over his freshly shaved head and breathed deep. "Good. He may not be ready, but his claim for the throne would be legitimate. He's the best chance we have."

The letter at his side burned. It was the only thing that could mess everything up. He could only hope to get Gibson out and set things in motion before one of Prince Eithan's letters found its way into Vera's hands.

It was time to remove the Matheris line from the throne.

Glossary

a li – my heart

aitanta – soul bonded mate

chinbi srol – baby king/princeling

daz – spirit/ghost

Mbi thothori trush zhu. – You're a female Magyki.

nlamb jekhna – horny idiot

nlayi – fine

Nlem Snadzend – Daughter to the Throne

Thyabathi zhe be. – Now use Thyabathi.

truik elixir – birth control

yinlanem dupye – holy fucking gods

zhumo dzind – stupid fool

zisdemyoz – guardian/personal guard

Acknowledgements

My first thank you could not be to anyone other than each and every single one of you who have been with me since the beginning and have patiently waited for this book. Postponing this release was, not only difficult, but nerve wracking.

I was absolutely terrified of disappointing all of you with pushing the release back, and I cannot say enough how much it meant for you all to be so understanding and supportive.

As much as I love the idea of rapidly releasing books, in the end, my main concern is delivering a book that is the quality you deserve. You all gave me that ability, and I cannot say enough how much it meant to me.

My second thank you goes to my mother, who has alpha read every one of my books for me in all their messy, typo glory. You are the best mother I could have, and I appreciate that you can read my smutty scenes without dying on the inside. You're a rockstar.

Next, to my editor, Elaine and sensitivity reader, Ruthie, both of whom squeezed me into their schedules. I'm a constant storm of chaos, and I cannot thank you two enough for working with me anyway!

My next shoutout goes to my best friend, who promised to beta read for me but didn't finish because she's "busy" and has a "job". Thanks for absolutely nothing. You're lucky you're pretty.

The final thank you goes to my husband, who took my rollercoaster of emotions in stride while I finished this book. Thanks for loving me even when I got so stressed out over the release that I cried about spaghetti. I love you too.

About the Author

Lilian T. James was born and raised in a small town of Kansas until she finished high school. Enrolling at a University on the east coast, she moved there with her son and obtained degrees in Criminal Justice, Social Work, Psychology, and Sociology. After graduating, she met her husband and moved to the west coast for a few years before they finally settled back in Kansas. She has three kids, one miniature dachshund, and has been an avid fantasy and romance reader her entire life. Lilian was finally able to publish her first novel, Untainted, in 2021 and has no plans of stopping.

Next in the Series

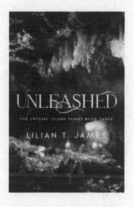

Something was stolen from the gods.

Something that never should have been taken.

And now *she* must pay the price.

Things are astir on Aleron.

Insanity clashes with revenge.

And a new name stakes claim on the throne.